A Sugarloaf Christmas

ROSEMARY WHITTAKER

A Sugarloaf Christmas

Rosemary Whittaker

Also by Rosemary Whittaker

The Cinnamon Snail

Sunshine State

The Wattle Birds

The Feijoa Tree

A Tale of Two Christmases

A Sugarloaf Valentine

A Sugarloaf Mix-Up

A Sugarloaf Surprise

Stopwatch Publications

First printing, 2023

ISBN-13: 978-1-922651-40-2

Published by Rosemary Whittaker
www.rosemarywhittaker.com

Cover design by 100 Covers.

For Rosie, with whom I have enjoyed discussing The Archers for many years.

Thanks too for the chess advice and for your consistent and generous support of my writing career.

Chapter One

The smell of gingerbread greets me as I open the bakery door. It's a good start. I haven't got on board with the holiday spirit this year, but I suspect that's about to change.

A woman appears from the back room and holds out a spoon to me. 'Taste that!'

I take a step back. Has she mistaken me for someone else?

'Go on!' she urges me. 'I need to know whether it's the right texture.'

The spoon is full of a dark brown substance. I can't tell whether it's melted chocolate or congealed gravy.

'Why do you need me to taste it?' I say, playing for time.

'Because it's the first batch of brownies I've ever made, and Abby will laugh at me if I mess it up. She says it's about time I learned to cook.'

'Abby?' I say, relieved. 'That's who I've …'

'Not until you've tried this!' she insists.

I take the spoon she hands me and examine it. It looks like brownie batter. It also smells like chocolate, which is an encouraging sign.

I taste it and nod. 'It's lovely.'

'Not too runny?' she says.

'I don't think so. But I'm no expert. Speaking of experts, is Abby –?'

'That's great!' she says. 'Thank you so much. I'll put the brownies in the oven, then I'll come back and serve you. I won't be a moment.'

Without waiting for an answer, she disappears. I sit at the nearest table and look around me. Abby described the bakery when she called me last week, but she didn't do it justice. The walls are painted in a soft palette of pink and cream. Twinkling fairy lights frame the large front window. Candles cast a warm glow over the tables, with their festive centrepieces of pinecones, holly leaves, and red berries. Even the menus are decorated with candy canes. Clearly, Christmas is a big deal at The Sugarloaf Bakery.

The woman reappears. 'Thanks for waiting. I'm Isabella. How can I help you?'

'I'm here to see Abby,' I say before she decides she'd like me to join her in the Great Flour Face-off or play a game of Pastry Pictionary.

She looks disappointed. 'You aren't a customer?'

'No. In fact, I –'

To my relief, Abby appears from the kitchen, wiping her hands on her apron. Her face lights up when she sees me. 'Grace! You made it!'

Isabella looks puzzled. 'Do you know each other?'

Abby comes over to hug me. 'Of course, we know each other! This is Grace.'

'I'd already reached that conclusion, based on your ear-splitting shriek of "Grace!"' says Isabella. 'But my question remains. Who is Grace? And what is she doing here, apart from giving her expert opinion on my brownie batter?'

She turns to me. 'You aren't by any chance a famous chef or an internationally renowned food critic?'

'I'm afraid not.'

Her face falls. 'What a pity. It would have been such a triumph to tell Abby my brownies had been approved by a Michelin-starred chef. She'd have had to stop teasing me about my lack of culinary skills. I might even have taken over her job.'

'The batter tasted very nice,' I say consolingly. 'Extremely chocolatey.'

Isabella looks pleased. 'I put in extra. I always say you can't have too much of a good thing.'

'You didn't use my imported dark chocolate?' says Abby.

'I wouldn't dare!' says Isabella. 'You've warned me and Lily about that often enough. You'd never think we owned this bakery from the way we allow our staff to treat us.'

'Which includes Grace,' says Abby.

'What does?' says Isabella.

'Your staff. She's working here over Christmas. You know that.'

Isabella frowns. 'I most certainly do not. What are you talking about?'

It's Abby's turn to look puzzled. 'You must have known she was coming. I fixed it up with her last week as soon as we won the hotel contract. Don't you remember me telling you I couldn't manage that on top of everything else, and we needed an extra pair of hands?'

'Vaguely,' says Isabella. 'But we'd spent the entire afternoon talking about desserts, so I may not have been concentrating properly. That still doesn't explain it. It's a big jump from saying you could do with some extra help to someone appearing on your doorstep. Were you specifically expecting Grace? She isn't some kind of a Christmas miracle?'

'She's more like a helper elf,' says Abby.

Isabella inspects me. 'You don't look like an elf. You're too tall, for one thing.'

'If there's some mistake …' I begin.

Abby grabs my arm before I can move. 'There's no mistake. Lily said I could call you, so I did. Grace is between jobs, Isabella, so she's kindly agreed to help us out. If you frighten her away, I'll never forgive you!'

'That explains it,' says Isabella. 'Lily never tells me anything.'

She gives me an apologetic smile. 'I hope I haven't made you feel unwelcome.'

'Not at all,' I say. 'I love being greeted with a spoonful of brownie batter. I hope it's a regular tradition here.'

'It isn't,' says Abby. 'But it's a common occurrence to find Isabella wandering around with a mouthful of cake. Raw or cooked – she's not fussy.'

The door opens, letting in a blast of cold air, and a woman wearing a bright red coat comes in. She pushes back her hood. 'Sorry I'm late. I had to drop Daisy off with Mum. They're making gingerbread people today.'

Isabella's eyes light up. 'I was thinking of dropping in to see your mum on my way home. Do you think my goddaughter will let me have one?'

'She's decorating one especially for you,' says the woman. 'It has rainbow hair, and it's carrying a bright pink handbag.'

'How well she knows me,' says Isabella.

'Lily, this is Grace,' says Abby. 'You remembered she was coming, didn't you?'

Lily gives me a stricken look. 'I'd forgotten you were arriving today!'

'That isn't all you forgot,' says Isabella. 'You forgot to mention her to me at all.'

'Are you sure?' says Lily.

'Not entirely,' says Isabella. 'But let's go with the idea of it having been your mistake.'

'Welcome to The Sugarloaf Bakery, Grace,' says Lily. 'We're grateful to you for stepping in at such short notice. Have you worked in a bakery before?'

'She's an advertising executive,' says Abby.

'For a bakery?' asks Isabella.

I'm not sure what to say. Does she think I'm an expert consultant in bakery management, and that I could step in and run everything at a moment's notice?

She smiles. 'I'm joking. Where are you staying while you're here?'

'With me and Chris,' says Abby. 'Grace and I got to know each other in London a while ago. The restaurant I was working in used Grace's company to boost their profile. She was the first person I thought of when you and Lily agreed we needed some help.'

'When Lily agreed,' Isabella corrects her. 'I still haven't decided whether I was in on that conversation.'

'When Lily agreed, then,' says Abby. 'Grace is here until the new year. Chris and I have a spare bedroom, so it's perfect. We have lots of catching up to do.'

'And if you get fed up with her,' Isabella says to me, 'there's a spare room at our house. You'd be very welcome to use it.'

'That's extremely kind of you,' I say. 'Especially as you had no idea I was arriving!'

'That's my story, and I'm sticking to it,' she says. 'Seriously, Grace, I'm happy you're here. It's going to be a frantic few weeks, and we can use all the help we can get. Did Abby tell you about this hotel thing?'

'Only briefly. I gather you have a contract to provide desserts for some Christmas party?'

'Not just any Christmas party!' she says. 'The Quayside Hotel Christmas ball is the event of the year in this part of the world. Anyone who's anyone will be there.'

Lily hangs up her coat. 'Who wants a hot chocolate?'

Isabella waves me to a table. 'We can sit here while Lily makes the drinks.'

'I have to get back to work,' says Abby. 'I'll see you at the end of the day, Grace. We can drive back to the flat together.'

She disappears into the kitchen. Isabella watches her go.

'She's working too hard,' she says. 'She seems permanently exhausted these days. It's good you're here, Grace. Can you bake too?'

'Not really. I've been working pretty long hours recently, so I've been eating a lot of takeaways.'

'Me too,' she says. 'The local delivery drivers know me well.'

Lily brings our drinks over. 'Has Isabella told you about this contract?'

Isabella drops a marshmallow into her hot chocolate and watches it melt. 'I was waiting for you.'

'It's an important contract for our business,' says Lily. 'Things have been tough for us financially this year. But it's been tough for everyone, so we aren't complaining. It could be a lot worse.'

'People are cutting back on non-essentials,' says Isabella. 'You wouldn't think cake could be classed as a non-essential, but you'd be wrong. Apparently, there are people in the world who treat it as an extra, a sort of afterthought. It's baffling, but it's true. So, we've been looking for ways to increase our profits and raise our profile in the local area.'

She stops to take a bite of mince pie.

'The Quayside Hotel put out a call to local caterers for the contract for their Christmas ball,' says Lily. 'They usually go with one outfit for the entire meal. But Isabella persuaded them to consider trying local businesses instead. I'm not sure how she managed it. I think blackmail may have been involved, but she won't tell me. It's a huge deal for us. It isn't only the profit from the party. It's a way of making ourselves more visible as a business. We're hoping that if we do well, we can go after other contracts in the area. We've been thinking for a while that it would be good to expand into different types of catering – weddings and parties and things like that. This ball could be a great springboard for us.'

Isabella finishes her mince pie and hands me the plate. 'Try one. They're excellent. I've never known anyone who could make pastry like Abby.'

I take a mince pie. 'Thanks. It will be my first one this year.'

'Goodness!' she says. 'It's at least my sixteenth.'

'And it's only mid-November,' says Lily. 'I fear the supplies of mincemeat across Hampshire may not last until Christmas.'

'There are plenty of other counties,' says Isabella dismissively.

'What will I be doing while I'm here?' I ask. 'Working in the bakery with Abby or serving in the shop?'

'A bit of both,' says Lily. 'We all have to be flexible at this time of year. Christmas is a busy period for us, even without this extra contract.'

Isabella selects another mince pie. 'Did you tell Grace about the TV thing?'

'Not yet,' says Lily. 'Unless Abby mentioned it?'

I shake my head, and she goes on. 'A TV company called Capital Productions has been making one of those fly-on-the-wall documentaries about the Quayside Hotel. The show went out over the summer. It was so successful that the producers thought it would be a good idea to send a team down to cover the Christmas party. And that includes us.'

'In what way?' I ask.

'They're sending their team to the bakery beforehand to watch us prepare the desserts,' explains Isabella. 'Poor Abby hit the roof when she heard. But she's calmed down now. I know it's a lot of pressure for her, but it should really put us on the map.'

'You can be in the kitchen that day,' I say. 'I'd rather not be on camera.'

'That's what I said,' says Lily. 'Luckily, Isabella likes nothing more than the sound of her own voice, so she won't mind doing it. She's also, although I hate to mention it because it's bad for her ego, extremely photogenic. The crew will be delighted to use her for that part of the programme. Grace and I will keep things going in the shop while Isabella charms the camera team into giving us all the best angles.'

'No wonder Abby is stressed,' I say. 'You're right. She does look tired. I hope she's taking a holiday after Christmas?'

'She and Chris are off to the Bahamas for a couple of weeks,' says Lily. 'He's a baker too, so neither of them can get time off over Christmas. They're really excited about their trip.'

'That's good,' I say. 'In the meantime, I'll do everything I can to make myself useful.'

'I know you will,' says Isabella. 'You radiate competence. "Now there's a woman we ought to recruit to the team," I said to myself as soon as you walked in.'

'Despite not having the faintest idea who I was?'

'Despite that,' she agrees. 'If you and Lily have finished scoffing all the mince pies, we'd better get to work. It may be the most wonderful time of the year, but it's also the busiest.'

'I'll find Grace an overall,' says Lily.

'And don't forget to tell her how to greet the customers,' says Isabella. 'It's important she gets it exactly right.'

'I know!' I say. 'We barely wait for our customers to get through the door before thrusting a spoonful of uncooked cake batter at them and demanding they try it.'

Isabella doesn't bat an eyelid. 'I knew you'd be a quick learner.'

'Don't let Grace do that when Mrs Ogilvie comes in,' Lily warns her.

'Of course not,' says Isabella. 'Although Mabel wouldn't mind. And Bernie would definitely be up for it.'

'Dogs can't eat chocolate,' says Lily.

'I know,' says Isabella. 'It's one of the reasons I'd hate to be a dog. Most of their lives look pretty appealing – sleeping for half the day, running around playing with a ball, and going for lots of walks. But that chocolate thing would be a deal breaker for me.'

Lily hands me an overall. 'Ignore her, Grace. Abby and I have learned not to encourage her. Anyway, put this on, and I'll get you started.'

I smile to myself as I pull on the overall and follow her over to the counter. This isn't what I expected to be doing this year, but that's not necessarily a bad thing. And from what I've seen this afternoon, working at this bakery will be a Christmas to remember.

Chapter Two

Abby and I arrive in Honeywell early the following morning. I drive, and she shows me the best place to park behind the shops.

'You need to get here on time if you want a parking space,' she says. 'We have some enthusiastic customers who stop at the bakery on their way to work for sandwiches and pies. The car park fills up quickly. Isabella is always complaining about it.'

'That suits me,' I say. 'I'm an early bird. I always have been. Which is lucky because I've been working ridiculous hours in London. It's become a sort of contest between some of the younger staff to show which of them is the keenest. They'd sleep at the office if health and safety didn't forbid it. But the competition to arrive first is fierce.'

'And as the office grandmother, that's been getting you down?' she says.

'Not quite that, but I'm one of the oldest in my department. I was thirty last month.'

'I'll ask Isabella to make reasonable accommodations for you each day,' she promises. 'I expect you'll need a nap after lunch, and a special reclining chair.'

'I'm not on my last legs yet. But you have no idea how cutthroat my line of business can be. I'll try to manage without the nap for the first few weeks. I have to impress my new employers.'

'Which is good,' she says, 'because you'd be fighting Isabella for floor space in the office. She says she's doing the accounts in there each afternoon, but I have my suspicions.'

She opens the bakery door, and Lily appears from the back room.

'I thought I'd get a head start,' she says. 'Daisy doesn't believe the day is worth living if it doesn't start at 5 a.m. Jack and I have tried everything we can to persuade her – reasoned argument, a sunrise clock, even outright bribery. But she's having none of it. No one warns you how exhausting parenthood can be. They don't dare, or the human race would die out.'

'I'm sure she'll grow out of it soon,' says Abby. 'In no time at all, she'll be a teenager, and you won't be able to get her out of bed in the mornings, no matter how hard you try.'

'She won't be a teenager,' says Lily. 'Jack and I have discussed it and decided to skip those years. We can barely cope with a toddler. We aren't remotely equipped to deal with the teen years. The memories are all too fresh for me. I don't want to re-live it all as an observer.'

'My mum says children of your own are karma for what you put your parents through growing up,' says Abby. 'Which means I'm in no rush to have children. I was a horrible teenager.'

'I had my moments too,' confesses Lily. 'I remember telling my mum that none of my friends' parents breathed in the same annoying way she did. If she kept it up, she'd have to stay in a different room whenever anyone came to see me.'

'How did she react?' I say.

'Oh, the usual way. She smiled and asked whether I was hungry, and would I like her to bake my favourite cake?'

'She sounds amazing,' I say. 'I got into the most awful shouting matches with mine.'

'I can't imagine Lily's mum getting into a shouting match with anyone,' says Abby. 'The woman's a living saint.'

'Don't say that to her!' says Lily. 'But yes, she's pretty great. Both my parents are.'

Abby pulls on her overall and reaches for a hairnet. 'I wish I could stay and chat, but I have bread to make and gingerbread batter to mix.'

'What shall I do?' I ask Lily.

She gives an enormous yawn. 'Sorry, I haven't woken up yet. Can you use a coffee machine?'

I look at the machine standing in the corner of the room. 'I'm afraid not. At least, not one like this. I have one in my flat at home, but all I have to do is choose a pod and switch it on.'

'You'll need to learn,' she says. 'But I don't have time to teach you now. I have to show you how to use the till.'

Abby disappears into the kitchen. A few minutes later, the door bangs open, and Isabella appears. 'Is someone making coffee? I timed that well.'

Lily hands her the scoop. 'You did, indeed. I was about to teach Grace how to use the till. You can make us all a drink while I do that.'

Isabella shrugs off her battered old duffel coat. 'You see how it is, Grace? Nothing gets done around here without me.'

'I've been here for half an hour,' Lily points out.

Isabella switches on the machine. 'Exactly! And you didn't start making coffee until now. Must I think of everything?'

The door opens again, and a woman comes in with a dog on a lead. He gives an enthusiastic bark when he sees Isabella.

'Hello, Bernie,' she says. 'Are you out for your morning walk?'

'Morning biscuit hunt, more like!' says the woman as she sinks into a chair. 'Are you making coffee? I'd love a cappuccino.'

The dog sits by the counter, looking hopefully up at me.

'Does he need some water?' I ask the woman.

'He wouldn't thank you for it,' she says. 'He knows where the dog biscuits are kept. That's what he's after.'

She wags a finger at Bernie. 'You can wait your turn. I can't think of anything else until I've had my morning coffee. People before dogs, that's my motto.'

'Don't let Mrs Ogilvie hear you say that,' says Isabella. 'She'd never speak to you again.'

'Oh, Edie's daft about that dog,' says the woman. 'I must say I'm rather fond of him myself. But when it comes to giving up my seat next to the fire because he looks cold, I draw the line. He has a nice fur coat, I tell my sister. When someone buys me one, I'll think about giving up my armchair, but not before.'

'What does she say to that?' says Lily, looking amused.

The woman takes the drink Isabella hands her. 'Nothing. She's given up trying to persuade me this dog is a canine prodigy and we should all cater to his every whim. She's a stubborn woman, but I'm just as stubborn. Which is hardly surprising, given we're twins.'

'I haven't introduced you to our newest member of staff,' says Lily. 'Mabel, this is Grace. She's helping us over the Christmas period. Grace, this is Mabel Watkins. She's recently moved to the village to live with her sister. Where is Mrs Ogilvie today?'

'She's still having her breakfast,' says Mabel. 'Bernie was climbing the walls waiting for his morning walk, so I said I'd bring him up here and pick up some nice bread rolls for us to have with our lunchtime soup.'

'Abby has just put them in,' says Isabella. 'I can smell them baking.'

'No hurry,' says Mabel. 'I still have my coffee to drink. Meanwhile, someone had better give that dog a biscuit before he jumps up and pulls the entire box off the counter. He may settle down with it for a while and allow me to enjoy my drink in peace.'

Lily reaches into the box. 'There you go, Bernie. You like this flavour, don't you?'

'Do you really bake dog biscuits?' I ask her.

'I don't, but Abby does. She dreams up all sorts of new flavours, and Bernie gives them the paws up or the paws down.'

'I've never seen him turn up his nose at any of them,' says Mabel. 'That dog has a healthy appetite. Just like his Aunt Mabel.'

'Could you pop into the kitchen and ask Abby whether she'd like a coffee?' Lily asks me.

'Of course. She may need someone to help her with the gingerbread. Would you like me to do that or stay in the shop with you this morning?'

'Whichever she'd prefer,' says Lily. 'Isabella and I can cope in here if Abby wants you.'

I stop in the kitchen doorway and take a deep breath. Abby has just taken out a batch of rolls. Freshly baked bread is one of my favourite smells in the world. But it's more than that. The entire kitchen smells like a spice bazaar – the scent of cinnamon and nutmeg mingling with the aroma of vanilla and citrus.

Abby is standing at one end of the long table in the centre of the kitchen, deftly rolling out gingerbread dough with a rolling pin. Her forehead is creased in concentration as she works it into a perfect rectangle.

'It smells amazing in here,' I say. 'Like a warm hug.'

She looks up and smiles. 'I didn't know hugs had a specific smell.'

'Well, they do, and this is it. How's it going?'

She gestures with her rolling pin. 'Flat out, as usual. It's always busy in here, but it steps up a notch around the holidays.'

'Lily sent me to ask whether you'd like a cup of coffee. And she wants to know if you'd like some help. Isabella has arrived, so there are three of us.'

'I could use an extra pair of hands,' she admits. 'If you're sure she can spare you.'

'I'm not doing much out there,' I say. 'There's only one customer in the cafe – a woman with a dog called Bernie.'

'That will be Mrs Ogilvie,' she says.

'I think she was called Mabel.'

She smiles. 'I keep forgetting there are two of them now. It's confusing when one of them brings Bernie into the bakery. They're identical twins, so it's difficult to tell who's who until they've taken off their coats.'

'Do they wear name badges?' I say.

'Not that I've noticed. But they dress differently. Mrs Ogilvie is quiet and restrained, and she wears lots of neutrals. Whereas Mabel is a fan of colour – the more, the better. She's been living in Australia until recently. Maybe they dress more brightly out there. But they've both bought themselves the same winter coat, so it's impossible to know which of them is which when you see them on the street.'

She finishes rolling out the gingerbread dough. 'The only real clue is how they speak to Bernie. If he misbehaves, and the woman he's with calls him a naughty boy, you'll know it's Mabel. Mrs Ogilvie worships the ground Bernie walks on. As far as she's concerned, he's terribly misunderstood. She's sure if people appreciated what a wonder he was, they would never believe he'd done anything wrong.'

'This one is definitely Mabel,' I say. 'She told Bernie he'd have to wait for his dog biscuit. I'll fetch your coffee, and you can tell me what you'd like me to do.'

Abby shakes her head. 'I don't feel like a coffee.'

'Are you sure? You didn't have breakfast this morning.'

'I didn't feel like anything to eat. I felt a bit sick.'

'You aren't suffering from morning sickness?' I say, surprised.

'Absolutely not! Although that was the first thing Chris asked me when it started a couple of weeks ago. But I'm definitely not pregnant. We aren't planning on having children for a few more years.'

'Have you seen a doctor?' I ask.

'I went to see my GP a few days ago. He thinks it may be IBS. He recommends I cut out gluten for a month or two and see how I go.'

'That can't be easy in your job,' I say. 'Don't you need to taste everything you make?'

'Generally, but it's an easy workaround in this place. As soon as I mentioned it to Isabella and Lily, Isabella volunteered to take on the job of official taste tester. She's been taking it terribly seriously.'

'It seems to be a subject close to her heart,' I say.

'Or her stomach,' says Abby. 'Anyway, I should be grateful she's willing to help.'

I spend the rest of the morning helping her as best I can. I don't know much about baking, but I'm happy to chop and slice and stir under her supervision.

Isabella appears at noon. 'Time for your lunch break, Grace. I can take over in here. I'm sure Abby has plenty of things for me to taste.'

'I'm not tired,' I say. 'I'm not even hungry. Smelling all these delicious scents seems to have filled me up.'

Isabella looks puzzled. 'I don't see how. Anyway, you'd better take your break now. Things will get busy in half an hour or so. People come into the bakery for lunch, and it's an excellent opportunity for us to show you the ropes.'

I leave them in the kitchen and go back to the shop. Mabel and Bernie are no longer here, but there's a line behind the counter, and several customers are sitting at the tables, chatting and drinking coffee.

Lily looks up when I come in. 'How's it going in there?'

'Fine, I think. I never realised how hard bakers worked. Abby hasn't stopped for a minute.'

'I know,' she says. 'She's looking exhausted, and the Christmas rush hasn't even begun. We need to take as much off her as possible. It's a pity none of us knows how to bake. Maybe she could teach us how to make the bread dough and prepare some of the more basic cookies and slices. Isabella made her first batch of brownies yesterday, but Abby said they weren't quite good enough to sell.'

'I'm happy to learn,' I say. 'Abby will be stretched thin with the Christmas ball on top of everything else.'

'Speaking of the Christmas ball,' says Lily, 'a member of the production team is coming over to the bakery this afternoon. They don't want to start filming yet, but we had a message to say they want to see the layout of the bakery and kitchen in advance.'

'It sounds exciting,' I say. 'It should be fun to watch them work, especially if Isabella and Abby are the ones on camera. I've never been involved with anything like this before.'

'Me neither,' she says.

A van pulls up outside the bakery, and Lily looks at her watch. 'I'm sure they said this afternoon. They must be running ahead of schedule. Could you let Isabella know they've arrived?'

A man gets out of the van and pushes open the door to the shop.

'It's cold out there,' he says, stamping snow off his boots. 'Hi, I'm Rob Marshall.'

'It is a chilly day,' says Lily. 'I had to scrape about ten inches of ice off my windscreen this morning.'

She holds out her hand to him. 'I'm Lily Carson, co-owner of the bakery.'

'Nice to meet you,' says the man.

Lily waves in my direction. 'And this is –'

The man looks at me in astonishment. 'Don't I –?'

'Yes, you do,' I say, just as Lily says, 'Grace Andersen.'

She breaks off and looks at us both. 'Do you two know each other?'

'In a manner of speaking,' I say.

Rob raises an eyebrow. 'You're the last person I expected to see when I walked in here today.'

Chapter Three

We stare at each other for a moment, then I clear my throat.

'Quite a coincidence. It never crossed my mind it would be your production company doing this thing. I thought yours was called something else entirely.'

'It is,' he says. 'I'm just free-lancing on this one because the editor of the original series had other commitments. The project wasn't originally supposed to last until Christmas. But they thought the Christmas ball would be a great way to round off the series. Our companies often help each other out, and the producer asked for me specially.'

'Do you two know each other?' says Lily curiously. 'I mean, obviously, you do. What I mean to say is, how do you know each other?'

I dart a quick glance at Rob. 'We met a couple of times in London. I haven't seen him for a while.'

I try to keep my tone neutral, but I'm not sure I succeed because she shoots me a questioning look.

'Grace and I went on a few dates,' says Rob.

Why did he have to say that? I gave Lily a perfectly reasonable explanation. He could have left it at that.

'Right,' says Lily. To my annoyance, it looks as though she's suppressing a smile.

'You have work to do,' I tell Rob and see a similar look of amusement pass over his face. I have no idea why. What's so funny about going on a few dates with someone? People do it all the time. Lily and her partner must have been on dates together when they first met. They can't have woken up one morning to find themselves with a baby, with absolutely no idea where she came from.

'This is the bakery and cafe,' Lily tells Rob. 'I hope it's ok for whatever it is you want to do. I'll take you to see the kitchen when you're ready. You'll want to meet Abby, our pastry chef.'

'Sure,' says Rob, pulling out a laser meter. 'Do you mind if I take some measurements first?'

He clicks the meter a few times and jots down some numbers. 'That's great. Lead on!'

'Will you be ok in here by yourself?' Lily asks me. 'I'll only be a minute. I can send Isabella to help you if you like.'

'I'll be fine,' I say shortly.

'Grace only started working here yesterday,' she tells Rob.

'Is that right?' he says. 'And what prompted this career change?'

'It isn't a career change,' I say, annoyed. 'I'm just helping out an old friend.'

'She means Abby,' says Lily. 'She and Grace knew each other in London. Like you and Grace, I suppose …' she trails off uncertainly.

'Not quite the same,' I say. 'I've known Abby for years, whereas Rob and I are barely even acquaintances.'

'Ouch!' murmurs Rob as he passes me.

I busy myself filling the macaron stand while he and Lily are in the kitchen. I can't help feeling a little uneasy knowing he's down here. I've been trying to forget about the dates we went on in London. Why did he have to turn up here when I was having such a good time? I haven't given him a thought in months. I hope no other casual acquaintance with whom I may or may not have gone out a few times turns up in Honeywell. It isn't really important, but I'd been looking forward to having a complete break until Christmas. Break may not be the correct word, but it's a change, which is supposed to be just as good.

I'm doubly glad now that I told Lily I didn't want to be involved with the filming. Rob and his team can spend all their time in the kitchen while I stay out here. It shouldn't take more than a few hours. What is there to film? Abby stirring a few dishes and telling the team about her secret ingredients, and Isabella giving them a potted history of the bakery and treating them to an exhibition of how to make several large cakes disappear in two bites.

Lily and Rob reappear a few minutes later. They're laughing about something, which is annoying. It doesn't seem very professional.

'You have a very nice set up here,' says Rob. 'I like the way you've decorated the place.'

Lily looks pleased. 'We did it ourselves. We didn't have the funds for a professional decorator. Building the cafe took all our budget, and then some.'

'It's always the way,' he says. 'I've never known a building project to come in on time or under budget.'

'You work in TV,' I can't help saying. 'You can't have been involved with much building work.'

'Not at work,' he says. 'But I had that extension done on my flat. Don't you remember?'

'No,' I say coolly. 'I don't think I ever went to your flat.'

'Are you sure? I could swear I cooked you dinner one evening.'

'You're mixing me up with someone else,' I say. 'An easy mistake to make.'

'Is it?' he says. 'I think you're fairly memorable.'

I flush. 'I didn't mean that. I mean you must cook dinner for so many women that you lose track.'

Lily looks surprised, and I remember where I am. I soften the sting by giving him a friendly smile. It's a little forced, but it will have to do.

'Chance would be a fine thing,' says Rob lightly.

I feel a fresh wave of annoyance. 'I somehow think you've had your fair share of chances.'

'Can I make you a drink while you're here?' says Lily before Rob can answer.

Why did she ask him that? He's here in a professional capacity. There's no need for her to worry about his hydration levels. I hope she means to charge him for it.

'That sounds great,' he says, and my heart sinks. Doesn't he have other bakers to go and annoy before he knocks off work for the day?

'Shall I go and help Abby in the kitchen?' I say hopefully.

'Isabella's in there,' says Lily. 'I need you out here.'

'What would you like to drink?' she asks Rob.

'I wouldn't say no to a latte,' he says.

'Grace?' she asks.

'I'm fine. Besides, it isn't my break time.'

'It's your lunchtime,' she says. 'And I've kept you waiting for it. Why don't I make you a coffee, and you can get yourself some food and catch up with Rob while you eat?'

I don't dare to glare at her while Rob is watching, but I could have done without this.

Lily doesn't appear to notice. 'Shall I make you a latte too?'

'I'll have a cappuccino,' I say grudgingly.

'Have you had lunch, Rob?' she asks.

I will him to say he's already enjoyed the eight-course tasting menu at the Quayside Hotel. But of course, he doesn't.

'Not yet. But don't worry. I have some sandwiches in the van.'

'Great!' I say. 'Perhaps you'd prefer your coffee to go?'

Rob gives me a confused look, but Lily is quicker. 'Nonsense. It's freezing out there, and Rob's driven all the way over to Honeywell. The least we can do is give him lunch. Abby's made some steak pies.'

'That sounds great,' he says. 'If you're sure it's no trouble.'

'Not at all. It's what we do,' she says, handing him his drink. 'Would you like a pie too, Grace?'

'No, thanks. I'm vegetarian.'

'Really?' says Rob. 'I could have sworn we went out for a steak together.'

'Like I said, that must have been some other woman. I've been a vegetarian for years.'

'I'll have to remember that,' says Lily. 'We have some vegetable pies if you'd like one of those.'

I'm about to politely refuse, so I don't have to sit and eat with Rob, but my stomach gives a huge rumble. I won't get through the afternoon unless I have something proper to eat. I can't subsist entirely on cake, although Isabella appears to. Still, she's had years of practise, while I'm a complete novice.

'That sounds good,' I say. 'But I can eat it while I work. Isabella says it gets busy in here over lunchtime.'

'I can manage,' she says. 'We can't fall foul of staff health and safety rules. Sit down anywhere, you two, and I'll bring your pies over.'

I almost pretend to misunderstand her and sit at a different table to Rob, but I don't want to risk looking petulant. I also don't want Rob thinking this is a bigger deal than it is. I barely remember him, let alone any of the dates we supposedly went on. Which means it won't a problem sharing a table with him for as long as it takes me to eat a pie and gulp down my coffee. If Rob finds it awkward, that's his problem.

He doesn't appear to. He pulls out a chair for me. 'Quite a surprise seeing you here.'

'So you said.' I catch Lily's eye and force a smile.

'How have you been?' he says.

'Since when?'

He gives me a half smile. 'Since I last saw you.'

'I can't remember when that was, so I'm not sure.'

'The fifteenth of August,' he says. 'We went to my firm's summer party.'

'Did we? Oh, yes, that rings a faint bell. Somewhere in Surrey, wasn't it?'

'Kent. My firm has a country house near Aylesford. It poured with rain, if you remember.'

'Vaguely,' I say. 'Was it really that recently?'

'I'm afraid so,' he says. 'So, how have you been since the fifteenth of August?'

'Fine, thanks.' I sense Lily's eyes on me again and add politely, 'And you?'

'Also fine. We seem to have lost contact after that. I hope it wasn't the rain. I put in an order for sunshine that day, but I may have got the date wrong when I filled in the form.'

'I wish someone would fill in a form for sunshine this week,' says Lily. 'My feet haven't thawed out in days. Here are your pies.'

She puts the plates in front of us and disappears to serve a customer. I stare at my pie, trying not to look at Rob.

'Well, this is awkward,' he says.

'Isn't it?' I agree.

He takes a sip of his coffee. 'Although I don't exactly know why.'

'Seriously?' I say, jerked out of my studied composure.

He looks puzzled. 'Seriously. It was your choice not to see me again, which is of course fine. You didn't owe me anything. But you're the one who stopped answering my messages, so I'm not sure why you seem so annoyed.'

'I'm not annoyed,' I say, trying to keep my tone light.

'The way you're gripping your cutlery would suggest otherwise.'

I glance down at my white-knuckled grip on my fork and force myself to relax. 'I'm not annoyed, but I'm not exactly thrilled to run into you like this.'

'I get it,' he says. 'But we're adults. We can be civil, right?'

'Of course,' I say, taking a bite of my pie. It's delicious, but Rob watching me eat makes me feel self-conscious.

'What are you looking at?' I say.

'It's just that I don't remember you being a vegetarian. We ate lobster tarts at my firm's party. They serve them every year. I could have sworn you had some because I remember you making a joke about it being shellfish of you to take the last one.'

'That doesn't sound like me. You must be thinking of someone else.'

'If you say so. Someone who was wearing a beautiful pale green dress.'

'How am I supposed to know what she was wearing?' I say, and he laughs.

'Fine, it wasn't you. You've never eaten lobster and steak in your life. And you wouldn't be seen dead in green.'

'Everything ok?' says Lily as she passes.

'Wonderful,' says Rob. 'This is far better than a packet of cheese and tomato sandwiches.'

'Why didn't you put something different in them if you don't like cheese and tomato?' I ask.

'Maybe the hotel made them,' suggests Lily.

'I bought them at a petrol station on the way over here,' he says. 'They were the last ones left. I could leave them here for you, Grace, as you're a vegetarian.'

'No need,' I say. 'I'm staying with two bakers while I'm here. I'm sure they both have a more adventurous repertoire than that. We had a lovely risotto last night.'

'Then I shall look out for some local ducks on my way home,' he says. 'They're also vegetarian, I believe. They may enjoy a sandwich. I doubt they get their beaks on much risotto.'

I pick up my plate and mug. 'It was nice chatting to you, but my lunch break is over. I should help Lily with … something or other.'

He pushes back his chair. 'I should get going too. It's been good to see you again, Grace. I've often thought about you since the party you and I definitely didn't attend together. Maybe we could –'

'I'm sure I'll see you around,' I say quickly. 'When you bring the film crew over to Honeywell, perhaps?'

I don't add that I'll do my best to make sure I'm out for a long lunch that day. I'll hack into the bakery computer and add a doctor's appointment if necessary.

He appears to get the message. 'Of course. I'll look forward to it.'

He tries to pay for his lunch, but Lily waves him away. 'Don't worry about it. Let us know when you want to start filming.'

'I'll give you as much notice as possible,' he promises. With a quick wave to me that I pretend not to see, he leaves the bakery.

Chapter Four

Lily watches him climb into the van and drive away. 'That was … unexpected.'

'I suppose it was,' I say. 'I hope I wasn't rude to him.'

'I've seen warmer icebergs. What's the story with you two?'

'No story.' I busy myself wiping tables, so I don't have to meet her eye.

'There must be something,' she says.

I feel a sudden wave of shame. 'I'm sorry, Lily. I didn't mean to make things uncomfortable for you. I had a few dates with Rob in London, that's all. It was a shock when he walked in today, but only because I wasn't expecting him.'

'I can see that. Did things end badly between the pair of you?'

'Not at all!' I say rather too quickly. 'I decided not to see him again, that's all. We weren't right for each other.'

She picks up a tea towel. 'That doesn't sound too bad. I'm glad it's nothing worse because we all have to work together. It won't be for long, but it's important we get along. Important for the bakery, I mean.'

She looks so anxious that I feel a fresh wave of shame. 'I understand that. No problem. It was strange seeing him when I assumed he was miles away. At least, that's what I'd have thought if I'd thought about it at all. Which I hadn't.'

Is that a gleam of amusement in her eyes? I hope not. There's nothing to be amused about. On the scale of things to which I should devote another minute's thought, this is a negative eight.

I half expect her to say something more about Rob, but she doesn't.

'I had a similar shock myself a few years ago,' she says. 'I'd just started work here at the bakery when my ex-boyfriend walked in demanding I decorate some Valentine's cookies for his new girlfriend. Who, by the way, just happened to be Isabella.'

'Seriously? That must have been weird for you.'

'That's one word for it,' she says. 'I could have come up with others. Luckily, my boss was there, so I was forced to be polite. I was too shocked to be anything else. To be fair, it was pretty awkward for Stephen too. He had no idea I was working here. Like you and Rob.'

'Not like me and Rob!' I say. I don't want her getting the wrong idea about us and passing her conclusions on to Isabella and Abby. Or, heaven forbid, the customers. Lily doesn't seem like a gossip, but it's best not to take any chances.

'I meant that Stephen didn't know I was working here,' she says. 'Can you imagine a more awkward situation than that?'

'Not outside a novel. What happened, if you don't mind me asking?'

'I made the cookies,' she says. 'He wanted them to spell Isabella's name. It was a struggle not to ice a rude message onto them instead, but I told myself I was a mature professional. I also needed the work. I'd been made redundant from my job in London, and I was desperate for the money.'

Her face crumples into laughter. 'Isabella would happily have eaten them even if they'd said *Hands off my man!* or *Get lost, witch!*

'Isabella would have eaten what?' says Isabella, appearing from the kitchen carrying a tray of gingerbread people. 'Don't these look amazing? I helped Abby to ice them, and I only ate one. He had a broken leg, so I put him out of his misery.'

'Was his leg broken when he came out of the oven?' says Lily.

'Unclear,' says Isabella. 'Anyway, I have to protect Abby from the gluten, so it was my moral duty to try at least one. And it's survival of the fittest where cookies are concerned. The gingerbread man I chose was the wounded one. He'd only have held the group back if they'd been planning to storm the bakery and escape.'

'They wouldn't have got far,' says Lily. 'I've just seen Bernie walking up the high street with one of his owners. I can't tell which one it is. Them buying the same navy winter coat was a mistake. Maybe we should give them each a brooch so we can tell them apart. Mabel would love a nice parrot.'

'What would Mrs Ogilvie like?' says Isabella.

'No idea,' says Lily. 'A cavoodle, maybe?'

'One of the gingerbread people is for Daisy,' says Isabella. 'I decorated it with a torch and a tiny tiara.' She holds up the cookie for us to inspect.

'A torch?' I say, and Lily laughs.

'Long story. It's gorgeous, Isabella! She'll love it. Come back to Mum and Dad's with me tonight, and the pair of you can do a cookie swap.'

Isabella lays down the tray. 'I'll put this in a box before I do anything else. Daisy would never forgive me if I allowed a customer to catch sight of it and buy it. What were you two talking about when I came in? Something about me eating something? You'll have to be an awful lot more specific than that.'

'I was telling Grace about you and Stephen,' says Lily, taking the gingerbread person and putting it into a pink and white striped box.

'I love that story!' says Isabella. 'Tell it to me again.'

'You know exactly how it ends,' says Lily.

'But Grace doesn't. It's a wonderful story. It has all the elements of a great novel – love, tragedy, kidnap, revenge, vampires, car crashes, and of course cake!'

'I don't remember the vampires,' says Lily. 'I'm not sure about the car crashes either.'

'Really?' says Isabella. 'The way you drive, I'm almost sure there must have been a couple.'

'And the revenge?' says Lily. 'I don't remember that either.'

'Of course, there was,' says Isabella. 'Haven't you heard the famous saying that eating cake is the best revenge?'

'That's living well,' I say.

'No, it's definitely that cake thing,' says Isabella.

'As long as any story contained cookies, you'd think it was a beautiful love story,' says Lily.

'I'm intrigued,' I say. 'I can't imagine an ex-boyfriend wandering in and asking me to make cookies for his new girlfriend. Did you kill him on the spot, Lily? Is his body under the bakery patio?'

'We don't have a patio,' says Isabella. 'Luckily for Stephen.'

Lily smiles. 'I was explaining to Grace that I behaved with my usual exquisite courtesy and professionalism.'

'Of course, you did,' says Isabella. 'It all seems a lifetime ago. Think how much has happened since then. Lily and I have bought the bakery and added on the cafe. Abby has joined the staff. Mrs Ogilvie now thinks we're the greatest thing since the invention of medium-thick sliced brown bread. And of course, my lovely goddaughter has been born.'

'I was wondering when you'd mention her,' says Lily.

'You haven't met Daisy yet,' Isabella tells me. 'She's the most adorable child you'll ever meet. Much like I imagine myself to have been at that age, only cuter, if that's possible.'

'I usually accuse Isabella of exaggerating,' says Lily. 'But in this case, she's telling the truth. Daisy is gorgeous. But it's difficult to appreciate her loveliness while she's going through her sleep allergy phase.'

'It gives you all the more time to enjoy her,' says Isabella. 'As her godmother, I have the best of both worlds. I get to spend as much time as I like with Daisy, but I can give her back at bedtime.'

'Having whipped her up into a frenzy,' says Lily. 'Isabella and Daisy have invented a wonderful new game called Twinkle Tag. I don't know which of them came up with it, but it's a nightmare when Jack and I are trying to get Daisy to bed. I'm not sure of the rules, but the game appears to involve a torch and glitter and a lot of crashing into furniture.'

'It's difficult for me too,' complains Isabella. 'I get overexcited, and I can't sleep. Lily has to make me a mug of Ovaltine to calm me down. Anyway, we're getting off the subject. Why were you telling Grace the story of the Valentine cookies?'

My mind jerks back to reality. I'd forgotten we were talking about Rob.

'I used to know the guy who came in here earlier,' I say with forced cheerfulness. 'That must have triggered the memory for her.'

Isabella looks interested. 'Was he the love of your life?'

'Not remotely. Not even an ex-boyfriend.'

'Did he by any chance ask you to make him cookies?' she says. 'I could help you if he did. I'm excellent at spelling long names.'

'No, he didn't,' I say shortly, and she and Lily exchange glances.

'Grace met him in London,' says Lily.

'He didn't mention it to me,' says Isabella.

'We barely knew each other, so there's no reason he should,' I say before she can get any ideas. Isabella strikes me as a woman with a vivid imagination, and one she holds on the loosest of reins.

'It's a terrible name to ice onto cookies,' she says. 'ROB. It's barely a mouthful.'

'But the cookies would be for his girlfriend,' Lily points out. 'For all we know, she may be called something like Georgiana Westwood de Montclair.'

'In which case, you're on your own,' says Isabella. 'My spelling has its limits. Hopefully, his girlfriend is called something long yet easy to spell. If he even has a girlfriend.'

'I would imagine that's a given,' I say. 'From the little I know about him, he's never without one – or several.'

'Is that right?' says Isabella. 'It shows you can never tell. He doesn't look the type. But if he did look the type, women would run a mile, so he's wise to keep his wolfish tendencies under wraps. Rather good-looking wraps, too, I must say.'

'Are you planning to discover his hidden shallows for yourself?' I ask.

She shakes her head. 'I never play second fiddle to anyone. If someone is dating me, they'd better not have eyes for anyone else. My mother always says the moment you notice your boyfriend's attention wandering, dump him and move on. You should never do the pick-me dance.'

'Is that a real thing?' says Lily.

'Of course!' says Isabella. She sashays from side to side like a penguin on melting ice, before spinning around several times, apparently strumming an air guitar.

I wait until she's whirled herself into the coffee machine, rubbed her elbow, and collapsed breathlessly into the nearest chair.

'How did the Valentine's story end?' I ask. 'You can't leave me hanging like this.'

Isabella smiles. 'Let's just say that Lily and I discovered friendship is more important than any man. Even one who orders cookies with your name on. We Sugarloaf bakers have to stick together. That includes you too, Grace, now you've joined us. So, if the pair of you would like to be upstanding, I propose we all raise a doughnut to Mates Before Dates!'

Chapter Five

Abby comes into the bakery mid-afternoon.

'Are you ok?' I say when I see her. 'You're looking even paler than you were this morning.'

'I don't feel too good,' she says, sitting down at a table.

'Have you had any lunch?' asks Isabella.

'Not yet. I haven't felt like it.'

'But you didn't have breakfast either,' I say.

'No wonder you're feeling awful,' says Isabella. 'I should have checked on you earlier. What can I get you? The sandwich press awaits your orders. Or would you prefer a pie?'

'I'm fine,' says Abby. 'I'll get myself something to eat when I've finished making the Danish pastries.'

'You'll have something now,' says Isabella. 'I'm not having you pass out in the kitchen. You might squash the pastries.'

Lily switches on the coffee machine. 'One latte coming up. And you must have something to eat. You look exhausted.'

'I haven't been sleeping too well,' says Abby. 'I'm not convinced the doctor is right about this gluten thing. But it's probably something I've been eating. I always feel worse after dinner. I get this sharp pain, and indigestion tablets don't seem to help. I expect I've been overdoing it. I'm glad you've arrived to take some of the day-to-day stuff off my hands, Grace. It will make a big difference, especially now we have to prepare for the Christmas ball.'

'You ought to see the doctor again,' says Lily. 'Why not call the surgery now while I prepare your toasted sandwich?'

'I'll do that in a while,' says Abby. 'I'd love a cheese and tomato toastie. You'd better use the gluten-free bread, so I can tell the doctor with a clear conscience I've been following all his rules, and they're making no difference.'

Lily makes her a toasted sandwich while Abby sips her coffee.

'Thanks,' she says when Lily hands her the plate. 'I just needed a break.'

'That's what we're here for,' says Isabella.

'Except we're the ones who got her into this state in the first place,' says Lily. 'I'm sorry, Abby. We'll try to take more of the work off you. Would you like us to go back to ordering in our bread again, at least until Christmas?'

'Not yet,' says Abby. 'I'm feeling better already. This toastie is hitting the spot. I should get back to work soon. Danish pastry day is Isabella's favourite day.'

'First, call the surgery and find out how soon they can see you,' says Lily. 'And when you've done that, you're going home. The bakery won't fall down if you leave an hour early.'

Abby starts to protest, but Isabella stops her. 'I wouldn't, not when Lily is using her Mummy voice. She doesn't use it often. But when she does, Daisy and I know better than to argue with her. She used it last week when we were in the middle of a game of hide and seek in the dark. I was terrified I'd be sent home with a note.'

'You would have been if I hadn't been sure you'd lose it in a puddle on the way home,' says Lily.

'It does sound tempting,' says Abby. 'A nap might do me good and get me back into a decent sleep pattern.'

'I can drive you,' I offer. 'It's only ten minutes each way.'

'No need,' says Abby. 'I'll text Chris. It's his half day today, so he can give me a lift. He didn't want me to come into work this morning. He'll be delighted to have been proved right.'

'I'm sure he won't,' I say. 'Not when he sees you looking like that.'

'Mildly smug, then,' she says.

Isabella heaves an enormous sigh. 'Men! I don't know how we live with them.'

'You don't,' says Lily.

'I prefer not to parade my superior judgement in front of you,' says Isabella. 'But you're right. I've made the correct call.'

'Can someone put those cookies into the oven for me?' says Abby.

'We'll look after everything,' promises Lily. 'It won't ruin our business if we don't have Danish pastries today. No one except Isabella will notice. And it will do her good to learn some patience.'

'There's that Mummy voice again,' says Isabella. 'But she's right. And I noticed you made Bakewell tarts this morning. Don't worry about me. I'll muddle through.' She gives us what is clearly intended to be a brave and self-sacrificing smile.

'How much extra work does Christmas make for you?' I ask, and they all laugh.

'More than you can imagine,' says Isabella. 'I almost quit on the spot during our first year.'

'It's all go in the kitchen,' says Abby. 'We're pushed to our limits keeping up with the Christmas rush in the bakery, let alone having to supply the hotel with desserts.'

'It will be a challenge,' agrees Lily. 'I sometimes wish we hadn't bid for that contract. I don't want to take on so much that we start dropping balls all over the place.'

'What do you usually do for Christmas?' I ask.

Isabella considers. 'We provide seasonal products – festive cookies iced with holly leaves and gingerbread house kits. Last year, we held a cookie decorating workshop for the children and a mulled wine and mince pie evening for the adults. We also make up special gift boxes. Our snowflake cookies are always a hit.'

'And we don't have to ice letters onto them,' says Lily.

Chris arrives a few minutes later. He takes one look at Abby and shakes his head. 'I called the GP before I left. They're fully booked today, but they can see you first thing in the morning.'

'Not any earlier?' says Isabella.

'I was lucky to get an appointment so soon,' he says. 'I had to lay it on thick with the receptionist. I told her how bad Abby has been feeling. Looking at her now, I'm not sure I gave the full picture.'

He helps her on with her coat. 'They told me to take you to the hospital if it was an emergency.'

'Which it isn't,' says Abby. 'I just need a rest.'

'Don't let her come in tomorrow if she isn't feeling better,' says Lily.

'I won't,' he promises.

We watch him help Abby into the car and drive away.

'You don't think I'm about to become a godmother for a second time?' says Isabella.

'She told me she isn't pregnant,' I say. 'And she should know. Don't suggest that to her.'

'I wouldn't dream of it,' she says. 'Tact may not be my middle name, but I would never ask someone such an intrusive question. That's why I asked you!'

'Hopefully, she'll feel better after a good night's sleep,' says Lily.

'And if she won't settle down for a nap,' says Isabella, 'Grace can let you know, and you can go over there and use your scariest Mummy voice. That ought to sort her out.'

Chapter Six

I go straight back to the flat after work. I'm eager to find out how Abby is doing. She opens the door to me, and I'm pleased to see she has a little more colour in her cheeks.

'Did you have a nap?' I ask.

'I crashed out as soon as I lay down on the sofa. I slept for almost two hours, and I feel much better for it.'

'That's good, but I don't think you should go into work tomorrow.'

'Nonsense,' she says. 'I'll be fine after a good night's sleep. Chris is making gluten free ravioli tonight, which should complete the cure.'

'I'm glad you're feeling hungry again. Isabella was quite concerned. I don't believe she'd worry about a compound fracture as long as you hadn't lost your appetite.'

'She wouldn't,' says Abby. 'I've never known someone to eat so much yet remain perpetually hungry. She could make good money as a medical test subject.'

'I'm glad you're seeing your GP tomorrow,' I say. 'There's no sense in running yourself into the ground, especially with

Christmas coming up. I'll go and see whether Chris needs help with dinner. You stay here and rest. Doctor's orders. At least, until you can talk to the real thing tomorrow morning.'

Chris comes into the living room. He's wearing an apron saying, 'Doughnut Disturb', and his hands are covered in flour.

'You're making the ravioli yourself?' I say. 'I'm impressed.'

'You didn't expect me to open a tin?'

'Why not? That's what I do. On a good day. On a bad one, I call and order a pizza.'

'I'll assume you're joking,' he says.

'You're welcome to think that if it makes you feel better.'

'Dinner in five,' he says and disappears back into the kitchen.

'Chris is a stickler for making everything from scratch,' says Abby. 'He says it's his training. But he and I have the same qualifications, and there's nothing I enjoy more than tinned soup or frozen pizza after a hard day at work. But if he's happy to cook, I won't argue.'

'I'm not sure I've ever had homemade ravioli,' I say. 'I thought it came out of a tin, filled with some meat adjacent product and swimming in an iridescent orange sauce that resembles the runoff from a nuclear waste facility.'

'You won't last long around here if you keep talking like that,' says Abby. 'I'll have to buy Chris a fainting couch. He takes his food seriously.'

'I'll be sure to make appreciative noises,' I promise. 'But that brings me to something I've been meaning to discuss with you. It's several more weeks until Christmas. I can't stay with you and Chris for the entire time.'

'Why not?' she says. 'Does his snoring bother you?'

'Does he snore?'

'Not that I'm aware of. But I'm usually asleep the moment my head hits the pillow. I like to tell him he does. It stops him thinking he's too perfect.'

'He seems almost perfect to me,' I say. 'Pleasant, easy-going, polite, and an amazing cook. Plus, he clearly adores you. I think you've done pretty well for yourself.'

'He's great,' she admits. 'And my parents love him too, which is nice. He and Dad play golf together each week.'

'How is your dad? You told me when you called last week that he was doing much better. Is he back to normal now?'

'He gets tired more easily than he used to,' she says. 'But so does Mum, and she hasn't had a stroke. She says he can be grumpy when he's tired. Chris told her so can I, and the solution is always a good meal and a hot bath. Dad says he doesn't dare snap at Mum nowadays because he'll hear the sound of running water a minute later. Mum can be quite literal at times.'

'I'm glad he's doing well,' I say. 'It must have been an anxious time for you all.'

Chris puts his head around the door. 'Dinner's on the table. I hope you're both hungry.'

'I know I am,' says Abby, pulling herself to her feet. She winces as she stands, and Chris looks concerned.

'I'm fine,' she says. 'I've been sitting in one position for too long. I'm not used to spending my afternoons napping on the sofa. It feels all wrong.'

I wait until Chris has served the ravioli before raising the subject of my accommodation again. 'I was telling Abby I need to find myself somewhere to live while I'm here.'

'Is Abby's snoring disturbing you?' he says, and she laughs.

'You may both snore like the Niagara Falls for all I'm aware,' I say. 'The point is that it's almost six weeks until Christmas. I can't stay here for that long. You know what they say about houseguests and fish.'

'They both like to spend a long time in the bathtub?' he says.

'Very funny. But it's true. They both stink after a few days. I should look for some alternative accommodation, so we don't end up falling out. Where would you suggest?'

'Here!' says Abby stubbornly. 'Chris doesn't mind, and I'll enjoy the company. We barely see each other in the run up to Christmas. Our shifts never seem to coincide, and we're too tired to talk in the evenings. Even Chris resorts to the odd ready meal when I'm out. He thinks I don't know, but I always discover the evidence in the recycling bin.'

'She has a vivid imagination,' says Chris. 'But Abby's right. We don't see much of each other in December. It will be nice to have you here to keep her company. And I can't let you go until I've persuaded you of the merits of cooking from scratch. My mission is for you to run screaming from the sight of a tin by the time you leave us.'

'I look forward to taking part in the experiment,' I say. 'But I think we should see how it goes. Isabella says she has a spare room too. Maybe I could alternate weeks and give you all a break.'

'Isabella can't cook,' says Chris. 'As far as I can tell, she lives off baked goods, takeaways, and whatever the Red Lion has on special that week. You'll be better off here.'

Abby says good night after dinner and goes to bed.

'There's nothing wrong with her,' says Chris as we clear the table and pack the dishwasher. 'She's just trying to get out of clearing up. It's a drastic way of going about it, but surprisingly effective.'

'Let's hope the doctor agrees with you,' I say.

I go to bed early too. I'm tired after my first couple of days at the bakery. The work itself isn't too exhausting, but it's full on. Isabella has assured me it will get far worse over the next few weeks, but I don't mind. I haven't come here to sit around all day. And it's a great place to work. I've always got on well with Abby, and Lily and Isabella are fun co-workers. There are worse places to spend Christmas than Honeywell. Not being in London is a bonus, having to watch everyone rushing off to work each morning. I'm glad to be out of the city for a while.

That may be the reason why I was so taken aback to see Rob this afternoon. It wasn't him – it was what he represented. He's a part, albeit a tiny one, of the life I'm temporarily trying to avoid. It was annoying when he appeared, forming a connection between my two worlds.

I wish now I hadn't been so snippy with him. He may have taken it to mean I had a personal problem with him and the way things ended between us. Not that they ever really started, but men are vain. Isabella is right to say Rob's good looking, with his wavy brown hair and deep brown eyes. I expect he thinks every woman he meets is ready to fall at his feet. He'll assume women like me, who've chosen not to see him again, are regretting their decisions and longing for another chance.

I fall asleep thinking about this and dream of snorkelling over a coral reef that bears a distinct resemblance to Chris and Abby's bathtub. Soft music plays as I drift over the coral. It gradually turns into a shrieking noise. I'm about to tell the nearest fish to turn down the volume when it turns and swims towards me. It flashes a torch into my eyes, emitting a faint blue radiance.

I roll over and sit up, wide awake. That noise isn't underwater muzak. It's a real-life siren. The torch is real too, only it's a flashing blue light. I jump out of bed and run over to the window. There's an ambulance outside. As I watch, the siren stops, and two women appear from our building wheeling a stretcher. I don't need to see the shock of brown hair to know it's Abby. Chris is standing on the pavement talking to the paramedics.

I grab my coat and run down the stairs in my bare feet, scarcely noticing the cold as I reach the street.

'What's happening?' I gasp.

'Abby woke up half an hour ago in a terrible state,' says Chris. 'She tried to sit up, but she passed out. I'm going with her to the hospital. I'll call you when I know anything.'

He jumps into the back of the ambulance. The paramedic slams the door shut, and they speed away.

Chapter Seven

I'm waiting outside the bakery when Lily arrives the following morning.

'It's nice to see our newest member of staff so punctual,' she says as she unlocks the door.

I follow her inside and pull off my coat.

'Are you alright?' she says. 'You're almost as pale as Abby. I hope you haven't caught whatever she has.'

'I haven't. I –'

'Did you drive in alone, or did you drop her off at the surgery on your way in?'

I sink into a chair, and she studies me more closely. 'Grace, what's wrong?'

'It's Abby.'

She looks alarmed. 'She isn't feeling worse, is she?'

'You could say that. She was rushed to the hospital in the middle of the night. It was awful, Lily. I woke up to hear an ambulance outside the flat. I looked out to see Abby on a stretcher. They raced away with the sirens going and the blue lights flashing.'

Her eyes are wide with horror. 'Did Chris go with her?'

'Yes. I arrived downstairs as the ambulance was leaving. He didn't call me for several hours. All I could do was sit and wait.'

'You poor thing,' she says. 'What was it?'

'Peritonitis. Chris called eventually to say they'd rushed her into surgery the minute she arrived at the hospital. He said they only just made it in time. Her appendix had burst, and sepsis had set in.'

Lily looks aghast. 'That's terrible! But they managed to operate ok?'

'Just in time, by the sounds of it. Chris said the surgical team was amazing. They had her out of the ambulance and into the operating theatre in less than fifteen minutes. But the surgery itself took a long time.'

'I can hardly imagine,' she says. 'Daisy was in hospital this summer, which was grim. But she was never in danger. Is Chris still there?'

'I think so. I doubt he had any sleep.'

'Neither did you, from what I can see. You look done in.'

'I slept for a few hours before the ambulance arrived at about three a.m.'

'Have you had any more updates?' she says.

'Not since Chris called to say the surgery had been successful. But Abby isn't out of danger. She's in the high dependency unit. He says she'll be there for some time.'

Lily switches on the coffee machine. 'First things first. You could do with a drink.'

'I could,' I say gratefully. 'I didn't even think about it this morning.'

'And something to eat,' she says.

'I'm not hungry, just caffeine deprived.'

'It wasn't a question,' she says. 'Choose some food for yourself, or I'll choose it for you.'

'Channelling your inner Isabella?' I say with a slight smile. 'Fine, I'll have a cheese roll. I don't often feel like eating sweet things in the morning.'

'You definitely aren't channelling *your* inner Isabella,' she says. 'Here you are. Eat that while I make our drinks. You'll feel better when you've eaten something.'

'Is this what Isabella refers to as your Mummy voice?'

She smiles. 'Yes, but it's my nice Mummy voice. It's the one I use to make suggestions I expect to be followed, while giving the illusion of choice. It works with Daisy, so I thought it might work with you too.'

I sip the latte she hands me. 'I don't take sugar …' I begin.

'You do today,' she says.

I'm too tired to argue, so I drink it obediently. The sugar, plus the jolt of caffeine, revives me.

Lily selects a mince pie and sits down. 'First things first. What can we do for Abby and Chris? Do her parents know yet?'

'Chris rang them while the ambulance was on its way, and they met him at the hospital.'

'I hope her father is alright,' she says. 'You know he had a stroke a while back?'

'Yes, but Abby says he's almost back to normal now. And I'm sure the hospital will have his records if there's any problem.'

'Abby's mum will make sure of that!' she says. 'She's a lovely woman, but she can be fierce when it comes to protecting her family.'

'Chris said they were magnificent. They're coming home to have a nap this morning, then going back to the hospital to give him a break. I imagine they'll tag team each other for a while.'

The door flies open and Isabella bursts in.

'Drat!' she says when she sees us. 'I was hoping to get here ahead of you for once. I planned to be sitting in the office doing the accounts when you all arrived. I would have been politely surprised to see you.'

Noticing the look on Lily's face, she stops. 'What's wrong?'

'They rushed Abby to hospital last night with peritonitis,' I say.

All traces of laughter disappear from her face. 'That's awful. Is she alright?'

'She made it through the surgery. But the sepsis means she'll be in the high-dependency ward for a while.'

She drops into a chair. 'I can't believe it. She was fine yesterday. Not fine, exactly, but not at death's door. How did she go downhill so quickly?'

'Maybe she felt worse than she would admit,' says Lily. 'You know how Abby is. She never wants to let anyone down.'

'It's our fault,' says Isabella. 'We knew how much pressure we were piling on her, but we didn't do anything about it.'

'Yes, we did,' says Lily. 'We got Grace here to help us. And thank goodness we did.'

Isabella doesn't look convinced. 'We should never have taken on this Christmas thing. What were we thinking?'

'That's nonsense!' I say. 'I'm not saying Abby hasn't been busy. Clearly, she has. But even without much medical knowledge, I know overwork doesn't cause appendicitis. Otherwise, half the country would be in hospital most years.'

'No, they wouldn't,' says Isabella. 'If half the country had their appendixes removed one year and the rest had them removed the following year, there'd be no work at all for the doctors.'

'And a lot of jars on mantlepieces,' says Lily. 'Do people still do that?'

'I hope Abby doesn't intend to,' I say. 'It would put me off my ravioli completely.'

'Grace is right,' she says. 'We didn't give Abby appendicitis. All we can do is hope she recovers as quickly as possible and offer Chris and her parents any help they need.'

'I don't suppose we can see her?' says Isabella.

'I doubt it,' says Lily. 'But there must be plenty of other things we can do. The moment my mum hears about it, she'll be filling all their freezers, so they don't have to cook for a month.'

'What about the Christmas ball?' I ask.

'We'll have to cancel it,' says Isabella. 'Not the ball itself. That can still go ahead. But they'll have to find someone else to do the desserts. We should let them know as soon as possible.'

Lily frowns. 'You may be right.'

'Of course, I'm right,' says Isabella. 'We can't manage something like that by ourselves. It's a shame because we were counting on the extra money. Things are tight enough as it is without us losing another source of income. And it isn't just the money. It's the publicity. We wanted to be in a good position to bid for their Valentine's ball. It isn't as big an affair as the Christmas one, but it would have been a great opportunity for us.'

'Could you outsource it?' I suggest. 'The contract is only to provide the desserts. The organisers won't care who prepares them, as long as they're well made.'

Lily shakes her head. 'That won't work. We have the camera crew coming over to watch us prepare. Or rather, they're coming to watch Abby prepare. We can't pass off someone else's work as our own. It wouldn't be ethical, anyway. Whoever makes those desserts deserves the credit for them. It's bad luck it won't be us. But there's always next year.'

She tries to speak cheerfully, but I can see it's a blow.

'Not if whoever gets the contract makes a success of it,' says Isabella. 'Maybe we can sabotage whoever it is, like that awful bakery did to us during the Mix-up.'

'What?' I ask.

'It's a long story,' says Lily. 'We aren't sabotaging anyone, Isabella. That wouldn't be in the Christmas spirit, and you know it. We'll have to drink Christmas spirits instead and make the best of it.'

'Killjoy!' says Isabella. 'But you're right that we don't want to stoop to Dave Collins' level. We'd have to take yoga lessons to get that low. I'll give the hotel a call now and explain what's happened. It will be difficult enough managing our usual Christmas work without worrying about the ball too. As you say, it's lucky we have Grace. That shows considerable forethought on my part.'

My phone rings, and I jump. 'It's Chris!' I mouth to the other two, and they watch my face intently as I speak to him.

I switch off my phone. 'It's good news. He says Abby is awake and doing as well as can be expected.'

'Thank goodness!' says Isabella with no trace of her usual levity.

Lily nods. 'That's wonderful. Did Chris mention anything we could do to help?'

'He wasn't too coherent,' I say. 'He hasn't slept at all, so that's not a surprise. I didn't want to bother him with questions. He says Abby's parents may pop in here on their way back to the hospital. They should be able to give us more news.'

'I'll call the hotel now,' says Isabella. 'After that, I'd better get onto our old suppliers and see if they can help us out. They may not have much availability left in the run up to Christmas.'

'Don't call the hotel straightaway,' says Lily.

'They need to know,' says Isabella. 'The more notice we can give them, the less annoyed they'll be.'

Lily flushes. 'I know I'm being ridiculous, but an extra half a day can't hurt. I want to think about this some more and make sure we've exhausted all available possibilities before telling them.'

'Fine,' says Isabella. 'Although what you think you can come up with beats me. None of us can cook, at least not to a professional standard. That's Abby's job. Maybe we shouldn't have put all our free-range, locally sourced, organic eggs into one basket. But it's too late to worry about that now. You aren't thinking of roping Jack in? I can tell you right now that would never work.'

'I'm not stupid,' says Lily. 'Not unless we think we can get away with serving scrambled egg *au fromage* and baked beans *en croûte* to the cream of Hampshire society. But he could be useful for odd jobs. He's always willing to lend a hand.'

'Chris?' suggests Isabella. 'No, that wouldn't work. He'll be looking after Abby for the foreseeable future. We can't ask him to do anything else. And when she's home again, he has his own bakery to run. They must be as busy as we are over Christmas.'

'Definitely not Chris,' agrees Lily.

'So, shall I call the hotel?' says Isabella. 'My mum always tells me you should rip off the plaster in one go. She may be talking about men who've wronged you, but it also applies here.'

'Not right now,' says Lily. 'Give me until tomorrow morning. If I haven't come up with anything by then, you can make the call.'

Chapter Eight

We don't have much time to talk for the rest of the day. Lily deals with the cafe while I look after the bakery. Now that I've worked out how to use the till, it isn't too difficult. Most people come in for bread, but our mince pies and gingerbread have almost sold out, and Abby isn't here to make any more. I can still hardly believe what's happened. Yesterday, she was making Danish pastries, and today she's in intensive care.

A middle-aged couple comes in just before closing time. I'm about to ask what I can get for them when Lily sees them.

'Mr and Mrs Dowling! How's Abby doing?' she asks, dropping her tea towel and rushing over to the counter.

This must be Abby's parents. She has her father's chin, but she's got her wavy hair and dark eyes from her mother.

Mrs Carson gives a wan smile. 'They say she's doing as well as can be expected. I'm not sure what that means, but it's better than saying she's doing worse than expected.'

'Of course, it is!' says Lily, enfolding her in an enormous hug. She stretches out her hand to Abby's father, who squeezes it. He looks even more exhausted than his wife.

'I still can't believe it,' says Mrs Dowling. 'I was telling Chris I knew Abby had been more tired than usual, but I never dreamed it was anything more than that.'

'None of us did,' says Lily. 'Poor Chris. How's he holding up?'

'He doesn't know if he's on his head or his heels,' says Mrs Dowling. 'It was awful sitting there last night while she was in surgery. None of us knowing what was going on, or whether –'

'I can imagine,' says Lily. 'But she's obviously in excellent hands. Thank goodness they caught it in time.'

'Only just,' says Mrs Dowling. 'The doctors said she was in a bad way when she arrived. There was nothing any of us could do but sit and stare at each other. It brought it all back –'

She breaks off and gives her husband a guilty smile. 'But everything turned out well then, and I'm sure it will be the same with Abby.'

'Do you have time for a coffee?' asks Lily. 'I expect you could both do with something.'

'I'm afraid not,' says Mr Dowling. 'We told Chris we'd be back at the hospital before dinner so he could go home and have a shower and take a break. He didn't want to, but we insisted.'

'He agreed in the end,' says Mrs Dowling. 'He's a sensible lad.'

'And he's still a bit frightened of you,' says her husband with a smile.

'Nonsense!' she says. 'No one is frightened of me. And it was you who threatened to stop taking him to the driving range if he didn't do as he was told.'

'Poor Chris,' says Lily.

'And you threatened not to let him come over to watch the World Cup on your new TV,' adds Mrs Dowling.

'Please tell Chris we'll do anything we can to help,' says Lily.

'I'm so sorry,' Mrs Dowling says to me. 'I haven't said hello to you yet. I'm Carolyn, and this is Geoffrey. You must be Grace.

I knew you were arriving this week, but it went clean out of my head.'

'Which is no surprise,' I say. 'After everything that's happened, I'm surprised you even remember who I am. Please let me know if you need anything. I have plenty of free time when I'm not at work. And I have my car down here, so I can pick up shopping for you or whatever.'

'Everyone's been so kind,' she says. 'News travels fast in Honeywell. We were only home for a few hours today, but the phone has been ringing non-stop. Your mother brought us a stack of meals, Lily. I don't know where she found the time.'

They say goodbye and go out to their car.

'I told you so!' says Lily. 'My mum's amazing. She must keep her freezer full of meals especially for this sort of thing. As Carolyn says, it's only been a few hours.'

'I look forward to meeting her,' I say. 'You three seem to have wonderful parents. Abby told me her mother was incredible when her father had a stroke. She held the whole family together. Yours sounds as though the village would come to a complete halt without her. And Isabella's sounds fascinating, from the little I know about her. Isabella's always quoting her.'

'The famous sayings?' says Lily. 'Mrs Campbell seems to have one for every occasion. But they seem to apply equally to men.'

'Is Isabella seeing anyone at the moment?' I ask.

'Loads of people,' says Lily. 'She could be out with someone different each night if she wanted to.'

I'm not surprised to hear this. Isabella is more than attractive. She's beautiful. She's also lively and intelligent and amusing.

'Has no one ticked all the boxes on her mother's list?' I ask.

'I'd like to meet the man who could,' says Lily. 'Chris and Jack are great, but they would both have fallen at the first hurdle. Isabella's mother would have banned them from the house, if not the entire village.'

We lock up the shop, and I walk to the car park. Lily sets off in the other direction towards her parents' house. I'm feeling increasingly uncomfortable about the idea of staying in Abby and Chris' flat. It feels even more of an intrusion now she's in hospital. Chris won't want an extra person hanging around, especially one he barely knows. He'll need space and privacy whenever he's taking a break from his shifts at the hospital. And Abby will need peace and quiet when she comes home. Maybe I can book myself into an Airbnb for a few weeks. I don't like to ask Isabella about her offer of a room. From what I know of her, it could have been a joke. She appears to have, if not an overdeveloped sense of humour, at least one that's more inflated than most.

There's nothing I can do about that tonight. I'll have to go home, do whatever I can to help Chris, then stay out of his way as much as I can. I can worry about it more when we know what's happening with Abby. I can't imagine what he must be going through. He and Abby are such a close couple and seem perfectly suited. He also gets on well with her parents, which must be a bonus.

I rarely see my own parents. They've been living in Scotland since taking early retirement. Mum grew up there, and she's always wanted to go back home. But Dad's job with a London property developer kept them in the south of England until they retired. I'm happy they're living their dream, but I miss them – especially around the holidays.

They invited me to stay with them for Christmas, and I almost accepted. I had visions of myself striding over the moors and drinking whisky by the fire with Dad in the evenings. But things changed unexpectedly, and I was glad when Abby called and gave me an excuse not to go. Families are great, unless you're trying to hide anything from them. In which case, forced proximity can be trying, especially when there's whisky involved.

I walk towards my car, deep in thoughts of grouse moors and why Scottish men don't get cold knees when they wear kilts in the snow. Maybe they use flesh-coloured knee-warming devices or buy huge stocks of Highland Heat Cream.

'Grace?' says a man's voice, making me jump.

I peer through the gloom, half-expecting to see Chris. My heart skips a beat as I wonder whether Abby is worse. But he wouldn't be here if she were. He'd be at the hospital.

'Hello?' I say, keeping my hand firmly on my car keys. I'm sure Isabella's mother has taught her a way to quickly fashion your keys into a throwing star, but it's too late for that now.

'Grace?' says the voice again, and my heart sinks when I realise it's Rob.

'What are you doing here?' I say accusingly.

'Looking for you.'

'And now you've found me. What can I do for you?'

'I'm not here as a customer,' he says, a hint of laughter in his voice. 'You don't have to be polite if you don't want to.'

'I wasn't terribly polite to you when you were a customer,' I say. 'I'm sorry about that. I was just surprised to see you down here.'

'I wondered what I'd done,' he says. 'I hoped you were mistaking me for someone else at first, but you can't have been. You remembered I worked for a production company.'

Why didn't I think of that? I should have given him a look of polite bewilderment when he arrived and insisted we'd never met. That would have showed him! Not that there was anything to show him, but it couldn't have hurt.

'Of course, I remembered you,' I say. 'You forced me to go to a boring work event in the depths of the countryside, and I ruined my sandals in the rain.'

'So, it was you!' he says. 'I'm glad we've got that straight. I was starting to think it had all been a bad dream.'

'Thank you,' I say politely.

'You know what I mean. So, if you were there, maybe you can remind me who was eating all those lobster tarts?'

'I can't help you there,' I say. 'Anyway, we've established we knew each other slightly in London. So, what brings you here this evening? It's cold, and I need to get home.'

'I was hoping you might have a drink with me.'

'The cafe's closed. You'll have to get here before five o'clock another time. Except on Fridays, when we stay open until seven.'

'I know it's closed,' he says. 'I searched for the bakery online. Nice website, by the way. I like all those pictures of your cakes.'

'That's nothing to do with me,' I say. 'I only arrived here a few days ago.'

'True,' he says. 'Anyway, I meant a proper drink. With alcohol in it.'

'Come in sometime when Isabella's on duty. She'll be happy to oblige. I'm sure she'd add a shot of something to your latte – for a price.'

'I'll bear it in mind,' he says. 'But that's still not what I meant. I'll try again. There's a nice-looking pub across the road. I was wondering whether you'd like to accompany me there for a drink?'

Chapter Nine

I almost say no. There's no reason for me to have a drink with this man, and several reasons why I shouldn't. But I've been dreading going home, and I'd like to delay it for as long as possible. I feel mean even thinking this. I should be there if Chris needs me. And I'm happy to be. But I suspect he'll see me as very much in the way, even if he's too polite to say so. And I'm quite likely to bump into Rob again over the next few weeks. If there's any air that needs clearing, now seems as good a time as any.

'I don't have long,' I say.

'Hot date?' he says teasingly.

'What?'

'Do you need to get home to do whatever it is you do before going on a date?'

'Do you want this drink or what?' I say.

He looks surprised. 'I didn't mean to offend you.'

'And you didn't. As I say, I don't have much time. Maybe it would be better to do this another night.'

'If you like,' he says. 'But I'm here now, and so are you. Who knows whether our paths will cross again in the foreseeable future? I vote we take this unexpected meeting as a sign the universe wants us to spend the evening together.'

'I don't believe in signs,' I say.

'A divine hint then,' he says. 'A very gentle one. Practically a whisper.'

I follow him towards the high street. 'What brings you to Honeywell again so soon?'

'What do you mean?'

'You said our paths had crossed unexpectedly. Which means you must have been in the village today for some other reason when we bumped into each other.'

He looks embarrassed. 'When I said unexpected, I meant I wasn't sure you'd be working today. I took a chance and came into Honeywell anyway. I recognised your car in the car park, so I waited for you here.'

I stop abruptly, and he nearly cannons into me.

'Are you saying you were stalking me?' I ask.

He looks horrified. 'No! I wouldn't dream of it.'

I almost let him off the hook, but something drives me to pursue it. 'So, you just happened to be in Honeywell, and you thought you'd hang around the car park in order to scare a random woman almost out of her wits?'

'No!' he says again. 'At least –'

'Please go on. I'm fascinated to hear what you were about to say. Were you waiting for an elderly resident to walk past with heavy bags so you could perform your good deed for the day and carry them home?'

'I'll happily carry heavy bags if anyone needs me to,' he says.

I'm starting to enjoy myself. 'Or were you lying in wait in case a gang of teenagers arrived with spray cans, ready for an evening of desecrating the local buildings and besmirching the reputation of the historic village of Honeywell?'

'Not exactly. I'm a bit out of practise at tackling teenage gangs. I once stopped my sister from spray painting her hair green the night before our cousin's wedding, if that counts. She was about fifteen at the time.'

I fix him with a steely gaze. 'So, you were waiting for me?'

'You or anyone else who came along looking thirsty. I just wanted to have a drink with someone. When I saw you striding along the street, I thought, "That woman looks as though she could drink me under the table. She'll do."'

'I'm driving,' I say. 'I won't be engaging in any drinking contests.'

'Spoilsport! But you'll do to start with. Maybe I'll bump into someone more fun at the pub, and I can ditch you for them.'

'I wouldn't be surprised,' I say, my amusement evaporating. I ought to be impressed he knows himself so well, yet all I can feel is annoyance that I've been so easily persuaded into having a drink with him. But I'm too tired to make a scene, and it would be nice to put a little distance between the day I've had and the evening ahead of me. I don't have to stay long. I can have a drink, decompress, then go home and see how best I can help Chris. And Rob can pay for the drinks.

'Are you ok?' he says. 'You've stopped in the middle of the pavement. I'm afraid if we stand here much longer, one or both of us will turn into a pillar of ice.'

I start walking again. 'It's not that cold.'

'It depends on what you're comparing it to,' he says. 'If you're talking about caribou wandering around the Arctic Tundra or penguins bobbing on ice floes, it's practically tropical. But on a scale of one to ten, with one being cool and brisk, and ten meaning me turning into that aforementioned pillar of ice, I'd say it was fast approaching an eight.'

'Typical soft Londoner!' I say.

'And what do you call yourself? You only started working here a couple of days ago. You're hardly a local. Is this a permanent move, by the way? Is there a top-secret advertising firm starting up in the area who saw your obvious talent and headhunted you?'

'No.'

I don't say any more. It's none of his business where I choose to live or work. With his apparent stalking tendencies, I'd be well advised not to give him any more personal information than he unfortunately already possesses.

'Here we are,' he says, holding open the door to the Red Lion.

I step into the welcome warmth. Whatever I may have said to Rob, it's freezing tonight. I'm glad to see a fire at the far end of the room.

'What would you like?' he says. 'Are you still drinking mojitos?'

'No,' I say. 'I've never liked those.'

'Are you sure? I could swear we drank those when we went to –'

'Quite sure. I'll have a glass of mulled wine, please.'

'Good idea. Just the thing for a tropical winter evening. I'll join you. Find yourself somewhere to sit, and I'll be with you in a moment.'

I walk towards the fireplace where a young couple is standing up to leave. I grab their table and sink into a chair. Rob arrives a minute later with our drinks.

'Well done on getting a seat near the fire,' he says. 'How did you manage that?'

'A couple was leaving when I arrived.'

'Of their own volition, or did you treat them to your famous Grace Andersen stare and terrify them into it?'

'I don't have a stare,' I say. 'At least, I don't think so. No one's ever told me I do.'

'So, you reserve it just for me?' he says. 'Interesting.'

'You're talking nonsense. That couple was leaving as I arrived. I didn't have to hang around stalking them.'

'Touché,' he says. 'I'm sorry if I startled you in the car park. It was thoughtless of me. Thanks for giving me another chance.'

'I'm having a drink with you, not giving you another chance,' I say without thinking.

'I understand,' he says. 'It's nice to see you again, anyway. Quite a coincidence us running into each other like this, isn't it?'

I take a sip of my mulled wine, which is spicy and comforting. 'Maybe.'

He looks confused. 'Isn't it?'

I give him an enigmatic look. 'Or did you track me down and follow me to Honeywell?'

He looks even more confused. 'Of course not. Oh, you're back on the theme of stalking.'

I shrug. 'I'm not rushing to judgement either way. It's either that or the work of this divine whoever it is you mentioned earlier. And I'm not convinced it was him, even if he was whispering.'

'Perhaps he had a sore throat,' he says.

'Then you should buy him some cough drops.'

'You aren't really annoyed, are you?' he says.

'Not really, but only because this mulled wine is so good. But take it as a warning. If I hadn't recognised you in time, I might have given you a roundhouse kick, and you'd have deserved it.'

'In the future, I'll only wait for you under a streetlight,' he says. 'And not until I've called you and confirmed our meeting by text. Possibly by fax, too.'

'I doubt we'll meet like this again,' I say. 'So, it won't be an issue. Seriously, Rob, you should remember what isn't an issue for men may well be one for women.'

'I get it,' he says. 'I really do. Thanks for the reminder. But I hope you're wrong about us not meeting again. I'm coming over to the bakery with the team soon. I'm bound to see you then.'

'Maybe. But we've agreed Abby and Isabella should be the ones on camera –'

I break off. How could I have forgotten about Abby? I shouldn't be drinking mulled wine with an annoying man. I should be at home supporting Abby's husband. I know it's what she'd want me to do if she could speak to me.

'Rob, I have to go,' I begin.

'But you haven't finished your drink. Is there something wrong with it? Shall I get you something different – a whisky sour, perhaps?'

He flashes me a teasing smile, but I don't smile back.

'Grace?' he says. 'What is it?'

I try to shrug it off and tell him it's nothing, but I can't. To my horror, I feel the tears start to my eyes. I look away, but it's too late.

'Grace?' he says again.

'I'm fine,' I say in a choked voice. 'I have to … I forgot that I …'

I can't go on, or not without crying, which would be embarrassing enough in a crowded pub, let alone in front of Rob Marshall.

'You're clearly not fine,' he says gently. 'You don't have to tell me. It's none of my business. But is there anything I can do to help?'

I pick up my serviette and wipe my eyes. 'It's been a difficult day, that's all.'

'The customers?'

I shake my head. 'They're great, at least the ones I've met so far. It's the staff.'

'They aren't giving you a hard time, are they? They both seemed so nice when I met them.'

'Not at all. They're lovely.'

'Abby was telling me you two have known each other for a while,' he goes on, seemingly to give me time to recover my composure.

'We have,' I agree. 'Which makes what's happened all the more awful. She was rushed to the hospital in the middle of the night with peritonitis.'

His face snaps in shock. 'That's pretty serious, isn't it?'

'It is. And to make it worse, she has sepsis.'

'I'm so sorry,' he says. 'Will she be alright?'

'I hope so. She got through the operation, but she's in intensive care. Chris says he doesn't know how long she'll be there.'

'That's her partner, is it?'

'That's right. They've been together for a while now. I'm staying with them while I'm working in Honeywell.'

I seem to have forgotten my earlier resolution not to give him a shred more information than I have to.

'So, you were there when it happened,' he says. 'That must have been tough for you.'

'Not as tough as it was for Abby. And Chris, of course. He was at the hospital all last night and most of today. I should get back home and see what I can do for him.'

'Is he there now?' he says.

'I don't know.'

I pull my phone out of my bag and see I have several messages. The first is from Chris, saying he's spending the night at the hospital, and he hopes I'll be alright. If I don't have my key, I should call Isabella, and she'll give me Abby's parents' number so I can collect a spare key from them. The second is from Isabella telling me she's spoken to Chris, and he won't be there tonight, so I should give her a call if I need anything. The final one is from Lily, saying much the same thing.

I lean back in my chair. 'Chris won't be home tonight. Maybe I'll finish my drink after all.'

'Good idea,' he says. 'And how about something to eat?'

'I'm not hungry.'

'When did you last eat?'

'I have no idea. Lunchtime, maybe?'

'Maybe?' he says. 'Can you be more specific?'

'I don't remember. It's possible I didn't think about lunch today.'

'How about breakfast?' he says.

I give him an exasperated look. 'I had a cheese roll.'

'I'm not trying to annoy you,' he says. 'I'm trying to look out for you. I remember what it was like when my dad had a heart attack. I barely ate anything for several days, then ended up passing out on the cardiac ward. They had to revive me with tea and toast.'

I can't help smiling at the image. 'Are you trying to revive me with tea and toast now?'

'I doubt they serve it here. But it might be a good idea for you to eat something, especially if you're drinking alcohol. They'll be scraping you off the floor otherwise.'

'I can make myself some dinner back at the flat,' I say.

'You could,' he says. 'Or you could let me get you something now, in case you forget about it again between Honeywell and wherever it is Abby and Chris live.'

'Brambling,' I say without thinking. It shouldn't matter. I haven't given him the exact address.

'I'll get us a couple of menus,' he says, and I'm too exhausted to argue.

He returns in a minute and hands me the menu. I stare at it unseeingly.

'Don't worry,' he says, taking it from me. 'I'll find you something that looks good. I was thinking of having their game pie, but you won't want that now you're a vegetarian.'

To my annoyance, my stomach gives a loud rumble, and I'm suddenly aware of how hungry I am. Game pie sounds delicious. There's bound to be something equally delicious in the vegetarian part of the menu, but I can't think what.

I throw caution to the winds. 'When I told you I was a vegetarian the other day, I meant I was mostly vegetarian.'

'Mostly?' he says.

'That's right. I'm on a … journey.'

'I see,' he says. 'A vegetarian journey?'

'That's right.'

'Like a quest?' he suggests. 'An odyssey, or a pilgrimage, but with vegetables?'

He doesn't crack a smile, but his eyes are alight with laughter.

'Just order me the game pie!' I say.

'If you're sure. I wouldn't want to interfere with your quest for inner enlightenment.'

'Right now, I'd settle for inner fulfilment,' I say. 'One portion of game pie, please. And don't forget the chips!'

Chapter Ten

Half an hour later, I push away my plate with a sigh of contentment. 'I needed that.'

'I could see that,' he says.

If he's waiting for me to tell him he's my hero, he can forget it. But it was nice of him to notice.

'I'm sorry about your dad,' I say.

'My dad?'

'You said he had a heart attack.'

'Oh, that. It was a couple of years ago. He's doing better now that my mum has bullied him into taking early retirement. I think she'd been waiting for the opportunity for a while, but he's a stubborn old thing.'

'What did he do?'

'He was a defence barrister. He was excellent at what he did, but it took a toll on him. He always said it was an immense responsibility having someone's liberty and happiness depend on how good you were at your job that day.'

'I doubt he'd have wanted to do anything else,' I say. 'I've noticed people in the caring professions often push themselves to burnout.'

'The caring professions?' he says. 'I've never thought of his job like that before.'

'I expect he did. Being a nurse or a doctor is important. They save people's lives. But so do people like your father. They prevent people's lives being lost in another way.'

'It's nice you see it like that,' he says. 'I grew up hearing people ask him how he could live with himself doing what he did. They also said it to me and my sister at school.'

'What did you say?'

'Not much. I used to argue. I even got into a couple of fights in the playground when I was younger. Some of the kids were telling me what their parents were saying about my dad. He was defending someone in a high-profile murder case at the time. I thought Dad would be pleased when he heard what I'd done, but he wasn't. He said if I was arrested and charged, I needn't think he'd be defending me. He would instruct the most inexperienced junior on his team and let them practise losing their first case on me.'

'That's pretty harsh,' I say. 'I assume he was joking.'

'I was never quite sure. But it taught me to keep my fists to myself from then on. Dad told me a lack of self-control had got most of his clients into trouble in the first place, and I should remember that whenever I felt tempted to lash out at someone.'

'I'd have been the same in your position,' I say. 'Maybe not the fist fights, although you never know. But why would the other children have a go at your dad? He wasn't the one who'd committed the crime.'

'I suppose they read the newspaper headlines. *Sinister developments as TV star faces trial. Have they finally crossed the line?* That sort of thing. No one could understand why someone like my dad would try to put a person like that back on the streets. I asked him once whether that bothered him. He was so good at his job,

I thought he must worry it could happen. But he told me the prosecution barristers were equally good at theirs. And if they weren't, the person deserved to be let off because the case against them wasn't sound.'

'He sounds like a decent person,' I say.

'He is,' agrees Rob. 'Although I didn't think so the day he told me he wouldn't defend me in court. I didn't realise at the time it was unlikely an eight-year-old would land up in the dock over a playground scuffle. And, as I say, it taught me self-control.'

'I wouldn't have thought that was your defining characteristic,' I say without thinking.

'What do you mean by that?'

'Nothing.' As he continues to stare at me, I add. 'I was watching you eat your pie just now. It was like watching a ravening wolf descend on a sheep fold.'

His face relaxes. 'You didn't do so badly yourself.'

'I was hungrier than I realised. I hadn't eaten properly since last night.'

'I could ask the chef whether there's any left,' he says. 'They may have a roast ox on the spit if we're lucky. I could request for the haunch for you.'

'I'm fine,' I say. 'It was delicious, but you can have too much of a good thing.'

'I'm sure you can manage one of their desserts,' he says. 'I looked at the menu while I was waiting for our drinks. You like tiramisu, don't you?'

'I love it,' I say before catching his eye. 'I mean, it's ok, I suppose.'

'I know!' he says. 'I'm thinking of someone else entirely. You are, in fact, allergic to sugar and have never allowed a morsel of anything sweet to pass your lips. Likewise, lobster tarts, steak, and any kind of fish.'

'That's right,' I say. 'Also, when I told you earlier I was a vegetarian, I meant vegan. Gluten-free and organic too.'

He smiles. 'So, why did you really tell me you were vegetarian that day in the bakery?'

The meal and the mulled wine have relaxed me, and I no longer feel the need to watch my words. 'Truthfully? I didn't want to have lunch with you, and I didn't realise we served vegetable pies.'

He smiles, but there's a faint trace of hurt on his face. 'Was there a particular reason for that? I thought we hit it off in London. I was never quite sure why we lost touch.'

'I don't remember. It was all so long ago.'

'Three months,' he says. 'I know we both have busy lives, but I can remember the past couple of years in a reasonable amount of detail. What happened, Grace? Did you start seeing someone else?'

I'm no longer feeling so relaxed. Maybe it's the effect of the alcohol wearing off. 'What does it matter?'

'It would help me to understand,' he says. 'I thought we were getting on well.'

'We were,' I say. 'I mean, it was fine, as far as it went. We saw each other a few times. Then we didn't. There's no need to make it into something it wasn't.'

'Sure,' he says.

'About this dessert,' I say. 'A haunch of sticky toffee pudding sounds great if they have it.'

'I'll check the menu,' he says.

I feel a sudden wave of guilt. 'Thanks for this, Rob. I really needed it.'

'No problem.' He hesitates. 'I don't want to keep dragging up the past, but did I say or do anything? If nothing else, it would be good for me not to do it again. We've already addressed the issue of me appearing without notice in car parks. Is there anything else it would help me to know?'

I almost tell him to drop it, but he looks genuinely eager to hear what I have to say. I don't want to give him the entire truth.

But I can tell him enough to satisfy him without embarrassing myself.

'If you must know,' I say, 'I stopped contacting you for a reason. When we met at my firm's launch party back in July, I thought you were a nice guy.'

'Never a good start,' he says. 'The next sentence always starts with "*But* ..."'

'This one doesn't,' I say.

'I'm glad to hear it.'

'*However* ...' I say, and he laughs.

'I should have seen that one coming. Go on. I can take it.'

'There's nothing to take. I was teasing you. I'm saying we got on well together. It was a relief to meet someone who didn't spend the entire evening talking about synergies.'

'As I recall, we spent the evening talking about pizza toppings,' he says. 'And we continued the conversation over drinks later on. It can't have been too bad. You agreed to have dinner with me a few days later.'

'I probably hadn't eaten in a while,' I say.

'And we went roller blading the following week. That can't have been because you were hungry. We only had an ice cream.'

'I stopped for a burger on the way home,' I say. 'I had no idea roller blading was such hard work.'

'I cooked you dinner in my flat the following week to make up for it,' he says. 'It was in your pre-vegetarian days, so I had a freer hand. I made you my famous spaghetti and meatball surprise.'

'Famous?' I say. 'Is that because you make it for all the women you take back to your flat?'

'Cards on the table, I'd never made it before,' he says. 'I found a recipe on one of those supermarket cards while I was wandering around wondering what on earth I could make to impress you.'

'It was very nice,' I say.

'I don't know who these other women are that you keep talking about,' he says. 'They must have heard rumours of my culinary skills – you know how news spreads in London – and broken in to raid my fridge while I was out. But the joke's on them. I only made it once. I hid the recipe card so you wouldn't see it, and I couldn't find it again.'

'I doubt they broke in,' I say. 'You probably gave them a key.'

'That's against our tenancy rules. We can get thrown out for that.'

'We're getting off the subject. You asked me why I didn't want to keep seeing you.'

'I'm starting to regret that now,' he says. 'You look so stern.'

'That suits me,' I say. 'I'm happy to put it all behind us and chalk it up to experience.'

'You'd better tell me,' he says in a resigned tone.

'Soon after you'd made me your world famous in London meatballs, you asked me to your firm's annual summer thing.'

'You owed me that,' he says. 'I'd suffered through yours. I thought you should return the favour.'

'I didn't invite you to ours. You just turned up. That was on you.'

'My bosses ordered me to go,' he says. 'Contrary to what you appear to believe, I don't wander around London, randomly gate crashing excruciatingly boring work functions.'

'It would make a wonderful book,' I say. '*Gatecrashing for Pleasure and Profit.*'

'Shall we write it and make our fortunes?' he says.

'Don't forget it would involve us having to attend all those functions,' I remind him.

'I'm up for it if you are.'

'I'm afraid I have a job at the moment,' I say. 'And I hear it will only get busier in the run up to Christmas. Another time, perhaps.'

He nods. 'Anyway, you graciously accompanied me to my firm's summer extravaganza. Is that what put you off? Did you suffer from a bout of food poisoning after your over-consumption of shellfish in pastry?'

A look of comprehension flashes across his face. 'Is that when you decided to make the switch to your new life of Zen vegetarianism? Shall I sue the catering company for you?'

'Your dad would only come out of retirement and defend them,' I say. 'And no, that's not when. I've already told you that was a mild fabrication.'

He smiles. 'The very words my father used in court when his clients' statements were proven false.'

'I'll bet he did. Anyway, the food was lovely, as I remember. It almost made up for the speeches.'

'That was Julian Simpson,' he says. 'He never uses one word when fifteen will do. He'd be a billionaire by now if he charged by the hour.'

'I'm glad I don't work for him,' I say. 'Isabella is one of the chattiest people I know, but at least she's entertaining. She's never once talked about regulatory compliance in relation to pension funds.'

'So, we've established it wasn't the food,' he says. 'And it wasn't the speeches. That narrows it down to … what? I'm out of ideas.'

'I talked to a few of your coworkers while you were chatting with your manager,' I say.

'That sounds ominous. What dark secrets of mine came to light? I've told you about the punching incident when I was eight, and you didn't recoil in horror. That's the worst thing I can think of.'

'They didn't tell me any dark secrets,' I assure him, wondering for the first time whether I've been making something out of nothing. 'But they mentioned … one of them in particular … that you were … shall we say, socially active?'

'You mean I'm friendly?'

'Not entirely.' I wish I hadn't started this conversation. He must know what I mean.

'That you had … have … a pretty active dating life,' I finish. Surely, he understands what I mean now.

He doesn't seem to. 'An active dating life?'

'That's right. Meaning that you go out with a lot of women. You play the field. Not that there's anything wrong with that. You're young and single, and you're entitled to do anything you like in your spare time. But that wasn't what I was looking for.'

'But I don't!' he bursts out. 'I meet people, and I go out on dates with some of them. But it's never anything serious.'

'That's my point,' I say. 'I'm not looking for marriage and babies in the next three months. But when I start seeing someone new, I like to know there's at least a possibility it may go somewhere. It usually doesn't, which is fine. But I don't waste time dating people who are only after a good time with as many people as possible.'

'Neither do I,' he says.

'You just told me you aren't looking for anything serious.'

'No, I didn't. I said I'd never found anything serious,' he says.

'It comes to the same thing. One person's serious is another one's playing the field. Anyway, your co-worker said enough for me to realise you and I weren't on the same page.'

He pushes his hand through his hair. 'I'd really like to straighten this out. Why don't I order our desserts, and we can discuss this further?'

I want to say no, but it can't harm to give him a chance to tell his side of the story. Besides, I really want that sticky toffee pudding.

'Fine,' I say. 'Can you order me a coffee too?'

'Good idea.' He goes off to the bar.

I stare into the fire, wondering what just happened. I didn't expect to see Rob again, let alone discuss why our relationship never progressed further than a few dates. It was one of those things. It happened, and I didn't intend to waste valuable time thinking about it.

But Rob appears to have other ideas. I should listen to what he has to say, although it won't make any difference. He and I barely know each other. Even if we rectified that, it's unlikely we'd have anything in common. It would fizzle out like most of these things do. However, in the interest of our two businesses working together harmoniously, I may as well hear him out.

My eyes close, and I don't fight it. I barely slept last night, and it's been a busy day at work. An anxious one too. I'll relax for a few minutes before Rob returns.

'Grace?'

That isn't Rob's voice, not unless he's been sucking on a helium balloon.

I slowly open my eyes and look up into a familiar face. It takes me a moment to place her. When I do, I freeze.

'You are Grace, aren't you?' says the woman.

I sit bolt upright in my chair. 'That's right. And you're …'

'Vanessa,' she says, sitting down at my table. 'We met a while back at the Capital Productions summer party.'

Chapter Eleven

I struggle to recover my composure. I was almost asleep when this woman arrived. With any luck, she's nothing more than a bad dream. I close my eyes, then open them again. She's still there, smiling down at me in that supercilious way I remember so well.

'Do you remember me?' she says.

'You're a producer of some kind?'

'That's right. And one of Rob's close colleagues.' She gives the tiniest of smirks as she says this.

I'm too tired to play games. 'You hinted at something like that when we first met. Are you two together?'

She shrugs. 'You think in cliches, don't you?'

'It's a simple enough concept. Not that I care either way.'

'Why would you? We're all adults.'

I'm not sure what relevance this has to this conversation. Of course, we're all adults. We wouldn't be in a pub if we weren't. But I can't be bothered to ask for clarification. I remember her from the party. She was full of cryptic hints and smirks then, and she doesn't seem to have changed. Maybe that's her manner. She may not even realise how she comes across.

'What are you doing down here?' I ask. 'Are you a part of the film crew?'

Her eyes flick towards the bar, where Rob is trying to catch the bartender's eye. He looks as though he'll be some time. I could have managed a micro nap if she hadn't disturbed me.

'I'm the producer,' she says. 'It's my job to make sure everything is running smoothly. And to spend time with Rob.'

'Mentoring him?' I ask. I don't know what's wrong with me. My brain seems to have turned to fluff, and I can scarcely remember where I am, let alone what job this woman does.

She arches an eyebrow. 'That's one way of putting it. Yes, let's say I'm mentoring him.'

Something about the way she says mentor grates on me. I hate it when people take quite ordinary words and concepts and add raised eyebrows and meaningful silences. Why can't they say what they mean? It would make things an awful lot simpler.

'Look, Vanessa,' I say. 'I've had a tough day after a night with almost no sleep. If there's something you're trying to say, why don't you say it before I fall asleep?'

'Have I upset you?' she says. 'I can sit somewhere else if you'd prefer.'

'Not at all. I'm letting you know I'm exhausted and in no mood for puzzles.'

'Nor am I,' she says. 'I'm not sure why you're being so hostile.'

Her eyes flicker towards Rob again, and her face snaps in understanding. 'Are you and Rob …? I didn't mean to intrude.'

'You aren't intruding. As I say, I'm tired. And no, Rob and I aren't whatever it was you meant to say. I bumped into him this evening quite by chance, and we decided to come here for a drink.'

My eyes fall on our plates. 'And some food.'

'Wonderful,' she says. 'I was a little concerned after we met at the party last summer that I'd inadvertently said something to upset you. I asked Rob one day how you were, and he said he had no idea.'

'That was the truth,' I say. 'I didn't see him again after that day.'

'You broke up?'

'No, because there was nothing to break up. We went out a couple of times. Neither of us was feeling it, so we stopped seeing each other. It happens all the time.'

'I'm glad to hear that,' she says. 'I'd hate to think it was because of anything I said.'

'Then you can put your mind at rest, because it wasn't.'

This may not be the strict truth, but I have no intention of discussing my personal life with her.

'Yet you're down here having dinner with him,' she pursues. 'You're a fair way away from home, aren't you.'

'If you mean London, yes, I am. But I'm working here temporarily, so you could say this is my current home.'

She doesn't look convinced. 'And it just happens to be somewhere you might expect to bump into Rob?'

'If I'd had the faintest idea he'd be working here, which I hadn't.'

A tiny smile plays around her mouth. 'I'll take your word for it.'

I'd like to argue, but I'm too tired. This woman's opinion of my life is irrelevant. Hopefully, I won't see her again. If I allow myself to doze off in front of this fire, I may not even have to see her tonight. It's tempting, but it wouldn't be polite.

'How long will you be in the area?' I ask as politely as possible. I look at my watch – eight o'clock. Hopefully, she'll say she's catching the eight ten train from Honeywell because she has to be at Gatwick airport tonight to fly out to her new life in Australia.

She looks surprised. 'As long as Rob's here, of course.'

'Because you're supervising the project?'

'That too,' she says with a catlike smile. 'Although I daresay I could project manage from a distance if I wanted to. But neither of us wanted to be apart for long, so I booked into the hotel, and here I am.'

'So, you and he are together?' I say.

'We don't like to put labels on it,' she says. 'Neither of us is the sort to relish being tied to one person. But it feels as though things may be moving in that direction. Somewhat to my surprise, I must say.'

'Congratulations,' I say, trying to keep a note of sarcasm out of my voice.

'You're alright with that?' she says.

'With you and Rob dating? Why wouldn't I be?'

'Marvellous,' she says. 'And here comes the man himself.'

Rob walks over to the table. He doesn't notice Vanessa until he gets closer.

'Hi, Van,' he says. 'I didn't know what time you'd arrive.'

She jumps up and kisses him on both cheeks. 'I came as quickly as I could after this afternoon's meeting. Thank goodness, I saw your text about coming here before I got to the hotel. Otherwise, I might have sunk into a deep bath and not emerged for hours. The room has a bath, doesn't it? I asked for one specially.'

Did she just wink at him?

'Er, yes,' he says. 'If there's one thing the hotel isn't short of, it's hot water.'

'Do you remember when that pipe burst?' she says. 'We got absolutely soaked! I had to strip off and spend the afternoon in your dressing gown while they dried my suit.'

'It's all fixed now,' he says. 'Although if it gets any colder, the pipes may freeze, and there'll be no hot water for anyone.'

She gives a delicate shiver. 'Everyone will have to snuggle up together under their quilts to survive.'

That was definitely a wink she gave him. Rob looks embarrassed. 'They have plenty of log fires. I doubt anyone will die of hypothermia.'

I push back my chair. 'I should be going.'

'Already?' says Rob. 'Didn't you say you were going home to an empty flat?'

'That's all changed,' I say. 'I've had an … er … text.'

'What a shame,' he says. 'You haven't eaten your sticky toffee pudding.'

'I don't have time. I'll settle up, and then I have to get going.'

'Nonsense,' he says. 'I invited you, not the other way around. And I practically had to force the food down your throat. I don't expect you to pay for the privilege too.'

'Well, thank you,' I say. 'Maybe Vanessa would like to eat my pudding when it arrives.'

'It sounds tempting,' she says. 'But I have a strict rule about never eating dessert on a weeknight. It's alright for you, Grace. You're so tall and lanky. I expect you can eat whatever you like and stay bony. But we mere mortals need to watch our figures, or no one will want to watch them for us. Isn't that right, Rob?'

'Sorry,' he says. 'I wasn't listening. I was wondering whether you'll be alright getting home, Grace. If you need a lift …'

'What a good idea!' says Vanessa. 'My car's outside. I haven't taken off my coat, and I haven't started drinking. I'm willing to bet Rob has, haven't you, darling?'

'I'm fine!' I say a little too quickly, and her lips curve into a faint smile.

'It isn't far, and I've had something to eat now, thanks to Rob,' I say more calmly. 'You two stay and enjoy your evening. I can recommend the game pie if that's not on your banned list for weekdays, Vanessa. By the way, Rob, I'd appreciate it if you could keep what I told you tonight to yourself for a few days.'

'Of course,' he says. 'If you won't let me take you home, at least let me walk you to your car.'

'Don't you mean stalk me?' I say. 'It's a three-minute walk. I'll be fine. You don't want to leave Vanessa here on her own now she's arrived.'

'I'd suggest sending you a text to check you'd got home safely,' he says. 'Only …'

'You don't have my number,' I finish for him. 'So, that won't work either.'

'Do stop fussing, darling!' murmurs Vanessa. 'Anyone would think she was crossing the Sahara on a camel, not walking across the road in a sleepy English village. Stop being such a Neanderthal. Women don't like it. At least, not under most circumstances.'

I don't dare look at her to see whether she gives him another wink. Third time lucky, and all that.

I pick up my bag, pull on my coat, and wave goodbye before Rob can come up with any more reasons why I can't be trusted to be out alone after dark.

'See you around,' I say, and walk quickly towards the door before he decides to follow me.

Chapter Twelve

I arrive at the bakery the following morning in a more cheerful mood. Chris came home last night, looking a lot happier. He told me Abby is now officially stable and the doctors are pleased with her progress. I slept like a log and woke ready to face the world again.

Lily arrives a minute after me. 'Any news?' she says, pulling the key out of her pocket.

'Chris says things are looking more positive. He left again before I was up this morning. Have you heard from him today?'

'Just a text last night saying much the same thing. Thank goodness Abby is doing better. He says we won't be able to see her for a while, but I told him to pass on our best wishes and tell her things are going fine at the bakery, and she isn't to worry. It would be typical of Abby to stress about that instead of concentrating all her energies on getting better.'

'It would. I'm glad you told her that. But everything isn't fine, is it? Isabella was saying yesterday we'll struggle with the Christmas rush without Abby, let alone the Christmas ball.'

'I know,' she says. 'But I couldn't tell Abby that. She needs to think everything is fine here, and we're coping well.'

'Have you decided what to tell the hotel?' I ask. 'Isabella's right – we need to let them know as quickly as possible if we're pulling out. Have you had any more thoughts about it?'

'Jack and I talked about nothing else last night. At least, after we got Daisy to sleep. She was shouting about Twinkle Tag as soon as I put her into her cot. I almost called Isabella and told her to get herself over to our house and deal with it. She's the one who started it, so she should cope with the fallout.'

'You should have,' I say, and she laughs.

'I know her too well. She'd have come straight over, armed with her torch and a bag of glitter. And I'd have had a call from her mother later that night, telling me she'd taken hours to settle Isabella and not to overexcite her like that again.'

'I'm eager to meet Mrs Campbell,' I say. 'I've heard a lot about her from Isabella, but I don't know whether she's exaggerating. What's she really like?'

'She's mildly eccentric. Like her daughters. I think you'll get on with her. Isabella's father is much quieter. I expect it's self-preservation. Georgia is quite similar to Isabella. Imagine living with the three of them!'

'Isabella on her own seems pretty full on,' I say. 'I can't imagine multiplying that by three. It's a good thing I didn't accept her invitation to stay. They'd be bound to think I was terribly dull. So, did you and Jack come up with a plan or were you forced to admit defeat?'

'Not a plan, as such. But I still think it could be done. Jack isn't so sure. He's happy to help, but he thinks it will be too much for us. He may be right.'

'Not necessarily,' I say. 'I was thinking about it when I drove in this morning. I know none of us can cook as well as Abby.'

'That's a pretty big obstacle,' says Lily.

'Possibly, but I doubt Abby could cook until she could. She had to start somewhere. Everyone always does.'

'True,' she says. 'But she took a two-year qualification, which included plenty of work experience. We have less than six weeks. And we're running a busy business at the same time.'

'I can see that's a problem,' I say. 'But is it insuperable? Isabella mentioned yesterday that she planned to contact your old suppliers to see whether they could supply you with basics for a while. That means they'll be covering most of what Abby does. It won't be as good, but I'm sure your customers will understand once they hear what's happened.'

'Most of them will,' she agrees. 'We've built up a pretty loyal clientele over the past few years.'

'So, that leaves the three of us. You only brought me in to help Abby because of all the extra work this Christmas ball would give her. She's no longer here, but neither is her regular work. Which means I can devote all my time to the ball. Or I could cover for one of you while you do it. It doesn't matter. The point is we have a superfluous member of staff until Christmas. If you decide not to go ahead with the contract, it makes no sense to me to stay here. I won't be offended if you send me home. You can't afford to pay an extra staff member to do something you can do yourself.'

'We'd hate to lose you right after you've arrived,' she says. 'But …'

'But you need to think of your business,' I say. 'I've worked with too many companies that put their hearts over their heads and made emotional decisions. It never ends well.'

'Do you really think we could do it?' she says. 'It would mean a tremendous amount of work, with no guarantee of success. That's what really worries me. Failure would be far worse than not doing it in the first place. The Christmas ball isn't a run through. It's the real thing. We won't get a do-over if we get it wrong. And it isn't fair on the people attending. They'll have paid for their tickets. Quite a lot, I believe. They're entitled to expect a certain degree of professionalism.'

'I get that,' I say. 'I'm not saying we could definitely pull it off. But it seems worth exploring. We'll need to get Isabella on board too.'

'On board with what?' says Isabella, who has opened the bakery door and is standing watching us.

'With our plans for a giant game of Twinkle Tag in the bakery on Christmas Eve,' says Lily. 'We thought you might like to organise it.'

Isabella shrugs off her duffel coat and throws it behind the counter. 'I'd be delighted. I'm glad to see you've come around to the wonder that is Twinkle Tag. May I ask what occasioned this change of heart? Has my goddaughter been putting in a good word for me?'

'I was joking!' says Lily. 'For goodness' sake, don't start planning it. Grace and I are discussing the Christmas ball.'

Isabella picks up a Bakewell slice and takes a bite. 'Have you decided yet what you want to do?'

'We can't do it without you,' says Lily. 'But we've both agreed it may not be impossible.'

Isabella switches on the coffee machine. 'I'm all ears.'

'Grace has pointed out we have three staff members doing two jobs,' says Lily. 'Her idea is that one of us – or a part of each of us – concentrates on the contract by doing – what, exactly, Grace?'

'That's where I'm a little hazy,' I confess. 'We'll have to learn to cook. Abby's bound to have left a record of what she planned to make, so we can focus on that. We don't need to learn all the basics like sausage rolls and pies and pastries, just the desserts for the ball. I don't mind working extra hours. I have nothing else to do in my spare time, especially now that Abby's in hospital.'

'We can ask Chris what she was planning to do,' says Lily. 'And we should find out whether she's given the hotel a final list. If not, we may be able to simplify things.'

'Good idea,' says Isabella. 'I'm not against this plan if you think we can make it work. But we can't afford to lose money over it.'

'I know,' says Lily. She pulls out a notebook from her bag. 'It's quite exciting, isn't it?'

'Not as exciting as a bakery wide game of Twinkle Tag,' says Isabella. 'But I'll take what I can get. We need a name for our plan. What shall it be? Mistletoe Mayhem?'

'Holiday Havoc?' I suggest.

'We don't want anything that suggests it might be chaos,' says Lily. 'We want a name that reminds us all we are approaching this challenge with professionalism and military precision.'

'Why didn't you say so?' says Isabella. 'I vote for Operation Festive Fury or Operation Sugar Rush.'

'Dessert Storm?' I say.

She gives a snort of laughter. 'We could call ourselves The Bakers Dirty Dozen.'

'If you don't plan to take this seriously –' says Lily.

'Sorry,' I say. 'I take it exceptionally seriously. Perhaps we should steer away from the military metaphors and go for something festive.'

'But with a hint of espionage,' begs Isabella.

'Operation Christmas Bauble,' I say.

'Excellent,' says Lily, picking up the pen and opening the notebook to the first page. She writes the heading carefully, then looks at us. 'Operation Christmas Bauble has officially begun. Now all we need is a plan to go with it.'

I sigh. 'That's the difficult part.'

'Nonsense!' says Isabella, sprinkling chocolate onto her cappuccino. 'We're three intelligent women. We can come up with a plan of campaign. And we have the name now, which is the main thing.'

She raises her mug solemnly and clinks both of ours. 'Here's to Operation Christmas Bauble. God bless it, and all who sail in it.'

Chapter Thirteen

The cafe fills up steadily throughout the morning. Lily pushes two of the tables together at the far end.

'Ready for the poker club,' she says. 'They should be here soon. A little sleet never stops them.'

'A full-scale blizzard wouldn't stop them,' says Isabella as she wipes down the table nearest to the door.

'It's a good idea to meet at a cafe,' I say. 'You need to keep your blood sugar up if you want to concentrate on full houses and royal flushes.'

'Even more so if you plan to cheat,' says Isabella. 'I'm sure there's some jiggery-pokery going on with Diane Bold and Jemima Higgins. They've scooped the pool three times in a row. I haven't worked out how they're doing it, but I will.'

'Please don't slander our customers,' says Lily. 'They're the only thing standing between us and financial disaster.'

'I wouldn't dream of it,' says Isabella. 'But it's only slander when someone is in the same room as you. Otherwise, it's just gossip.'

'I'm no lawyer, but I'm pretty sure you're wrong,' I say.

'She is,' says Lily. 'But don't bother trying to persuade her. Isabella can talk the hind leg off a donkey. And we don't have time for that today. I need to check the dog biscuit situation. Tuesday is one of Bernie's regular days.'

'I don't know how he manages it,' says Isabella. 'I know for a fact Mrs Ogilvie keeps her calendar next to the front door about the hall table. Bernie can't reach that high to read it. Yet every Tuesday at eleven o'clock, in he comes. That dog is a wonder!'

'The vet says Bernie has the best internal clock of any dog he's ever seen,' says Lily, and they both laugh.

I don't have time to ask for elucidation because my attention is diverted by a woman wearing a bright orange coat that clashes with her hennaed hair.

'Excuse me!' she greets me in a tone that lets me know in no uncertain terms she plans to have her say, whether or not I excuse her.

'How can I help you?' I ask.

She pulls a loaf out of her bag. 'I bought this yesterday afternoon.'

She pushes the loaf towards me so aggressively that I take an involuntary step backwards. She isn't exactly brandishing it. But she's giving the impression she knows perfectly well this loaf could function as a serviceable weapon in an emergency, and she isn't averse to using it. Maybe she's the undisputed All Counties Loaf-Poking champion, and I'm the only one here who isn't aware of it. I don't see a badge, but she may be wearing one under her coat. Two crossed baguettes rampant on a sable and vert background, with a heraldic scroll saying *Panis Pugilatus*.

'It's a loaf,' I say to get the conversational ball rolling.

'Don't talk to me as though I'm a fool!' she snaps.

I take a deep breath. 'Is there something wrong with it?'

'You can see as well as I can what's wrong with it! Don't play games with me, young lady! I'm in no mood for it.'

I don't know what game she thinks I'm playing – the Under-Fifty Focaccia Face-off? Neither am I sure why she thinks I should be in the mood for it. It seems a niche kind of activity, and one best played after a few too many drinks one evening. But she's a customer, so I'd better not be rude.

'I'm new here,' I say. 'Would you mind telling me what the problem with is with your loaf? That way, I'll know for next time.'

She picks up the loaf and waves it menacingly. I can't take another step backwards because the wall is behind me. I look out of the side of my eye at the trays of bread to my left, sizing them up. A baguette would make a good short sword, although its thin crust means it would snap easily – a distinct drawback if it comes to a full-fledged fight. It may be better to grab an armful of rolls and hurl them at random. One of them would be bound to hit her somewhere. They're yesterday's rolls too, so their crusts should be at full strength.

'This is a currant loaf!' she says. 'Now do you see the problem?'

My mind races. What could possibly be wrong with a currant loaf? Did Abby mess up and put raisins in it instead?

'I'm not sure I do,' I say. 'But I'm listening.'

She almost audibly grits her teeth. 'It doesn't have any currants in it.'

I stare at the loaf, bemused. 'How do you know? A currant loaf keeps its currants on the inside. And you haven't started this one.'

'Are you as stupid as you look?' she says.

My grip on my temper is loosening fast. 'I can't answer that because I don't know how stupid you think I look,' I say curtly. 'But I'm definitely not as stupid as you are rude. As you see, we have several customers waiting to be served. Either tell me what you'd like me to do for you or step aside so I can serve them.'

'I want my money back!' she says, her jaw jutting dangerously.

No one has mentioned the bakery's policy on refunds. But I don't care. I pull out my purse. 'How much was it?'

'£3.50.'

I hand her a five-pound note. 'There you go. Now you can buy yourself a nice sliced loaf from the supermarket and still have enough change for a bag of currants.'

A woman waiting in the queue gives a shout of laughter. 'That's told you, Wendy Protheroe! You should be ashamed of yourself, coming in here and talking to the young lady like that.'

She leans forward to inspect the loaf more closely. 'And that's a Sally Lunn, you daft woman. It isn't supposed to have currants in it!'

Several of the customers snigger, and Wendy looks discomposed. She recovers herself, snatches up both the loaf and the five-pound note, and stalks out of the shop.

'Cheeky beggar!' says the woman. 'She didn't even leave the loaf. I'm glad you put her in her place. She's always doing things like that. She'd ask for a refund from the collection plate if the vicar wasn't already onto her.'

'It doesn't matter,' I say. 'We wouldn't have been able to resell that loaf. I hope I haven't offended an important customer.'

She snorts. 'Important customer, my hat! She's a pain in the proverbial, that's what she is.'

Lily finishes serving coffee to a group of women and comes over to the counter. 'Is everything alright here?'

'It is now,' says the woman before I can speak. 'Wendy was in making a tremendous fuss, as usual.'

'Didn't she like her Sally Lunn?' says Lily.

'She thought it was a currant loaf and came in to complain it didn't have any currants. Still, she's gone off with five pounds of this young woman's money, so she's happy enough.'

Lily opens the till and hands me a five-pound note.

'Don't do that!' I say. 'It was my decision. I could have asked you what your policy was about this sort of thing. But it seemed like too much effort.'

'Take it,' she says. 'I'd have had a long argument with her and ended up refunding her anyway. You've saved me the trouble.'

'Have I lost you one of your regulars?'

She shakes her head. 'She comes in about once a week, and she returns half of the things she buys. Isabella says everyone needs a hobby, and this seems to be hers. Why don't you finish cleaning the tables while I deal with this queue?'

Isabella appears a few minutes later and points towards the high street. 'What did I tell you? Right on time!'

Two women in identical navy-blue coats are walking down the street with a dog. As they get closer, I see it's Bernie.

Isabella opens the door to them. 'Good morning, ladies! Good morning, Bernie. Your usual table awaits.'

Bernie makes for the table next to the door and settles himself under a chair.

'You'll have to wait until the queue dies down,' one of the two women tells him as she sits down.

'But he's hungry!' says the other one. 'He's had a long walk here in the cold.'

'So have I,' says the other woman. 'And no one's offering me preferential treatment.'

I'm fairly sure which woman is which by now. This impression is confirmed when they remove their coats. The first woman is wearing a striped coral and cream jumper, and a pink tweed skirt. The other is more soberly attired in a dark green woollen suit.

'Hello, Mabel,' I say to the woman in the striped jumper. 'Hello, Bernie. And this must be Mrs Ogilvie?'

I'm not sure what to call her. I've only heard her referred to as Mrs Ogilvie by Lily and Isabella.

'That's right,' she says. 'Are you new?'

'She's the one I told you about,' says Mabel. 'One of Abby's friends. She's helping out over the Christmas period.'

Mrs Ogilvie looks anxiously at Bernie. 'I wonder whether …?'

'Would he like a biscuit?' I say.

She gives me a grateful smile. 'If you wouldn't mind. He's had nothing since breakfast, and it's cold out there today.'

'Dirty queue jumper!' Mabel tells the dog, who grins.

She shakes her head at him. 'No one ever offers to give me biscuits when I'm cold. But all you have to do is give one wag of your idiotic tail, and Edie's convinced you're at death's door. I should try it sometime.'

'I'll get your tea,' says Isabella. 'And perhaps one of those brownies you like so much?'

'Now you're talking!' says Mabel.

'I'll have a slice of your lemon drizzle, please,' says Mrs Ogilvy. 'Abby makes that very nicely.'

I'm about to tell her the news when Isabella catches my eye and slightly shakes her head.

'Grace, could you help me with the tea?' she says.

She waits until we're out of earshot to whisper, 'Don't mention Abby to anyone yet. We'll discuss it later.'

I'm not sure what to make of this, but I barely have time to think about it as the lunchtime rush begins.

It isn't until about four o'clock that the queues die down enough for the three of us to stop and chat.

'I'll make us all a drink,' says Isabella. 'Then we can talk about our plans.'

'Isabella told me not to mention anything about Abby,' I say to Lily. 'Have her parents asked us not to? She isn't worse, is she? I spoke to Chris this morning, and he said she was doing better.'

'Not that,' she says. 'It's the other thing.'

'You mean Operation Christmas Bauble?' I say. 'Do the bakery walls have ears? Should we give the operation its own codename, so no one ever hears its real name?'

'That would be fun,' says Isabella. 'But it isn't our most pressing concern. I popped over to Lily's house yesterday evening to rile up my goddaughter before bed. It's all part of a godmother's duties.'

'I think someone sold you the wrong handbook,' says Lily.

'I don't think so,' says Isabella. 'But while I was doing that, I realised we have a bigger problem than making these desserts.

The contract doesn't specify who should make them, just that they should be of a high standard.'

'Which they will be,' I say.

'We know that, but the TV crew doesn't. They're coming over to the bakery next week to see us in action. They want to film us baking our Christmas goods.'

'You think if they get wind of the fact our head chef isn't here, they'll assume we aren't able to fulfil our side of the deal?' I ask.

'Exactly,' says Lily. 'Either they'll tell the hotel, who are bound to call us in and interrogate us about our non-existent expertise. Or they'll see a chance to make us look ridiculous on camera. They won't care about the quality of our products. They're after gripping footage.'

'Which means what?' I say. 'Is this the end of Operation Christmas Bauble? It's a shame after Lily's bought the notebook and everything.'

'Not at all,' says Isabella, a mischievous gleam in her eye. 'All it means is that we have to keep Abby's illness a secret until after the team has been and gone. It won't matter if it comes out after that because there's nothing they can do about it.'

'I don't see how that's possible,' I say. 'News like that always gets about. Especially in a small village. Isn't that what they're famous for? Half the murders of Miss Marple's village were solved by elderly women gossiping.'

'And knitting,' adds Isabella. 'That village could have started a cottage industry for crocheted shawls. It would be like cutlery coming from Sheffield, or cotton from Manchester.'

'We should be alright,' says Lily. 'It's only for a couple of days. Abby's parents won't be around the village much. They'll be spending most of their time at the hospital. Chris doesn't live in the village, and I've told my mum to keep it quiet for now and to ask people not to spread the news. We should be able to keep it under wraps until next week. The TV crew is staying at the hotel, filming their Christmas preparations. They won't be spending much time in Honeywell.'

The phone rings in the office, and Isabella goes to answer it.

'When I agreed to come down here for Christmas,' I say, 'I had no idea I was about to be pitched into such a nest of intrigue. I hope this doesn't really turn into a Miss Marple story. I'd hate to arrive at the bakery one morning and find a pile of dead bodies stretched out on the floor.'

'Only one at a time,' says Lily. 'Miss Marple tripped over bodies. She didn't clamber over them. Anyway, there won't be a murder. Not even a jewel robbery. All we have to do is keep one small secret for two days. To use a bakery-related metaphor – it's a piece of cake!'

Isabella appears in the doorway. Her usual smile has disappeared.

'What is it?' says Lily. 'Not Abby?'

'It's nothing to do with Abby,' says Isabella. 'At least, not directly. That phone call was from someone called Vanessa. She was calling from the Quayside Hotel. Apparently, she's heading up this TV production. To cut a long story short, she has to be back in London sooner than she expected. So, the team is coming here tomorrow afternoon to start filming!'

Chapter Fourteen

Lily and I stare at her blankly.

'Coming tomorrow?' says Lily. 'But they weren't supposed to start before Monday.'

'That's all changed since this Vanessa woman has arrived,' says Isabella. 'She wants to get the establishing stuff done as early as possible in case of any hiccups. It makes sense, but it's awkward for us.'

'Do you think if we told them about Abby in confidence, they might be alright with it?' suggests Lily. 'They must know how difficult this sort of thing can be.'

'That wouldn't work,' I say. 'Not with this woman. You'll have to take my word for it.'

'Do you know her too?' says Lily. 'Is she also a friend from London?'

'I've only met her a couple of times. But I've seen enough of her to know she isn't the kind of woman to be motivated by sympathy. She'd be more likely to go straight to the hotel, tell them what was going on, and suggest they cancel our contract.

Worse still, she might insist on coming back here every week to film us making fools of ourselves.'

Lily sighs. 'What about Rob? He seems like a nice guy. Is there any point in appealing to his better feelings?'

'No,' I say. 'He and she are … together. He isn't likely to keep anything we tell him in confidence.'

'I thought you didn't know whether he was in a relationship?' says Isabella.

'I didn't. But I bumped into them both at the pub last night. She told me then.'

There's no need to go into the entire story of how I met Rob and how Vanessa turned up. It isn't relevant to this professional conversation.

'That's a shame,' says Lily. 'It seems we're out of options.'

'Not necessarily,' says Isabella. 'I told you I'd come up with some ideas, and I will. I'm having dinner with my uncle and his family this evening, so I must go. But I'll do some hard thinking between courses.'

'As long as it doesn't involve anything that will give the TV crew food poisoning,' says Lily.

'I'm a seasoned professional,' says Isabella. 'I wouldn't dream of it.'

Lily doesn't look convinced as we close the shop and prepare to leave.

'I'll text you after dinner and let you know what I've come up with,' says Isabella as we step outside into the chilly night air.

'Otherwise, we'll have to tell them what's going on and throw ourselves on their mercy,' says Lily.

'There'll be no need for that,' says Isabella. 'I'll eat some fish tonight. It's good for the brain.'

'I wonder what custard tarts are good for?' says Lily as we watch her walk to her car and drive away.

I go straight back to the flat, avoiding the temptation to stop at the pub for something to eat. If Chris is home, I should make him some dinner. It won't be homemade ravioli, but I can heat up some soup and stick a sprig of parsley on it if need be.

The flat is empty when I arrive. There's a note on the fridge.

I won't be back until late. Angela Carson has put several meals in the freezer with instructions for heating them. Help yourself. Abby is still stable but exhausted. Chris.

I don't take him up on his suggestion. Those meals weren't meant for me. Mrs Carson made them for Chris, which was nice of her.

Instead, I order a pizza and collapse onto the sofa to wait for it to arrive. I don't know why I'm so tired. I slept well enough last night. It must be the stress of all this uncertainty. First, we didn't know whether Abby would be alright, and now there's this worry about losing the contract. So much for a peaceful Christmas break.

My phone buzzes, and I look at the screen, expecting it to be from Chris. But it's from Isabella.

I told you I think better with food. I've had some salmon linguine, and it did the trick. I haven't got time for more or I'll miss the lemon souffle. But I'll see you tomorrow x

What does she have up her sleeve? Is this one of her usual jokes or does she have a workable plan? I hope so. I don't like the thought of us throwing in the towel so easily. Especially not in front of Vanessa. I'm not sure what it is about her that rubs me up the wrong way, but something does. It isn't the fact she and Rob are together. That has nothing to do with me. It's more to do with her manner. And her habit of winking lasciviously at him. It feels like watching a Benny Hill show. Still, he must like it, or he wouldn't be dating her.

I get the distinct impression she doesn't like me either, despite all the gushing charm. It can't be anything to do with Rob. She's perfectly aware he and I only dated a few times and haven't seen each other since. But there's definitely an undercurrent.

She may be the type of person who isn't keen on other women. I'll have to watch how she is with Lily and Isabella tomorrow. Isabella, especially. She has the kind of looks someone like Vanessa might resent. Vanessa looks nice enough – tall and willowy, with long, shiny hair. But Isabella is something more. If Rob shows the faintest interest in her, which he may well do if his womanising reputation is accurate, Vanessa is bound to resent it. And she's the kind of woman who'll let it show, whether or not she intends to. She'll find some way of putting Isabella down in a way that's hard to pinpoint, just as she did last night when she called me bony and lanky.

I don't really care what she calls me, but it's obvious she did it on purpose. It's equally obvious there's no point calling her on it. She'd only throw up her hands and appeal to 'Rob, darling!' telling him she couldn't understand why I was overreacting when she meant to compliment me by saying how slim I was. It will be interesting to see how Isabella deals with that behaviour if it occurs. I'm sure her mother has given her lessons on it.

My pizza arrives, and I spend the rest of the evening watching rubbish reality TV, then have a hot bath and go to bed. Isabella hasn't texted with further details, and I'm too tired to wait up in case she does. She'll have eaten enough to feed a family of boa constrictors, washed it down with a bottle of wine, and passed out. If so, there's nothing we can do, short of letting down the tyres on the film crew's van, and I don't know where it's parked.

I wake early and tiptoe out of the flat in case Chris is sleeping. I haven't seen him to talk to since Abby was rushed to the hospital. I need to find myself somewhere else to stay as soon as possible and leave him in peace. It will be easier to think once the film crew has been and gone, and the question of the contract has been settled one way or another. If the worst comes to the worst, and we lose it, it's best to know at once. Then we can concentrate all our energies on maximising our income stream in the run up to Christmas.

I smile as I realise I'm using the word 'we'. What Lily and Isabella decide to do is none of my business. I'll never see them again once I leave Honeywell in the new year. But I like them both, and I want to see their business succeed. If I'm being honest with myself, I'd also like to see Vanessa's face when she realises she's been tricked.

Chapter Fifteen

To my surprise, Isabella is already waiting when I arrive at the bakery the following morning.

She laughs when she sees my face. 'I'm tempted to tell you that you're an hour late and threaten to dock your wages.'

'I'd probably believe you,' I say. 'I seem to be losing track of time at the moment.'

She looks at the clock. 'Lily should be here at any minute. She told me last night her mum was happy to take Daisy an hour early today so we can get on with things here.'

'I don't know what we're supposed to be getting on with,' I complain. 'Have you had any wonderful ideas?'

'Hundreds,' she says with a complacent smile. 'Not only did I eat all my salmon linguine last night, but I finished off my aunt's bouillabaisse.'

'What did you come up with? Hopefully, nothing fish related.'

'I'll tell you when Lily arrives,' she says. 'I see her coming up the high street now. She must have walked in today.'

Lily bursts in a minute later and throws her coat onto a chair. 'You didn't text me back last night!'

'That's because I was busy,' says Isabella.

'How long did the meal last?' says Lily. 'You told me your table was booked for seven.'

'We had a lot of catching up to do. Besides, I wanted to concentrate on the food. We went to The Oasis, and it would have been a shame not to have done it justice.'

'Couldn't you have put your stomach on one side for once?' says Lily. 'This is important.'

'I didn't need to,' says Isabella calmly. 'I fed both my body and my brain, and I came up with several ideas.'

Lily sighs. 'You should have let me know what they were, however late it was. I was up half the night worrying. Jack didn't help. He made all sorts of suggestions, each one more ludicrous than the last. Daisy would have been more useful than he was if she hadn't chosen last night to fall asleep in her dinner. She refused all my attempts to wake her up and give her a bath. It left me with too much time to worry.'

'You should have suggested a game of Twinkle Tag,' says Isabella. 'That always gets her going. If she didn't want to play, I'm sure Jack would have enjoyed it.'

Lily picks up her mug and takes a gulp of coffee. 'We have exactly four hours until the film crew arrives. I still think we should put them off. Can't we close the bakery for the afternoon and tell them we're doing staff training, or that one of the customers has typhoid and we have to do a deep clean?'

'No need,' says Isabella. 'We don't want to lose half a day's profit if we can help it.'

'What's the plan?' I ask.

'I need an hour in the office if you can spare me,' says Isabella. 'I have to make something. And then there's this!' She waves her phone at us.

'You're making a phone call?' I hazard. 'Who are you calling?'

'I'm not,' she says. 'But you're close. Abby has called me!'

'She has?' Lily and I say simultaneously.

'How is that possible?' I add. 'Chris told me Abby's still in the high-dependency unit. How could she have got hold of a phone without anyone knowing, and why would she have called you?'

'I expect she misses me,' says Isabella. 'But I didn't say she called me today. I said she'd called me. And so she has. Several times. Thank goodness I always forget to switch on my phone, so everything goes to voicemail.'

'You mean she left you a message?' says Lily.

'Several. And they're going to get us out of this mess today.'

'I don't see how,' says Lily. 'Not unless she called you at some point saying, "Hi, Isabella. I'm absolutely fine and definitely not in the hospital with peritonitis. I'll be in bright and early tomorrow to make a start on the Christmas desserts. Please apologise to the film crew for my unexpected absence."'

'That would have made things a lot easier,' says Isabella. 'I'll have a word about her thoughtlessness when I next see her. Maybe we should do something like that for the future. We could come up with a list of possible emergency situations. Each of us could record our voices saying them, along with some of the most common words in the English language. If we're ever faced with a similar situation, we can splice together a plausible sounding message.'

'Is that what you've done with this one?' I say.

She beams at me. 'That's right. I have a sixteen-year-old nephew who's good at this type of thing. It only took a small bribe and a promise to buy him as much beer as he likes as soon as he's legally allowed to drink it. I gave him all the messages I have from Abby, and he made them into one long one.

She switches on her messages, and we hear Abby's voice. *'Hi Isabella, I just wanted to give you a heads up I won't be able to stay late tomorrow. I have a family dinner. Sorry about that.'*

There's a click, and the next message plays.

'Don't forget you promised to come in at eight o'clock tomorrow morning. We have a meeting with the supplier. I have to talk to them about the Christmas orders. It's important to get it done early. I'll call you again to remind you.

The phone clicks again.

'Me again. Do we have any updates about the hotel contract? We should sort it as quickly as possible. When I was over there yesterday, Daniel told me he'd get the paperwork done by the weekend. We don't want them changing their minds.'

Isabella grins at us and presses another button. We hear Abby's voice, sounding a little crackly but clear enough. *'Hi, Isabella. I won't be able to come in tomorrow. Important family meeting. I'll call you by the weekend when I have any updates.'*

Lily gives a shout of laughter. 'That's pure genius! I'm sorry for doubting you.'

'As you should be,' says Isabella. 'I'm off to the office now while you two open up the shop. See you in an hour or so.'

She disappears, and Lily picks up an overall. 'Do you think it will work?'

'I'm past thinking,' I say. 'All we can do is go with the flow and hope for the best.'

Isabella reappears a while later, holding a large sheet of card. 'This week's rota!'

'For what?' says Lily.

'For our workflow. We need to memorise it and remember what we're all supposed to be doing, and when. Abby's a stickler for organisation and routine.'

'She is?' I say, fascinated.

'Of course, she is! You know how scary she can be. Chef Abby is a talented individual, but she's a tyrant in the kitchen, and we all live in fear of her. Remember when she hurled the saucepan at my head only because I asked the time, Lily? And the time she chased you into the bakery, waving a carving knife, because you put pink sprinkles on the doughnuts instead of purple?'

'I'm afraid I don't,' says Lily.

'That's understandable,' says Isabella. 'Trauma is a complicated thing, and the memories often disappear entirely. Still, one of us remembers it, which is all that matters.'

'Take care you don't say any of that on camera,' warns Lily. 'Abby could sue you for slander and take the bakery. I wouldn't blame her.'

'It's exactly the sort of thing Chef Abby would do,' agrees Isabella. 'I'll be most circumspect. I'll drop the odd hint here and there and hope they get the picture.'

I look at the chart she's drawn up. It's a wonderful creation – full of cryptic abbreviations. She's written all our names and tasks in different colours and added a complicated zigzag of lines joining the various elements.

The morning flies by, and none of us has the chance to talk further about the film crew's visit. We debate closing the shop while they're here, but Lily points out it may be better to have as much activity going on as possible. We can blame the commotion if we find ourselves unable to answer tricky questions.

The van pulls up outside the bakery right on time. I'd been hoping it might break down. Failing that, that the team would get themselves lost in the wilds of the Hampshire countryside and spend the afternoon driving in circles until they ran out of petrol in a remote area.

Sadly, neither of these things appear to have happened. So, it's on to Plan B – blinding them with Isabella's intricate chart. And if that fails, dazzling them with Abby's phone message.

Rob climbs out of the driver's seat, and my heart sinks when I see Vanessa climb out of the passenger seat. Doesn't she have a meeting to manage or autographed photos of her wearing Rob's bathrobe to sign?

A young woman emerges from the back of the van and stares at the bakery. She walks to the street, turns and looks at the frontage, making a rectangular shape with her two forefingers and thumbs. She says something to Vanessa, who laughs.

Lily sees me watching them and nudges me. 'That table over there asked for coffee five minutes ago. Could you deal with their order while I find Isabella?

I'm happy to stay in the shop all afternoon. The last thing I want is to appear on camera. I don't want to be the one who speaks out of turn and gives the game away. And I know almost nothing about the business, so I have no idea what should or shouldn't be discussed with the crew. I send a silent message of good luck to the others and walk over to the coffee machine.

The shop door opens, but I don't turn around. Lily has asked me to serve these customers, and she's my boss.

'Hi Grace,' says a voice, and I turn to see Rob smiling at me.

'Oh, hi!' I say. 'I'd forgotten you were coming in today.'

'I'm sorry it was such short notice,' he says. 'But Vanessa is going back to London this weekend, and she's eager to get started as soon as possible.'

'No problem,' I say, hoping my expression gives nothing away.

Vanessa follows him inside. 'Is this it?'

There's a hint of scornful contempt in her voice which makes my hackles rise.

'It's great, isn't it?' says Rob. 'I had lunch here the other day. This place is quite a find.'

'Marvellous,' she says. She catches sight of me. 'I didn't think you'd still be here.'

I don't answer. I have as much right to be here as she does. More right, in fact. I'm performing a useful function, whereas she's only getting in the way and annoying everyone.

'You're here until Christmas, aren't you, Grace?' says Rob.

'That's the plan.'

'Can you get me a cup of coffee before we start?' says Vanessa.

I want to point out we have a string of customers waiting, all of whom arrived before she did. But it's important we don't get off on the wrong foot today, so I give her my politest smile. 'What would you like?'

'I don't suppose you can manage a latte?' she says.

'Of course. What kind of milk would you like?'

'What do you have?'

'Full fat, half fat, skim, lactose free, soy, almond, and oat,' I rattle off. I'm tempted to add yak's milk or unicorn tears, but I refrain.

'I'll have a skinny decaf latte,' she says. 'If you could hurry it along a bit, that would be great. Time is money in this business.'

Why would she think it's any different here? Does she imagine Lily and Isabella run the bakery as a little side project to keep them busy and stop them getting bored in this sleepy backwater?

I busy myself with making her coffee in the cleanest cup I can find. I don't want to give her anything to criticise.

The camera woman comes in. 'It will be difficult to get a decent shot of the frontage. That lamppost is in the way.'

'What would you like us to do about that?' I say.

She rolls her eyes. 'I'm not asking you to move it. I'm just saying.'

I finish preparing Vanessa's coffee and hand it to her. 'I'll be quite busy in here this afternoon. If you need anything else, maybe it's best to ask Lily and Isabella.'

'Fine,' she says dismissively.

'Would you like a coffee?' I ask Rob, who shakes his head. 'You look pretty busy. We should let you get on with it.'

'How about you?' I ask the young woman.

'I'll take a turmeric iced latte,' she says.

I glance at Rob and see he's grinning.

'I don't know where you'd find one of those around here,' I tell her.

She swings around to face me. 'Are you serious? How about a matcha?'

'Sorry. But I can do you a pot of Earl Grey.' I almost laugh at the look of disgust on her face.

'I'm good, thanks,' she says. 'Where do you want me, Vanessa?'

'In the kitchen,' says Vanessa. 'We need some footage with this Abby woman. Can you show me where it is?'

I lead them towards the kitchen, where Isabella is standing at the far end with Lily, deep in conversation.

She turns when we walk in. 'Welcome to The Sugarloaf Bakery! I'm Isabella, and this is my business partner, Lily. Nice to meet you. Hi, Rob. I didn't expect to see you here today.'

'I asked him to come,' says Vanessa. 'He and I work as a team.'

I flicker a look at Rob, who doesn't speak.

'I'm Vanessa, and this is Bryony,' she goes on. 'Can we get down to business? We want to get some establishing footage. Most of it will be in the kitchen, but it would be good to get shots of you serving in the shop, making coffees, that sort of thing.'

'Although not turmeric or matcha,' I say.

Vanessa waves a dismissive hand. 'No one cares what you serve. They'll barely be paying attention. All this scene needs to say is, "We've switched over to The Sugarloaf Bakery."'

'Sounds good,' says Isabella. 'Would you like to do that now?'

'After we've had a proper look at the kitchen,' says Vanessa. 'Is this Abby ready? We need to see her preparing the usual Christmas stuff – gingerbread houses, candy cane cupcakes, whatever it is you do.'

'As it happens,' says Isabella, 'Abby isn't available today. But Lily and I are happy to stand in for her.'

'What do you mean she isn't available?' says Vanessa. 'It's the entire reason we're here. She needs to make herself available.'

Rob shoots a quick look at me, and I stare back at him defiantly.

'I'm afraid it can't be helped,' says Isabella. 'She's had to attend to a family matter. You didn't give us much notice.'

Vanessa looks as though she's bitten on a lemon. 'That's pretty inconvenient. Couldn't she have done that at some other time?'

'Obviously not,' says Rob. 'It sounds like an emergency.'

'That's right,' says Isabella. 'But only a very temporary one.'

'Will she be back tomorrow?' says Vanessa.

'It's unlikely,' says Isabella.

Vanessa sighs. 'How about Friday? I think we have a free hour in the afternoon.'

Isabella doesn't blink. 'What a shame. If only you'd said morning.'

Vanessa turns to Rob. 'We have that other thing on Friday morning, but we could switch them around.'

I catch Rob's eye and give him a pleading look.

'That won't work,' he says. 'I have to get back to London for an afternoon meeting, so it needs to be in the morning.'

I breathe a sigh of relief. Vanessa gives me a suspicious look. 'Did you say something?'

I shake my head, and she sighs again. 'I'm not happy about this. You knew we'd be here today. The least you could have done was make adequate preparations. Is this Abby woman ever coming back? How do you know this isn't some excuse? She may be interviewing for a job somewhere better.'

I hear Lily draw in a sharp breath. Isabella cuts in before she can say anything.

'I think you mean somewhere else. I'm sure that isn't happening. For one thing, there's nowhere any of us would rather work. For another, Abby isn't like that. It wouldn't occur to her to lie to us about an interview and leave us in the lurch. I doubt the idea would occur to most people.'

Vanessa doesn't appear to catch the subtext. She gives an impatient shrug. 'It would leave you in a difficult position if she did. Can any of the other staff cook?'

'Naturally,' says Isabella in such a haughty tone I have to choke back a laugh.

'Our establishment,' she goes on, 'prides itself on the fact that each staff member is highly trained in every area of our work. We could all step into each other's shoes at a moment's notice. It's part of running a professional business.'

I look at Lily. She's a full head shorter than me and Isabella. I doubt either of us could force our feet into her shoes.

'I'm glad to hear it,' says Vanessa. 'Because one of you will have to step in for her this afternoon. If we can't get the footage this week, we may as well not bother. Are you sure she's coming back this weekend?'

'I am,' says Isabella. 'As a matter of fact, I've just received a message from her.'

She waves her phone at Vanessa. 'Would you like to hear it?'

Without waiting for an answer, she switches on her voicemail and plays Abby's supposed message.

'You see?' I say to Vanessa.

'Where was she speaking from?' she says. 'It didn't sound clear.'

'I think she was on a train to her family's country house,' says Lily. 'I expect she was going into a tunnel.'

'In the meantime, which one of you will take over and do the baking this afternoon?' says Vanessa.

She notices the glances we give each other. 'You are qualified, aren't you? You told me you were.'

'Naturally,' says Isabella. 'It's all part of The Sugarloaf Bakery's policy to ensure the smooth running of our business.'

'I'm sure it is,' says Vanessa. 'In which case, let's make a start.'

Chapter Sixteen

I leave Lily and Isabella washing their hands and pulling on their hair nets and return to the shop, where I find Mrs Ogilvie about to leave.

'Bernie is having his claws clipped this afternoon,' she informs me. 'He doesn't enjoy it, but the dog groomer says he's always so well-behaved.'

'Are you both taking him?' I ask Mabel.

She snorts. 'Wild horses wouldn't drag me! The fuss that dog makes about a simple procedure. I cut my nails each week without one tenth of all that carrying on.'

'He has sensitive nail beds,' says Mrs Ogilvie defensively.

'He has sensitive everything,' says Mabel. 'If he were mine, I'd have sent him to military school years ago.'

'Don't you like dogs?' I ask Mabel when Mrs Ogilvie has left.

'I love them,' she says. 'Especially Bernie. He's a treasure. But he has Edie wrapped around his little finger. I suppose I should say his little toe. I can't help teasing her about him. It's revenge for all those years she used to play the older sister card.'

'But you're twins,' I say.

'Very true, but even twins aren't born at the same time. She's exactly twenty-one minutes older than me, and she's never let me forget it.'

'I'm glad you like Bernie,' I say. 'He seems a sweetheart.'

'He'll do,' she says. 'But don't let Edie know I said that. I'd never live it down. I'll take a couple of your wholemeal rolls if you have any left.'

I'm about to fetch her rolls when Lily appears, looking anxious.

'How's it going in there?' I say. 'Have you nearly finished?'

'It's a disaster!' she whispers. 'Vanessa has been asking all sorts of questions. I took some mince pies out of the oven. I thought Vanessa would be impressed when she saw them. But all she wanted to know was what we put in our mincemeat, and Isabella said –'

'Don't tell me,' I say. 'Mince?'

'Not quite. She said we used freshly chopped mint. When Vanessa queried it, she doubled down. She said it was a medieval recipe, and it was a well-known fact that Henry the Eighth refused to eat mince pies without it.'

'Vanessa can't prove that isn't true,' I say. 'With any luck, she'll forget all about it. What are they doing now? Have they finished filming?'

Lily looks even more agonised. 'No! Vanessa has just asked Isabella to whip her up some cheese straws. She said they're her favourite, and it won't take a moment. Neither of us has the faintest idea how to make them, so I came out here to look it up. Isabella is stalling by pretending to mix a cake and giving them a long lecture about the use of herbs in cooking through the ages. When I left, she was busy telling them Joan of Arc's visions were caused by overindulging in oregano fritters, and A Midsummer Night's Dream was written after Shakespeare's landlady mistakenly put basil into his special rice pudding.'

'Again, difficult to disprove,' I say. 'Please don't say she said any of this on camera?'

'I'm not sure. I hope not. But I was so busy trying to look as though I knew how to roll out pastry, I wasn't paying attention. Anyway, I need to look up how to make cheese straws before Isabella runs out of historical figures and their herbal foibles.'

'Can't you say there's no time to make anything else?'

'Vanessa is clearly becoming suspicious,' she says. 'I don't dare let her know we have no idea how to make something so simple.'

'It's either that or telling her the truth,' I say. 'This isn't going as well as we'd hoped. I thought they'd be here for half an hour, talk to a few customers, get some footage of you stirring a couple of things, and leave. What are you planning to do?'

Lily looks close to tears. 'I don't know. Tell them the truth, I suppose. What else can we do?'

'Right!' booms Mabel, making us jump. She marches over to the counter, snatches up an overall and pulls it on. She jams a baker's hat over her hair and makes for the kitchen.

I follow. 'What are you doing?'

'Never you mind!' she says and flings open the kitchen door.

Isabella is standing by the table briskly mixing something in a bowl. We hear her voice proclaiming, 'And then there was Galileo. It's common knowledge he was violently allergic to coriander. Well, one day, he was looking through his telescope –
'

'What do you think you're doing?' demands Mabel.

Everyone turns to face her. She points an accusing finger at Isabella and glares around.

'I arrive after my day off to find the shop understaffed and a long queue of customers. Then I come in here and find this!'

She gestures to the kitchen table, which is covered with flour and what looks like a map of England made of raisins. It must be one of Isabella's bright ideas. A tour of the British Isles as told by dried fruit.

'Someone had better tell me what's going on right now!' says Mabel, her hands on her hips and her cap askew. 'I take one day off, and I get back here to find everything going off like a frog in a sock.'

Isabella darts me a questioning glance, but I shrug.

'Who are you?' says Vanessa.

Mabel looks as though she's about to combust. 'Who am I? I'll tell you who I am. I'm Chef Mabel! What do you think of that?'

Vanessa looks puzzled. 'I've never heard of you.'

'Clearly, you don't know the first thing about culinary matters!' snaps Mabel, and I'm surprised to hear a faint Aussie twang in her speech, which grows more pronounced as she talks.

'Are you having fun with me?' she demands. 'The famous British sense of humour we hear so much about?'

'I have absolutely no idea who you are,' says Vanessa. 'But we're filming in here, so perhaps you could ...'

Mabel turns to Isabella. 'I hold you entirely to blame!'

Isabella stares at her feet. 'Yes, Chef Mabel.'

'Look at me when I'm talking to you!' barks Mabel. 'Are you responsible for all this?'

'Yes, Chef Mabel,' murmurs Isabella again. 'If you'd allow me to explain ...'

'I'm not interested,' says Mabel. 'If this has something to do with that ridiculous documentary, you'll do it in your own time. I want this kitchen cleared up and all these people out of here in ten minutes flat.'

'We're still filming,' says Vanessa. 'I don't know who you are, but we're working for Capital Productions, and we have every right to be here.'

Mabel fixes her with an icy stare. 'You may not know who I am, but I'll wager these two do. Or they will if they're halfway decent at their jobs.'

'You!' she snaps at Bryony, who jumps in fright.

'Yes?'

'You've heard of me?' says Mabel.

Bryony turns bright red. 'Erm ...'

'Give me strength! What about you?' Mabel demands of Rob.

Rob turns his head to where I'm standing in the doorway, trying to blend into the frame. I don't dare signal to him. It wouldn't do any good. He's on the opposite team.

His face doesn't change. 'Who hasn't? Chef Mabel of … er …?'

'Fremantle,' she says promptly. 'Not that I was born there, but it's where I was working when I hit the big time.'

'Where were you born, Chef Mabel?' says Isabella. 'You've never mentioned it.'

'In a tiny outback community in Western Australia,' says Mabel, her accent now giving Crocodile Dundee a run for his money. 'Wombat Wallow, it's called. You wouldn't have heard of it. Population fifty-eight. Fifty-nine when I came along, of course. I was almost born in the back of my parents' ute in the middle of Crocodile Flat, but they made it just in time. My old dad was a dingo whisperer there. What he didn't know about training dingoes wasn't worth knowing.'

'I wondered whether you were going to say he was a gold miner,' says Rob.

'That was my uncle Digby,' says Mabel. 'Gold, copper, opals. You name it, he mined it. I suppose you got that out of my autobiography?'

'I'm afraid I haven't read it,' he says. 'It was just a wild guess.'

'It was good training for my future career,' Mabel goes on. 'I could cook a five-course meal over a campfire when I was seven. By the time I was ten, I'd left school and was working as a sous-chef at a restaurant in Perth.'

'Ten?' says Vanessa.

'Different times,' says Mabel briefly. 'I worked my way up to head chef there. By the time I was fifteen, I was running the place. I stayed in Perth until I was eighteen, when I was spotted by a food critic from the Sydney Herald and given my own TV show.'

'That would have been in the fifties?' says Vanessa with a smirk.

'That's right,' says Mabel. 'It's very popular to put the colonies down these days, but we were way ahead of you when it came to that sort of thing. I remember having old Jake Judkins on the show one day, and he made emu burgers. Quite a stir it made. They sell them in all the supermarkets nowadays, but back then we thought it was haute cuisine.'

'I see,' says Vanessa. 'This is all absolutely fascinating. Do you mind if we get some of it on camera?'

'You don't catch me that way, cobber!' says Mabel. 'I've been burned too many times. That's a chef joke, by the way. I'm not signing any release without a proper contract and payment.'

'What a shame,' says Rob. 'But that's probably wise.

He turns to Vanessa. 'We should be making a move. We didn't intend to stay here for so long.'

She ignores him. 'You still haven't told us what you're doing here in Honeywell.'

'The staff didn't mention me?' says Mabel.

'Not a peep.'

Mabel glares at Isabella, who shuffles her feet. 'I'm sorry, Chef Mabel. We've been so busy.'

'Not too busy to make a mess in my kitchen,' says Mabel.

She surveys Vanessa more tolerantly. 'I'm visiting my sister who lives in the area, and I agreed to do a few days here as a consultant. This bakery is really going places. Honeywell is no Wombat Wallow, but it's not a bad place for all that. I see no reason why there shouldn't be a chain of Sugarloaf Bakeries right across the country in a few years' time. Who knows – if everything goes well, we may even think about franchising them in Australia.'

Vanessa looks from Mabel to Isabella, who still appears suitably chastened. 'How interesting. So, you're filling in for Abby this week?'

'That's right,' says Mabel. 'As soon as I heard she wouldn't be here for a few days, it seemed a great opportunity for me to come in and consult. It's better not to have two professional chefs in the same kitchen. You know what they say about too many cooks.'

'I do indeed,' says Vanessa. 'But I was under the impression the entire staff here is made up of professional cooks.'

'Fair dinkum,' says Mabel. 'But there's professional, and there's professional. These three girls can cook with the best of them. But Chef Abby is something else entirely. And I've done more laps around a kitchen than the drivers around Mount Panorama. Between the pair of us, we'll put this bakery on the map. In the meantime, I'd say we're finished in here. The girls and I still have to make a batch of Stollen before we close. So, we'll bid you a good arvo, folks, and catch you later.'

'We're sorry to have taken up so much of your time,' says Rob.

'No worries, mate,' says Mabel.

Vanessa looks as though she'd like to argue, but Rob is already helping Bryony pack up the equipment.

He stops in the doorway and looks back. 'It was a great pleasure to meet you, Chef Mabel. You always read about the greats, but you never expect to meet them in real life.'

'I don't suppose you do,' says Mabel.

'Nice to see you again, Grace,' he says.

I can't make him out. He can't possibly have heard of Chef Mabel because she doesn't exist. At least, I assume she doesn't. Maybe there's a real Chef Mabel swanning around the Australian outback, and Mabel is impersonating her, although it doesn't seem likely. But why did Rob try to help us? Surely, his job is to make the best television he can, even if that means making the three of us look like idiots on camera. It's a puzzle. Maybe he's biding his time, and he'll talk to Vanessa tonight and hatch a plan to expose us.

I can't do anything about that. I'm just grateful we've managed to get through the afternoon without total disaster. That will have to do for now.

I smile back at him. 'Oddly enough, it was nice to see you too.'

Chapter Seventeen

We shepherd the team out of the kitchen. Thank goodness for Bernie's claws. It would have been most inconvenient if Mrs Ogilvie had still been sitting in the cafe when they left. Vanessa might have noticed her and asked questions. I wouldn't put it past Mabel to have brazened it out and made up some ridiculous story about doppelgängers. But Bernie would have been bound to give things away by leaping up and licking her repeatedly like an old friend.

It's unlikely the team will see Bernie walking home from the groomer's. If they do, the chances are they won't associate a grey-haired, elderly woman in a dark blue coat with the flamboyant Chef Mabel of Wombat Wallow.

Where did she come up with all that? If I were forced to don an apron and cap and improvise a back story at a moment's notice, I'd fail miserably. I hope Wombat Wallow and Mabel's restaurant and TV show are too obscure for Vanessa to find online. Although Mabel will doubtless have some explanation ready to hand.

It was quick thinking on her part to refuse to sign a release. I must remember to do the same if there's any suggestion of me appearing on camera. I was careful to stay in the background today, so there's only the Christmas ball to worry about, and I doubt we'll be invited to that. We'll be confined to delivering our desserts to the servant's entrance and expected to stay out of the way of the paying guests.

Bryony has stopped to take some shots of the interior of the shop and cafe. Vanessa is busy directing her and moving tables and chairs about without asking Lily and Isabella.

'I haven't finished that!' says a woman indignantly as Vanessa picks up her cup and moves her table out of the way.

Vanessa gives her a dismissive look. 'They'll get you another one.'

I give the woman an apologetic smile. 'Sorry about that. If you could wait for just one moment, the team is about to leave, and I'll make you a fresh coffee. I'm so sorry for the inconvenience.'

Rob hasn't reacted. He must be used to Vanessa's ways. What I see as bossy and overbearing, he may see as strong and competent. Is this why I took such an instant dislike to her? She's a tough, resourceful woman who's made it to the top in a man's world? It's an unpleasant thought, but I don't really think that's why she rubs me up the wrong way. I would find her behaviour just as obnoxious in a man. Lily and Isabella have done pretty well for themselves by building up this business practically from scratch, and I never feel the urge to push either of them into a vat of custard.

'That's all I want for now,' Vanessa says to Bryony. 'I'll need you to get some shots out on the street. It's a pity it isn't snowing. It would be far better to see a cutesy English village in the snow, with its quaint, old-fashioned little bakery. People lap up that sort of thing.

'Old-fashioned?' says Mabel, who's still wearing her apron and lopsided hat and avoiding several of the customers' surprised looks.

'You haven't seen old-fashioned,' she goes on, 'until you've been to old Joe Spigot's in Kangaroo Crossing. He runs a bakery and cafe just like this one, but without any of these fancy herbal teas and lactose free milk. If you go to old Joe's, you're likely to get black coffee and dampers. And if you annoy him, he'll throw one of his boomerangs at you. He whittles them as a sideline.'

'Is that right?' says Vanessa.

'Strewth!' says Mabel. 'I've seen him bring down one of the shearers from the old Patterson place. Big man, too. And all because he passed a remark about the crusts on Joe's bannocks.'

'I'm sure that wouldn't happen here,' says Rob.

'Never,' agrees Isabella. 'Chef Abby puts us all through a strict training programme. She's thorough and extremely strict. She has this place organised with military precision, and woe betide anyone who steps out of line. Did you see her chart on the kitchen wall?'

'I did,' says Vanessa. 'It was most interesting. Especially the fact you appear to have eight days in your working week.'

She turns to me. 'Will you be undertaking this rigorous training programme too?'

'I'm afraid not. I'm only here until the end of the year.

'There's another feller up in Galah Gulch,' says Mabel. 'He used to wrestle crocs until he lost his second leg.'

Rob's lips twitch, but he doesn't say anything.

'We'd love to stay and listen to your stories all day,' Vanessa tells Mabel. 'But if you won't sign a release, there seems no point.'

'Too right, I won't,' says Mabel. 'But any time you and your team want to get together to sink a few tinnies and have a chinwag about my days in the outback, just give me a bell. I haven't told you about my time in Perth yet. And don't get me started on my first radio show.'

'We won't,' says Vanessa. 'We're off now. Thank you for a very … interesting afternoon. It's a pity we didn't meet Abby. That was the point of us coming here today. Still, we've got something.'

'That's good,' says Lily. 'Thanks for coming. We'll see you at the Christmas ball.'

'About that,' says Vanessa, and my heart sinks at the smug look on her face. 'We've been told we now have a forty-five-minute slot for this programme, rather than the original thirty minutes. This has been an unexpectedly popular series, so they want to make a big splash with the Christmas special to round it off in style. Which means we can add extra footage of the caterers. We'd like to come over the day you're actually preparing these desserts and see the entire team in action.'

There's the tiniest of pauses before Lily answers. 'No problem. We look forward to seeing you all.'

'I'll be in touch,' says Vanessa. 'Come on, Rob! Hurry up, Bryony!' She opens the door and motions them through.

'Thank you for giving us so much of your time,' says Rob. 'Especially when you're so busy.'

None of us moves until we've seen them safely into their van and watched them drive away.

Isabella collapses into a chair. 'That was a close thing!'

'Wasn't it?' agrees Lily. 'When Vanessa suddenly asked you to make those cheese straws, I thought all was lost. Thank goodness Chef Mabel arrived on the scene.'

Mabel pulls off her overall and smooths down her hair. 'I must say, I rather enjoyed myself. That producer woman isn't very nice, is she? Do you think she's like that with everyone, or has she taken a dislike to you for some reason?'

'She seems to be like that with everyone,' I say. 'I'm sure she's excellent at her job or she wouldn't hold such a senior position. But her bedside manner is a little lacking.'

'And I thought my chart was so good,' mourns Isabella.

'It was wonderful,' says Lily.

'You looked very professional making that cake,' I tell Isabella. 'What kind was it?'

'Goodness knows! I only had time to throw a few ingredients into a bowl before they arrived. I think I put in the usual things – sugar, some sort of flour, eggs, jam, a spoonful of lard. Oh, and a pinch of turmeric. I was dreading Vanessa asking me to put it in the oven so they could all have a slice before they left. They'd have woken up in the next bed to Abby.'

'Do you think they bought our story about where she is?' I ask, and she shrugs.

'No idea. Vanessa doesn't seem to buy much. But it's given us enough time to learn to cook, which is the main thing.'

'And it stopped them making us look like complete idiots on film,' says Lily. 'It's a pity they're coming back to watch us prepare the desserts. I wasn't expecting that, but we'll have to do the best we can. They're bound to have found out about Abby by then. But as long as we look competent and professional, we should be ok.'

'Will Chef Mabel have returned to Australia by then?' I ask. 'She was a welcome distraction today, but there may be people watching the programme who've actually been to Australia!'

Mabel laughs. 'Are you saying I didn't paint an entirely accurate picture of that great continent? I'm hurt.'

'I believed every word of it,' says Isabella. 'It's filled me with an intense desire to retrace the steps of Australia's favourite daughter – the plucky little battler. Do you think they run Chef Mabel tours? I'd pay good money to go on one of those. Starting in Wombat Wallow, cooking possum over a campfire, before moving on to the big city and eating at the restaurant where she got her humble beginnings. Is there a plaque?'

'I wouldn't be surprised,' says Mabel.

'There'll be a plaque for us in Honeywell one day,' says Lily. 'Once we've extended our chain of bakeries nationwide. First, we'll appear on Dragon's Den. Then we'll go global. Isabella and

I will write a book – *The Sugarloaf Shenanigans.* With a foreword by Chef Mabel.'

'Good on you!' says Mabel. She pulls off her overall. 'I should get going. I mustn't forget my wholemeal rolls. And you'd better throw in a biscuit for the mutt. There's always the faint possibility he behaved himself this afternoon. Even if he didn't, Edie will tell me he did, and I'll have to pretend to believe it.'

Chapter Eighteen

We sit down to review our plans after the bakery has closed for the evening.

'That didn't go quite as we expected,' says Lily. 'But it wasn't a complete catastrophe either.'

'I forgot to ask you about those mince pies you pulled out of the oven,' I say. 'Are they one of the few things you know how to make?'

'I wish!' she says. 'Pastry is a complete mystery to me. We have my mum to thank for those. I told her what was going on when I dropped Daisy off with her this morning, and she said she'd make us some pies and partially bake them. All I had to do was pre-heat the oven and pop them in for the last five minutes.'

'I didn't notice her arrive,' I say.

'Neither did the camera crew. Mum was lurking outside the back when they arrived. I waited until everyone was busy watching Isabella preparing her cake of doom before opening the door. I was terrified one of them would turn around and ask what I was doing. Luckily, Isabella was spraying clouds of flour in all directions, which diverted their attention. All I had to do was put the pies into the oven and open it again at the correct moment.'

'Your mum's the best,' says Isabella. 'I wasn't sure whether I wanted to try one when I thought you'd made them. But now I can eat as many as I like.'

'No offence taken,' says Lily. 'But you can't eat them all. We need them to sell in the bakery. They're our current bestseller, and we don't want our customers deciding to go elsewhere. Speaking of which, whatever possessed you to tell them Abby puts mint in our mincemeat?'

'I thought she did,' says Isabella. 'It isn't my fault. If chefs don't want people thinking there's mint in mincemeat, they should call it something else. It's like pecan pie. I was surprised to find it didn't have peas in it when I first ate it.'

'Abby won't be pleased when they air the programme and she sees what we got up to today,' says Lily.

'She may forget it's being shown,' says Isabella. 'If not, I'll have to tell Chris to break their TV. I'm sure he won't mind if it's in a good cause. Or Grace can put it in her car while he's out and tell him they've had burglars.'

'No, Grace couldn't!' I say. 'Chris would want to know why I hadn't called the police. What would I say?'

'They were having a doughnut break?' she suggests.

'No one is burgling Abby and Chris' flat,' I say. 'Not while I'm living there. I'm looking for somewhere else to stay, but in the meantime, I'll behave like a good guest.'

'Has Chris asked you to leave?' says Isabella.

'No, but it's time I moved on and left him in peace. I'm Abby's friend, not his. He must want the flat to himself. He's spending most of his free time at the hospital, but it can't be fun coming home and having to be polite to someone you barely know.'

'I agree,' she says. 'When will you be moving your things out? We can fetch them now if you like.'

'I haven't found anywhere to live.'

She clicks her tongue impatiently. 'I invited you to stay with us ages ago. You can move in as soon as you like. It will be fun.'

'You haven't asked your family yet,' I say.

'Yes, I have. I told them the night you arrived that you might need somewhere to stay and I'd offered you our spare bedroom. My mum said, "Marvellous, darling." My dad said he didn't realise you'd moved out. It took me a moment to realise he thought you were my friend Olivia who stayed with us for a few nights during the summer. Dad hadn't even noticed she'd left. My sister Georgia said you needn't think you were having her room. Otherwise, she didn't care. So, you can see it will be fine.'

'Don't be so pushy,' says Lily. 'Grace may have enough of you during the day without putting up with you in the evenings too.'

'I wouldn't have thought it was possible for anyone to have too much of a good thing,' says Isabella.

'But I'll be here for several more weeks,' I say. 'It might be better to find a place where I can stay until I leave.'

'You won't be in anyone's way. My family all does their own thing. Georgia was away for almost a month last spring, and I didn't notice. Come and try it for a few nights. You can always find somewhere else if you hate it.'

'If you're sure …' I say doubtfully.

'She is,' says Lily. 'She loves having someone else to talk to. I'll lend you a pair of earplugs, and you should be fine.'

'I'll let Chris know tonight,' I say. 'If you really don't mind, I'll bring my case with me tomorrow and go home with you after work.'

'Don't forget the television,' says Isabella. 'With any luck, Chris will be so tired he won't notice, or else he'll think they never owned one.'

Lily looks at the clock. 'I have to leave soon. Jack and I are having dinner with my parents tonight. But first, we should discuss our plans. Today was a success of sorts, but now the actual work begins. We have one month to learn how to cook well enough that the hotel doesn't sue us, and the camera crew doesn't make us look ridiculous on national TV. How are we going to do that?'

'We need to find out what Abby planned to make,' I say. 'I'll ask Chris tonight in case she told him. Otherwise, we should check with the hotel in case she's promised them anything like souffles or other complicated dishes.'

'I'll do that,' says Lily. 'I'll call their event planner and say I want to make sure we're all on the same page before we put in our order for supplies.'

'And I'll ask around to see if there's anyone who's willing to teach us to cook,' says Isabella.

Lily picks up her coat. 'Let's compare notes before work tomorrow. That means arriving early, Isabella. Do you think you can manage that?'

'Naturally,' says Isabella. 'But it would be so much easier if Grace was there to jump on my bed and pour cold water over me. Don't forget to bring an alarm clock when you come, Grace.'

Chris is making dinner when I arrive home. He greets me cheerfully enough. 'How's it going? I'm sorry I haven't been here much this week.'

'And I'm sorry I have,' I say. 'You must have been wishing me gone for several days.'

'Not at all.'

'That's polite of you. But in your place, I'd have been desperate to get the flat to myself again. I'm moving into Isabella's house tomorrow, so you only have to put up with me for one more night.'

He ladles stew into two bowls and sets them on the table. 'Are you sure? You're welcome to stay for as long as you like. You aren't a difficult houseguest.'

'It will be a good thing for me to be nearer the bakery. We have a lot to do over the next few weeks.'

I fill him in on everything that's happened while we eat the stew.

'I'm impressed,' he says. 'I thought you'd have told the hotel they needed to find someone else. No one would have blamed you.'

'None of us wanted to do that. I get the impression Lily and Isabella are counting on the money from the contract to keep them afloat until the new year.'

'So Abby said. They're doing ok, but it's been a tough couple of years for everyone, and no one can afford to turn down extra income. From what she said, they're particularly keen on this TV thing. Lily and Isabella think it could give them an edge in the local area and set them up to bid for other contracts.'

'Will it?' I ask.

He spoons some more peas onto his plate. 'I would think so. That hotel series was surprisingly popular. Plenty of people will tune in for the Christmas special. It should really raise the bakery's profile. Abby was so excited when they got the contract. She had to go over and make several desserts before their events manager would agree to take a chance on an unknown outfit. Until then, they'd been planning to go with some London caterer they use for most of their parties. But Isabella's uncle knows one of the local chefs, and he called the hotel and asked them to give Abby a shot. He reminded them it would look better if people saw them using local businesses. So, the manager called Abby with a list of dishes, and Abby went over there and knocked their socks off. They hired her on the spot.'

'I'll bet she did,' I say. 'That's the problem. It's a lot to live up to, and none of us knows how to cook.'

'I wondered about that,' he says. 'I'll do my best to help you, but …'

'Don't even think about it! You have enough on your plate at the moment. We aren't asking you to do anything practical. We should be helping you out, not the other way around.'

'I won't have time for much extra over the next month,' he says. 'Abby's doing better, so I'm going back to work doing reduced hours until she's out of the high-dependency unit. But she'll move into a regular ward after that. It will be a while before she's home.'

'I'm just happy she's recovering,' I say. 'Lily plans to call the hotel and find out whether we have any wiggle room or whether we're locked into a specific menu.'

'Get Isabella to do it,' he advises. 'She's a fast talker, and she can be very persuasive when she wants to be.'

'That doesn't surprise me. I wonder how we'll get on living together as well as working together.'

'You'll be fine. Speak up for yourself when you need to. The great thing about Isabella is that she's happy to take no for an answer. Maybe not happy. But she'll accept it if you dig in your heels and argue back loudly enough. And she never bears a grudge.'

'That's a great quality in anyone,' I agree.

'Abby says it's because she's always on to her next madcap idea,' he says. 'She doesn't have time for raking up past grievances.'

He suggests a list of desserts after dinner. 'I don't know exactly what Abby was planning to make but see if you can talk them down from anything too complicated. With any luck, you can get away with lemon tarts, chocolate mousses and crème brûlées, Christmas syllabubs, and something baked, like white chocolate and almond brownies. If they're well made, you'll be fine. They're all festive, but not too complicated. Given what the hotel charges for a ticket, there should be plenty of alcohol flowing. The guests won't notice minor imperfections.'

'If the worst comes to the worst,' I say. 'We can pour brandy over them all and set them alight.'

'Flambéed syllabub,' he says. 'It could become the new Acai bowls.'

'Unless we also set the ballroom on fire. It would make great television, but it wouldn't do much for the bakery's reputation.'

'Abby would hit the roof if she heard about that,' he says. 'Stick to those basic dishes and make sure you can prepare them perfectly. Don't try to run before you can walk. And whatever else you do, keep Isabella away from naked flames.'

Chapter Nineteen

Isabella is as good as her word. She's waiting in the shop when Lily and I arrive the following morning. She's made us both a coffee and looks more serious than usual.

'First things first,' she says. 'I've spoken to our old suppliers, and they're happy to help. They'll be here sometime this morning. That takes care of our day-to-day supply problems.'

'They're happy to help?' says Lily. 'So close to Christmas?'

'They were delighted,' says Isabella. 'They were falling over themselves to oblige us. They told me they'd never got over losing the custom of one of the most prestigious bakeries in the New Forest area, and –'

'Isabella!' says Lily.

'Fine! They said there was no availability. They'd taken on several new customers since we last spoke, and their schedule was packed. If I called again in the New Year, they might consider it. But they could offer us no guarantees.'

'So, why did you raise our hopes like that?' says Lily.

'Dramatic effect!' says Isabella. 'I wanted to give you a lovely surprise. You have so little faith in me, despite having known me for so many years.'

'Despite?' murmurs Lily.

'Yes, despite! It was a long phone call. It took me a while to persuade Mr Harville it was in his best interests to capitulate. But he was eventually persuaded to see things my way.'

'I'm not sure I like the sound of that,' says Lily.

'It sounds like something the Mafia would say,' I agree. 'Did you tell him he might be sleeping with the fishes if he refused to oblige us?'

'I did not,' says Isabella. 'Although a night locked in the fishmonger's might do him good. He was quite rude to me at one point. He didn't like me asking for an old and valued customer discount.'

'I'll bet he didn't,' says Lily. 'So, how did you persuade him? Did you tell him in an ominous voice you were … connected?'

Isabella looks delighted. 'How did you know? That's exactly what I said. I told him my uncle is close friends with the chef at The Oasis, and he also knows most of the other restaurant owners in the area. Mr Harville supplies a lot of them, and he knows my uncle, so he knows I was telling the truth. I can't believe I didn't think to play that card years ago.'

'Isn't that blackmail?' I say.

'What an unpleasant insinuation! It was a case of me working hard and employing my considerable charm and business acumen in order to persuade a fellow professional that our interests aligned. I didn't say one word about concrete boots or taking a dirt nap, and I resent the implication I did.'

I laugh. 'If you're looking for an apology, Don Isabella, you can forget it. But it's good news.'

'It's excellent news,' says Lily. 'We could probably have found someone else to supply us, but it would have cost us a lot more, which would have been disastrous for our bottom line. And the quality might have been worse.'

'Did you manage to get that discount?' I ask Isabella.

'Ten percent.'

'You didn't!' exclaims Lily.

'I did,' she says. 'I'd like to think he remembered what a pleasure it was to deal with us, and how my charming manner and cheerful smile always lit up his morning and made his entire day worth living. But I suspect it had more to do with the fact my uncle authorised me to dangle the prospect of supplying some of his future garden parties.'

'I don't care if you promised to dance the tango with him in the middle of the street while wearing a top hat,' says Lily.

'That would have been a treat for our customers,' agrees Isabella. 'Thankfully, it didn't come to that. But I'll keep it up my sleeve in case of last-minute emergencies.'

She takes a bite of her coconut and cherry slice. 'I've done my bit. How about the rest of you?'

'I talked to Chris last night,' I say, pulling the piece of paper out of my jeans pocket. 'He made a few suggestions. He also found me the number for the events planner. Would you like me to call them?'

'I'll do that,' says Lily. 'Thanks, Grace.'

She looks at the paper and pulls a face. 'Some of these seem rather complicated. I don't even know what a syllabub is. And he suggests making sixty of each dessert! Will the guests really eat that much? They'll already have eaten a buffet.'

Isabella studies the paper. 'That looks about right to me. Twenty people should easily be able to get through this lot.'

'Twenty?' says Lily. 'I thought Abby said it was one hundred and twenty.'

'She's joking,' I say. 'Chris told me all the tickets have sold, and there's a waiting list. It seems a popular event.'

'I may have been teasing you a little,' says Isabella. 'I personally feel the catering should be done with a more generous hand, but long association with Lily and Abby has led me to believe I eat a smidge more than the average person.'

'Chris says most of these desserts are simpler than they look,' I say. 'Especially after he suggested we switch Abby's souffle idea for chocolate mousses. He advised us to keep things as simple as possible and prepare everything well ahead of time. Then all we need to do on the day is put on the finishing touches.'

'Simple sounds good,' says Isabella. 'Could we get away with jam sandwiches, I wonder? I used to love those when I was small. We could tell the hotel we were going with the idea of British tradition and nostalgia. We may be able to persuade the other caterers to go with a wartime theme and serve spam fritters and corned beef hash. Do we know the likely age of the guests? If they're all over eighty, we may be in with a chance.'

'We'd better open up the shop,' says Lily. 'It's almost nine o'clock, and I see Mr Mason coming up the street with a purposeful look on his face.'

'Ask him whether he's attending the ball,' says Isabella.

I pull on my overall. 'In the meantime, have we decided how to turn ourselves into professional cooks in a month?'

'I talked to my mum about that last night,' says Lily. 'She's happy to come in after the bakery closes and give us some lessons. She knows a couple of silver surfers she thinks would help us too. One of them runs a part-time cake decorating business.'

'I didn't know we had competition in the village,' says Isabella.

'There isn't much overlap,' says Lily. 'She does one-off cakes for her friends' grandchildren – trains and mermaids and things like that. Mum showed me the photographs on her website. They're fantastic. There's no competition with us because we don't offer that sort of thing. Abby makes birthday cakes with flowers and iced messages when people ask for them, but that's all. Still, this woman may be prepared to give us some pointers. We need all the help we can get.'

'No argument there,' says Isabella.

Lily turns the sign around and opens the bakery door. 'Good morning, Mr Mason. How are you today? It's cold out there, isn't it?'

An elderly man wanders into the shop. 'Good morning, my dear. I wasn't sure whether you'd be open yet.'

'We open promptly at eight o'clock each morning,' says Isabella. 'Except for the weekends, when we open half an hour earlier. I myself am not always present at these opening ceremonies. Circumstances often lead to unavoidable delays. But my fully trained staff is competent to cover for me during my absences.'

'Please sit down, Mr Mason,' says Lily with a warning glance at Isabella. 'I don't believe you've met Grace, our new assistant.'

Mr Mason peers at me over his glasses. 'Another new assistant? How many does that make now? There's Lily and Imogen here, and Abby. Then there's Olivia …'

'She was only here for a few weeks,' says Lily. 'She left after Mrs Ogilvie's party, remember? She's in Bristol now, studying to be a surgical nurse. I had a text from her last week. Will has set up his own photography business there and seems to be doing well.'

'That's nice to hear,' says Mr Mason. 'And how is dear Abby? I hear she's been indisposed. Nothing serious, I hope?'

'She was pretty unwell for a while,' says Lily. 'But she's doing much better now.'

'I'm so glad,' he says. 'Give her Daisy and my best wishes when you see her.'

I leave him chatting to Lily and go to the kitchen to fetch the rest of yesterday's mince pies. I find Isabella eating one.

'Lily says we need those for the shop,' I say.

'No, we don't,' she says. 'I realised last night Mrs Carson had made them at home. She doesn't have a food safety certificate, and her kitchen hasn't been inspected by an environmental health officer. We can't sell her pies in the bakery.'

'Luckily for you,' I say. 'Does everything we sell have to be made on the premises?'

'Or else delivered by a registered supplier. It will make things more difficult for us, but we have to follow the rules.'

I leave her happily munching the remaining mince pies and return to the shop. The cafe is already half full, and Lily and I are kept busy fielding orders for the next couple of hours.

Isabella appears at lunchtime. 'How's it going in here?'

'Busy,' says Lily.

'I almost came to check on you,' I say. 'I had visions of you passed out on the kitchen floor after a surfeit of mince pies.'

Isabella looks scornful. 'It would take a lot more than that. But thank you for your concern. I've been doing the accounts. I called the hotel when I'd finished and spoke to their events manager. He was quite abrupt with me. I asked him what he was expecting us to make for the desserts, but he said it wasn't a good time to talk. He was nowhere near his computer, and he had to be somewhere before they closed for lunch. He told me he would be back in his office by three o'clock. He suggested one of us came over to see him if we had any questions.'

'I'll go,' says Lily. 'You and Grace can look after the shop.'

'Not this afternoon,' says Isabella. 'I'm having my root canal, remember? I've already put it off twice.'

'I can't leave Grace to handle everything alone here,' says Lily. 'It wouldn't be fair.'

'I can see that,' says Isabella. 'What if Wendy Protheroe comes in again? Could Grace drive over to see this Daniel person?'

'I'm not sure,' says Lily. 'We have to discover what we've promised him without letting him know we have no clue what we're doing.'

'I expect I could manage that,' I say. 'You don't work in advertising for years without learning how not to say what you mean.'

'Maybe,' says Lily. 'We need to find out what we're up against as quickly as possible so we can make a plan.'

She gives me directions to the hotel. 'Are you sure you can manage this?'

'She's asking for a list of desserts, not trying to inveigle the Allied plans from him,' says Isabella. 'She'll be fine.'

'Should I change into something smarter before I go?' I ask. 'I have my things in the car.'

'By all means,' says Isabella. 'You won't need a full-length gown. But if you have a cheeky little cocktail number in your suitcase, now's the time to crack it out.'

'You look lovely as you are,' says Lily. 'Make sure you don't have flour on your nose, and you'll be fine.'

'I still think you're sending her into the lion's den unprepared,' says Isabella.

'What a coincidence he should be called Daniel,' says Lily. 'But we can be reasonably sure he won't eat her, however grumpy he is. You worry about yourself, not Grace. You're having a root canal. That's far worse.'

'I know,' says Isabella gloomily. 'The last time I had one, my dentist told me not to eat until the anaesthetic had worn off. It took almost three hours! I'm way ahead of him this time. I've finished all your mum's mince pies, and I still have nearly an hour to eat my lunch.'

Chapter Twenty

I set off for the hotel after lunch. I drive out of Honeywell and past fields glittering with the remains of this morning's frost. The air is still and clear, and I feel my spirits lift. This feels about as far from London as I could get.

The road forks, and I take the left-hand turn past a small row of thatched cottages. I join the main road and pull up a few miles later outside the Quayside Hotel.

It's larger than I expected and, somewhat to my surprise, nowhere near the water. From an advertising perspective, I can appreciate The Quayside Hotel sounds a lot better than The Dual Carriageway Inn or The Roadworks Retreat. I walk across the gravel sweep to the main entrance. There's an enormous fireplace in the lobby, and I stop to enjoy its warmth before making my way over to the reception desk.

'Good afternoon. How may I help you?' says the receptionist with a bright smile. She sounds as though Isabella has trained her. I half expect her to add, 'I hope your experience at the Quayside Hotel is everything you hoped for.'

I assume my most professional manner. 'I'm here to see Daniel Carter. Is he available?'

She dials a number and waits for a moment. 'Daniel? It's Mandy in reception. I have a visitor waiting for you. I'm not sure.'

She covers the mouthpiece. 'May I ask for your name?'

'Grace Anderson. I'm here from The Sugarloaf Bakery.'

She repeats this, then rings off. 'He'll be down momentarily. In the meantime, please make yourself comfortable by the fire.'

A man appears a few minutes later. He's tall, with sandy hair and an unsmiling face. The receptionist points to me, and he walks over and holds out his hand.

'Daniel Carter. Sorry to have kept you waiting.'

'Not at all,' I say. 'Thank you for seeing me at such short notice.'

'Shall we go to my office?' he says.

I follow him through the lobby and up a flight of stairs. He opens a door and gestures for me to go inside.

It's a small room, but I can see why he's chosen it. The window at the far end looks out onto a wide sweep of lawn, which sparkles like a blanket of diamonds under the winter sun. The lawn leads down to a meandering river, which partially explains the word Quayside.

'What a lovely view,' I say. 'If I worked in this office, I'd never get anything done.'

'I'm barely ever here,' he says. 'What can I do for you?'

So much for small talk. I'd been hoping to chat for a while and gradually bring the subject around to the Christmas ball and the fact his star caterers don't have a clue what they're supposed to be making for him.

'This is a lovely hotel,' I say. 'I haven't been here before.'

'Weren't you here when we gave you the contract?'

'No. That happened before my time.'

He looks surprised. 'Three weeks ago was before your time? I thought you said you worked at The Sugarloaf Bakery?'

'I do, but only just. I mean, I've only recently arrived. They took me on to help them over Christmas. It's their busiest time of year. When they got this contract with your hotel, it meant a lot of extra work for them. Not that they couldn't cope, of course. They can. But in the interests of maintaining the utmost professionalism and … erm … expertise, they hired me. Out of an abundance of caution.'

I add this last bit because it's what all the politicians say. It doesn't mean much, but it sounds good.

'Sure,' he says, and I flush. Why didn't I just say yes?

'That's why I haven't been here before,' I finish.

He looks at his watch. 'And now you are here, how can I help you?'

'It's nothing,' I say. 'I mean, obviously it's something or I wouldn't be wasting your time like this.'

What's wrong with me? I deal with million-dollar contracts for a living and can make obnoxious executives quail and tremble. Yet here I am, unable to ask for a simple point of clarification about a two-bit contract.

'I was wondering about our contract,' I start again.

His brow furrows. 'What about it? Your chef signed it a couple of weeks ago. If there was any problem with it, that was the time to raise it.'

'No problem at all,' I assure him. 'It's a great contract. At least, I assume it is. I haven't actually seen it.'

He gives me an odd look. 'You haven't seen it?'

'No. As I say, I've only been here for a week. I work in advertising.'

'I don't understand,' he says. 'You said your bakery needed a temp over Christmas, which is why you're here.'

'Oh, I see. No, I'm not working for an agency. I'm here in the capacity of a friend. But a professional one. It's a very professional setup.'

He leans back in his chair and surveys me with a hint of amusement. 'I don't doubt it for a minute. Sending you here like this is ample demonstration of that.'

'I'm only here because Isabella had to have a root canal,' I say. 'And Lily couldn't trust me alone in the shop.'

'It's hard to see why,' he says politely.

I try again. 'What I mean is that I've only recently started work there, and Lily didn't think it was fair to leave me in charge.'

'Fair to the customers?' he says.

'Fair to me!' I say crossly.

'I see. And Isabella is one of the chefs at your bakery?'

'No, she's one of the co-owners. She works in the shop, and she also handles the business side. She eats a lot of cake, though,' I add honestly.

'Hence the root canal?' he says. 'So, is Lily a chef?'

'No, she's the other co-owner. She works in the shop and cafe.'

'And we've established you aren't the chef. I feel as though there's a missing piece of the puzzle.'

'That's Abby,' I say. 'She's our pastry chef.'

'I thought we might get there in the end,' he murmurs.

He opens a drawer and pulls out a sheaf of papers. 'Ah, yes. Abby Martin. I remember her now. She came over and wowed us all with her cooking. If she has a problem with the contract, she should have contacted me directly. Why isn't she here today?'

'She's otherwise engaged,' I say. 'As I mentioned previously, Christmas is our busiest time of the year. I'm here as her official spokesperson.'

He raises an eyebrow. 'Spokesperson? That sounds official. So, she has … people?'

I remember Isabella's conversation with the suppliers and am tempted to agree she has.

'I'm joking,' he says. 'What's the problem?'

'No problem. We wanted to clarify a technical point about how much latitude we may or may not have with the putative range of desserts you have engaged with us to supply.'

'With the what?' he says.

'Can we change the menu?'

He looks at the papers again. 'You're providing desserts for one hundred and twenty people. What did you want to change?'

'Nothing! We're happy with that concept.'

'So, what's the problem?' he says. 'The number of people?'

'No! If anything, it's not enough. Abby was saying only yesterday she wished there were more.'

'More?' he echoes, now looking thoroughly bewildered.

'Yes. She was saying what a small affair this is – hardly a challenge for someone of her capability. She's catered far larger events than this.'

I have no idea whether this is true, but this man is starting to annoy me.

'Has she, indeed?' he says. 'Most impressive. However, I'd be grateful if she could confine her activities to one hundred and twenty guests on this occasion.'

'Of course. I was just saying …'

'It may not be a large number to her,' he goes on. 'But it is to me. This ball will be televised, which only adds to the pressure. I don't have a moment to call my own. So, if you've got what you came for? What was that, by the way? I'm still not entirely clear.'

'To clarify a point of law,' I say. 'I mean, contract law.'

I throw caution to the winds. 'To find out what we've promised to make for you. Did we agree on anything specific?'

'Don't your managers have a copy of this contract?' he says.

'They do, of course. What I wanted to ask was whether you and Abby had verbally agreed on any particular dishes? As you know, verbal contracts are binding in the state of … I mean in Hampshire.'

'I wasn't aware,' he says. 'But I prefer to get everything in writing. It saves trouble. Doesn't Abby know? She's the one I had the conversation with.'

'She has a terrible memory. But not that terrible! She hasn't forgotten how to cook or anything.'

'I'm delighted to hear it,' he says dryly.

'What I meant to say was that she's out of the bakery for a couple of days.' Why didn't I say that at once?

'Is there no telephone connection in Honeywell?' he says, and I can't tell whether he's hiding a smile.

'Yes. But she doesn't have a phone.'

'How unusual,' he says. 'Or should I say charmingly old-fashioned?'

'She isn't!' I say. 'She's trained in all the most modern techniques. But she's at a … spa. No phones allowed.'

He looks surprised. 'At your busiest time of the year?'

'It's a … cooking spa. She goes there each year to prepare for Christmas. She always comes back with lots of new recipes, so it's worth her not being in the bakery for a few days.'

I stand and hold out my hand. 'We're both busy professionals, so I won't take up any more of your time. I should get back to the bakery. Lots to do.'

'Especially with your chef on her spa retreat,' he agrees. 'Will they be covering *sous vide* cookery, I wonder?'

'Covering what?'

'It strikes me a spa would be the very place for it. All those steam rooms …'

He breaks off. 'Forget it. Culinary humour is out of place for busy professionals such as us.'

I'm annoyed by the note of mockery in his voice. I'm aware I've made a complete fool out of myself this afternoon. He doesn't have to rub it in.

'Perhaps it would be better if you concentrated on this ball,' I agree. 'It sounds as though you may have bitten off more than you can chew.'

'More culinary humour?' he asks, and I flush.

'I'm saying that if one hundred and twenty people is too much for you …'

'Perhaps it would have been easier to keep it to fifteen or twenty,' he says. 'An intimate yuletide soirée. But it would have been rather less like a ball. Perhaps I should book myself into a spa next year to prepare.'

'A managerial spa?' I say.

'Exactly. A Yuletide retreat for Hampshire's overworked event planners.'

'Agendas and aromatherapy?'

'If only I'd met you earlier,' he says.

'I'm always happy to offer my professional advice. Although next time it will have to be on a consultancy basis. And I should warn you, I'm horribly expensive.'

'I'm surprised your bakery can afford you,' he says. 'They must be doing well.'

'I'm charging them mate's rates. But I'm afraid I can't extend that further afield. Exclusivity is the key to any successful business. You must realise that.'

'They didn't cover the subject at our last spa retreat,' he says. 'Perhaps I should buy myself a book instead.'

'I'll send you a copy of Event Planning for Dummies,' I promise.

He walks me downstairs and into the lobby. 'Thank you for coming. I enjoyed our … contract negotiations.'

'Contract clarification,' I correct him. 'I appreciate your time, Mr Carter.'

'Daniel,' he says. 'Nice to meet you, Grace. I look forward to seeing you again.'

'I expect we'll meet at your intimate yuletide soirée.'

'It's too late to change the arrangements now,' he says. 'But I'll bear your suggestion in mind for next year. I may see you before that. You say your bakery is in Honeywell?'

'That's right,' I say cautiously. 'But it's miles from anywhere – right out in the sticks. Most people get lost trying to find it.'

'That can't be good for business,' he says.

'The locals all know where it is.'

'I'm glad to hear it. I'm not a local. But, unlike your pastry chef, I have access to a phone. And I can download a map. I assume you're on the map?'

Should I tell him the Streetview cars got lost and never came back to cover the village? I suspect he wouldn't buy that. He looks the competent sort.

'Possibly,' I say in a noncommittal tone.

'Wonderful!' he says. 'The Sugarloaf Bakery sounds a fascinating enterprise. As soon as I can find a spare minute, I'll make a point of coming over to see it for myself.'

Chapter Twenty-One

I arrive back at the bakery half an hour later. It's lucky for me that Honeywell is on the map because I get lost several times and have to consult my phone. The connection is patchy, but I eventually see the church spire in the distance and drive in its general direction.

'How did it go?' Lily greets me when I walk in. 'Did you find out what we wanted to know?'

'I think so.' I don't mention that I also talked a load of nonsense, and we now have to face the prospect of the hotel's event planner turning up here without warning. She doesn't need the extra worry. With any luck, Daniel will forget all about it.

'How's Isabella?' I ask. 'Is she back from the dentist yet?'

'She's in the office. Apparently, she's dying. I offered to call for an ambulance, but she told me in a failing voice she wouldn't dream of adding to the burden of an already over-stretched medical service, and she'd take her chances.'

'Poor thing,' I say. 'Does she need anything?'

'She took a slice of chocolate mousse cake in there with her. I thought the dentist had warned her not to eat, but she said he only mentioned solid food, and this was practically liquid. Long experience has taught me not to argue. You can check on her if you like. But be prepared to beat a hasty retreat.'

I find Isabella leaning back in her armchair with her eyes closed. I'm about to close the office door again in case she's asleep, but she opens one eye. 'Hi, Grace.'

'Hi,' I say in a hushed tone. 'How are you feeling?'

'As though eight camels have kicked me in the face at once.'

'That's an odd metaphor.'

'I was going for a Christmassy image. Donkeys would work too.'

'I'm sorry,' I say. 'I had a root canal last year, and it was awful. Did they give you any pain medication? Myrrh or Frankincense, perhaps?'

'They gave me something or other,' she says. 'But it doesn't seem to be working. Now the anaesthetic is wearing off, I realise I've bitten the inside of my cheek. It's extremely painful.'

'Nothing to do with the chocolate mousse cake?'

She sighs. 'I knew Lily would make a fuss about that. It couldn't have been the cake. I ate it without chewing. It was either that or passing out for lack of food.'

'You should have something soft for dinner,' I say. 'Soup, maybe?'

'As a starter? Good idea. I could manage some cream of tomato. And something light to follow. Pie and chips? We could go to The Red Lion.'

She sits up, looking more cheerful. 'Their crème brûlée is to die for. And you don't need to chew it. I'm feeling better already. Let me know when you and Lily have closed up, and we'll pop over there.'

By the end of our meal at the Red Lion, Isabella has revived and is back to her old self.

'The cook here is almost as good as Abby,' she says, pushing away her plate. 'Her crème brûlées are amazing. I once asked her for the recipe, but she laughed.'

'You seem so keen on food, I'm surprised you never learned to cook,' I say.

'You aren't the first person to say that. But it doesn't follow. If someone's mad keen on Monet, they visit art galleries and exhibitions. They don't buy themselves a paint by numbers book and expect to produce wonderful art.'

'They could take lessons,' I say. 'Plenty of people do.'

'But they don't fill their houses with wonky pictures of their dogs or bowls of fruit and expect to get as much pleasure from them as *Woman with a Parasol.* It's a completely different experience.'

'You've given this some thought,' I say.

'It's a subject close to my heart. Anyway, we need a concrete plan. Are you sure this Daniel didn't want us to make anything specific?'

'He said Abby had wowed them all with her souffles.'

'We should stay away from those,' she says. 'He may not be as discerning a food critic as myself, but I expect he'd be able to tell the difference. It would be as though someone had made a finger painting of the Mona Lisa.'

'What do you think of Chris' suggestions?' I ask.

'They sound good. I expect we could learn to make crème brûlées without too much difficulty, even if Shelley won't give us her secret recipe.'

I pull out my phone and start taking notes. 'Are we in agreement about how many portions we need to serve?'

'Abby says two and a half for each person. Which makes Chris' calculations about right.'

'Who eats half a dessert?' I say.

'Not me, that's for sure! It's a complete mystery to me why people leave restaurants without finishing their food. Human beings are strange creatures. In another life, I'd have been an anthropologist.'

'Meanwhile, in a world where you're a humble bakery owner, could we finalise this list?' I ask.

'You sound like Lily,' she complains.

'My sympathy for her increases by the day. Abby, too.'

She clicks her tongue. 'I've heard that before, and it's nonsense. I'm a delight to work with – sunny, cheerful, and always willing to help with taste testing. I imagine it's like working with Pollyanna. I'm a beam of sunshine around the place.'

'I'll take your word for it. But I'm interested to know how Abby came up with this two-and-a-half portions idea.'

'She mentioned something about averages,' says Isabella. 'I'm not terribly good with numbers, so I just go along with whatever she says.'

'Aren't you an accountant?'

'Technically,' she says. 'I beaver away in the office with my little abacus each day. But financial numbers are one thing. Food numbers are quite another. They confuse me. I start thinking about what they represent, and my mind wanders. Even when I'm ordering basics like dried fruit and chocolate chips, I start wondering what Abby will use them for, and I lose focus.'

'Crème brûlée!' I say to bring her back to the present.

'I still think we could do something with jam sandwiches,' she says. 'If we make the theme of the ball Childhood Reminiscences, we should be fine. We can make stacks of them, showcasing a variety of local jams. My mum used to cut them into shapes with a cookie-cutter when Georgia and I were good.'

'I can see it now,' I say. 'All the bigwigs tucking into heart-shaped jam sandwiches. I assume we'll use white sliced bread to keep it traditional?'

'Of course! And we must have jelly and ice cream.'

'How about packet trifles?' I suggest.

She beams. 'I used to love putting the sprinkles on those. Georgia usually did it because she was the youngest, and she threw better tantrums than I did.'

'I find that hard to believe.'

'It's true,' she assures me. 'She still does. It's very sad. Anyway, if Daniel wants his ball to stand out, he'll have to come up with something more original than music and dancing. And what could be more original than sitting your guests down to jam sandwiches and ice cream?'

'He may have his own ideas about that,' I say. 'Do you know if this ball has a theme? Under the Sea or Hollywood Glamour? That sort of thing.'

'This isn't a high school prom from the 1950s,' she says. 'It's an upmarket Christmas ball.'

'So, what's the theme? Gilded affluence? My diamonds are bigger than yours?'

'We'll have to ask my uncle,' she says. 'He's bound to be there. He goes to all the local events. He lives in the manor house in our village and runs the family farm. People think he's far more influential than he is, so they invite him to everything. My family lives in the Lodge because we're the poor relations. My uncle sends his housemaid down the hill to us each morning with a basket of food containing the leftovers from their breakfast and last night's dinner. You needn't worry we won't look after you, Grace. Our family has a long tradition of hospitality to strangers. You'll get first dip in the basket.'

'I can hardly wait. If I could bring you back to earth for a minute, are we agreed on our list of desserts?'

'Probably,' she says. 'But I can't think clearly at the moment. I'm too full. We should go back to my house, and you can settle in. You have to meet my family at some point, and they aren't too awful. Even Georgia has her good points.'

She picks up her bag and pulls on her ancient duffel coat. 'Don't look so scared, Grace. You'll be fine. Don't forget I promised you first dip in the basket tomorrow morning. It's extremely generous of me, considering that Thursday is kedgeree day up at the Manor.'

Chapter Twenty-Two

I wake the following morning unsure where I am. The light is unfamiliar. I take a moment to realise why. My bedroom in Chris and Abby's flat has a small window facing west, so there's almost no sun on it in the mornings. This room has cream curtains, through which the sun appears to be shining.

Recollection comes rushing back. I'm at Isabella's house. We arrived here yesterday evening after our dinner at the Red Lion. Her family was friendly and welcoming, but it's always awkward staying in a new place with people you barely know. It was fine with Chris and Abby because she's an old friend. But I hadn't met any of the Campbells before last night. For all I knew, they had no idea I was coming. I wouldn't put it past Isabella to have forgotten to mention some random stranger would be arriving.

There's a knock on the door, and Isabella opens it. 'Do you have everything you need? I've saved you a bacon sandwich, but you'd better hurry. Georgia is on the prowl.'

We arrive at The Sugarloaf Bakery half an hour later to find the door already unlocked. Lily is inside, talking to a woman I don't recognise. A small girl is sitting on a booster seat eating a piece of toast.

Isabella makes a beeline for her. 'Dizzy!'

The little girl drops her toast onto the floor and holds out her arms to be picked up.

Isabella swings her out of her seat, gives her an enormous hug, and turns to face me.

'Grace, I would like you to meet my beautiful goddaughter.'

'And my daughter,' says Lily.

Isabella takes no notice. 'Daisy is one and a half. Haven't I done a good job of raising her?'

'Hello,' I say to the little girl. 'I'm Grace.'

She stops smiling and stares at me with wide blue eyes, just like Lily's.

'She's always shy with new people,' says the woman. 'Hello, Grace. I'm Angela Carson, Lily's mum. And Daisy's grandmother.'

'And did I mention I'm her godmother?' says Isabella, planting a huge kiss on Daisy's cheek before returning her to her seat.

'You've dropped your toast,' she adds. 'We'll have to make you some more. Perhaps I should make some extra. It's been a long time since I've eaten anything.'

'We had bacon sandwiches for breakfast!' I say. 'Even you can't be hungry again already.'

'Not hungry, precisely. But my motto is, "Always eat when you get the chance." You never know when you'll get another opportunity. It comes of growing up with Georgia. You only have to turn your back in our house, and all the food disappears. I don't know how she does it. It can't be good for her.'

'Bacon sandwiches?' says Lily. 'Isn't Grace a vegetarian?'

'Are you?' says Isabella. 'You never mentioned it. I'd have eaten your bacon for you if I'd known. I saw Georgia had her eye on it while you were eating. Greedy pig! Never leave your plate unattended when she's in the house. It only takes a second. You'll go to the fridge to get yourself some milk. When you turn around, your plate will be empty, and Georgia will be sitting there looking like a contented python.'

'Thanks for the warning,' I say.

'But I don't understand,' she says. 'Didn't you have game pie last night? Or did I pull a Georgia and eat it when you weren't looking? I'm sorry if I did.'

'I'm not a vegetarian,' I say. 'I only pretended to be because of Rob.'

'Why? Is he the founder member of the society of meat eaters? Or was he attacked by a vegan when he was young?'

'Possibly. But that wasn't why I said it.'

'Why did you care what he thought about your eating habits?' she pursues. 'You told me you barely knew him.'

'It was all rather ridiculous. He came into the bakery, and I didn't want to have lunch with him. I thought if I said I was a vegetarian, I wouldn't have to. He could sit in lonely splendour eating his pie, and I could make my escape. How was I to know Abby made such amazing vegetable pies? Anyway, that's all it was. I do, in fact, eat meat. So, there's no need for you to rescue me from whatever is on my plate.'

She looks disappointed, then brightens. 'But you could have a sudden change of heart at any moment – a road to Damascus conversion. I won't give up hope.'

'I'll let you know if I do. Aren't you supposed to be making toast instead of interrogating me about my food choices? The shop will be opening soon, and the opportunity will be lost.'

'I'm afraid we don't have time,' says Mrs Carson. 'Daisy and I are off to the farmers' market this morning. Aren't we, poppet? We're buying some lovely leeks for Grandpa's soup.'

'Save some for me!' says Lily. 'It's my favourite. And you always seem to make it when I'm not there.'

'I'll make an extra-large batch,' says Mrs Carson. 'Daisy loves it too. Which reminds me. I'd better buy us a nice crusty loaf while I'm here. She likes to make her bread into boats and sail them in her soup.'

'I taught her to do that!' says Isabella proudly. 'And how to use her spoon to make a storm.'

'I know you did, dear,' says Mrs Carson. 'It took me quite a while to clean the floor. Daisy and I pretend to sail our boats down a tiny stream now. It's far less messy.'

'I can see Mrs Ogilvie coming up the street,' says Lily. 'We'll have to open the shop. Mum only popped in to tell us she can give us a cooking lesson after work. She's suggested starting with lemon tarts.'

'That's an excellent idea,' says Isabella. 'Do you think we could learn to make them well enough for the ball?'

'Of course!' says Mrs Carson. 'There's nothing you girls can't do if you put your mind to it. Look what you've done with this bakery. It wasn't doing too well when Lily started working here. And now it's a thriving business in the heart of the village. If you can do that, you can learn to make a few desserts.'

'Enough for one hundred and twenty people,' Lily reminds her.

'It's all a matter of scale,' says Mrs Carson. 'It doesn't take six times as much effort to cater for one hundred and twenty people as it does for twenty. You'll see.'

'I hope you're right,' says Lily. 'Anyway, we appreciate you offering to teach us.'

'We do,' says Isabella. 'I know how busy you are. My goddaughter takes up plenty of your time without adding cookery lessons for incompetent women.'

'Nonsense,' says Mrs Carson. 'I love to keep busy. And you aren't incompetent. Merely inexperienced.'

She picks up Daisy. 'Come on, darling. Off to the market with you!'

'Don't get muddled up and sell Daisy by mistake,' Isabella warns her. 'It would be a simple mistake to make, wouldn't it, Dizzy?'

Mrs Carson walks towards her car with Daisy clutching her hand. A moment later, the door opens again, and Bernie rushes in, followed by one of his owners. He makes straight for the counter, looks up at the basket of biscuits, and gives a hopeful wriggle.

'You wait your turn, young man!' says his companion. 'I'm always telling you it's rude to beg. Besides, I want my coffee.'

'Good morning, Mabel,' I say. 'Just the two of you today?'

'Edie has a bit of a cold, so I told her to stay in the warm this morning. Bernie and I are capable of going for a walk by ourselves. She tried to argue, but I wasn't taking any nonsense. "We don't want it turning to pneumonia," I said. "Then I really would have my hands full, between you and Mr Attention Seeker here." She saw sense in the end.'

'One pot of tea coming up,' says Isabella. 'It's on the house. We owe you for saving us yesterday.'

'That was nothing,' says Mabel. 'I enjoyed it. But I wouldn't say no to one of those Portuguese tarts. And a biscuit for the mutt. He won't give us any peace otherwise, and I want to talk to you.'

'Do you call him that in front of Mrs Ogilvie?' says Isabella, handing her a plate.

Mabel winks. 'Only when I want to annoy her. I have a list of names for him – The Mutt, Mister Eats-Too-Much, Sir Good-For-Nothing. I like to keep her grounded. She spoils that dog beyond sense or reason.'

'Until you arrived, he was her only companion,' says Lily. 'I understand why he means so much to her.'

'So do I,' says Mabel. 'But I can't help teasing her. Goodness knows, she did enough of that to me when we were small. Anyway, I came in to see whether you girls need any help with this Christmas ball?'

'Wombat burgers and crocodile steaks?' says Isabella. 'Where did you come up with that back story, by the way? I have a vivid imagination, but even I would have struggled.'

'I surprised myself,' says Mabel. 'It came pouring out. Do you think they believed any of it?'

'Not a word,' says Isabella. 'But that isn't the point. You bought us some time. And you prevented Vanessa asking difficult questions. We'd hoped to hide Abby's illness, but Vanessa knew something was up. You came along in the nick of time and saved us.'

'Any time,' says Mabel. 'You may have put them off the scent, but that's only the beginning. Now you have to produce what you've promised. Are you able to do that?'

'I hope so,' says Isabella. 'But it's a bigger undertaking than we realised. Angela is coming in this evening to give us a cookery lesson. She'll have her work cut out for her.'

'That's where I can help,' says Mabel. 'I may not have been entirely accurate when I sketched out my culinary history for the team. But some of it was true.'

'Which part?' I say. 'The bit about you almost being born in the back of a ute?'

'That can't be true,' says Lily. 'Mabel and Mrs Ogilvie were born near Honeywell.'

'We were,' agrees Mabel. 'And if you tell my sister I suggested we first made our appearance in a tiny town in the outback, I'll never forgive you. She'd be horrified.'

'We won't,' I promise. 'So, what was true? The part about the man who throws boomerangs at you if you insult his bread?'

'Not that either,' she says.

'That's a shame,' says Isabella. 'I was thinking of introducing a similar system here. It might make that Wendy woman think twice before she complains about our products.'

'Opening your own restaurant in Perth?' I ask. 'The TV show in the fifties?'

'I only moved to Australia about six years ago,' says Mabel.

'We've ruled out all the best bits,' says Isabella. 'There's nothing left.'

'That depends on how you look at it,' says Mabel. 'They may not run tours to Wombat Wallow to look at the one-bedroom house in which I and my fifteen siblings grew up. But so what? The important thing is that I can cook.'

'You can?' says Lily.

'I helped a friend in Melbourne when they were opening a restaurant. I worked as her unofficial sous-chef for a while when she couldn't afford to pay someone else to do it.'

'What sort of restaurant?' says Lily.

'Italian. I learned to make all sorts of desserts – cannoli and tiramisu and pannacotta. You name it. And it struck me last night you might appreciate my help. So, first thing this morning, Bernie and I put on our coats and came up here to make the offer.'

She bites into her tart. 'Don't feel obliged to ask me if you have someone better in mind.'

Lily swoops down and kisses her cheek. 'I can't believe it! We've been desperately hoping for a miracle, but we didn't dare expect one. Then you come along and tell us not only do you know what to do, but you're willing to do it.'

Mabel looks pleased. 'No one has ever called me a miracle before. A lot of other things, but never that. Edie would laugh if she heard you.'

'You're *our* miracle,' insists Lily. 'If you'd walked in today wearing a pair of wings and a halo, none of us would have been surprised. If Bernie weren't already the bakery mascot, we'd commission someone to do a huge painting of you and hang it on the cafe wall.'

'I wouldn't want you doing that,' says Mabel. 'People would be bound to think it was Edie, and I don't want her taking all the credit. I'm surprised the mutt is your mascot. What did he do to deserve that?'

'It's a long story,' says Lily. 'If you won't let us paint your portrait, can we at least buy you lunch?'

'Another time, perhaps,' says Mabel. 'I should get back home and see how Edie is doing. And that dog will be pestering for another biscuit if I give him half a chance. When would you like to talk about this party?'

'How about tomorrow morning?' says Lily. 'Come in at ten thirty if you're free. We should have time to sit and chat before the lunchtime rush.'

'I'll be there,' says Mabel. 'But I can't promise the mutt won't be there too. It's difficult to sneak out of the house without him knowing.'

'We'd love to have him,' says Isabella.

Mabel raises an eyebrow. 'There's no accounting for tastes. I'll see you all tomorrow.'

She and Bernie set off home, and Lily lets out a huge sigh. 'Can you believe it? I'd started to despair that we could pull this off. Then, along comes Mabel.'

'Chef Mabel,' I say. 'She deserves her full title.'

'She does,' says Isabella. 'Isn't it lucky she worked in an Italian restaurant? It could easily have been something else – sushi or barbeque.'

'Hickory-smoked syllabub wouldn't have been ideal,' I agree. 'But Italian cuisine is perfect. I went to Rome last year and ate almost nothing except desserts.'

'It sounds my sort of place,' says Isabella.

She picks up Mabel's tray. 'We can't sit around talking all day. We have customers to serve. I hope your mum knows how to make dog biscuits, Lily. We're almost out, and I don't have a clue what Abby puts in them. I'd better call Chris and ask whether he has the recipe. Otherwise, Bernie will be stuck with my famous lard and baking soda surprise.'

Chapter Twenty-Three

Mrs Carson arrives as we're closing up after work.

'Daisy and I had a wonderful time at the farmer's market,' she says. 'She loves our trips there. Someone was demonstrating how to make cream, and they had some lovely samples of cheese. I bought some blue cheese for Martin. You know how much he loves that, Lily. You should have seen Daisy's face when I gave her the parcel to hold. She sniffed it, shouted Stink! and dropped it on the ground. I can't think where she learned that.'

'It's a mystery,' says Lily, glancing at Isabella.

'I expect it was Jack,' says Isabella. 'You should have a word with him, Lily. I don't want my goddaughter thinking it's alright to behave like that. It will hinder her chances of becoming the youngest Prime Minister in history.'

'Is that what you have planned for her?' I ask.

'I haven't quite decided. It's one possibility. Otherwise, I'm considering her becoming a rocket scientist or a brain surgeon. It's a tremendous responsibility being a godmother. You have no idea of the pressure.'

'Perhaps she'll become a famous chef, like Mabel,' I suggest. 'That way, it won't matter if she shouts rude things and throws food around.'

'Are you talking about Mabel Watkins?' says Mrs Carson.

'It was a silly joke,' I say quickly.

She smiles. 'Daisy can become a chef if she likes. She's clever enough for anything. But that won't be for a while yet. In the meantime, I need to teach her mother and her friends how to cook.'

'I can manage the basics,' says Lily. 'Just not award-winning desserts for hundreds of people.'

'How about you, Grace?' asks Mrs Carson. 'I'm sure you can cook a little.'

'Enough to survive,' I say. 'I can make an omelette and heat soup or beans. And I can prepare rice pudding and jam. That was one of my childhood favourites. But I only make it when I can remember where I put the can opener.'

Mrs Carson clicks her tongue. 'There's nothing easier to make from scratch than a nice rice pudding. It's so warming on a winter day.'

'Let's start with something simpler,' says Isabella. 'Grace and I thought we could make crème brûlées as one of the options. That comes out of a packet, doesn't it?'

'Oh no, dear!' says Mrs Carson, shocked.

'I hoped we could buy a box of crème brûlée mix and add water,' says Isabella. 'Or milk for a special occasion. But you said you wanted to start with lemon tarts. They don't come out of packets, do they?'

'I recommend you use pre-made shells,' says Mrs Carson. 'You'll want your desserts to be uniform in appearance. No one will mind if the bases are pre-made as long as the filling is excellent.'

'You mean we can't pour tinned custard into them?' says Isabella. 'This cookery thing is turning out to be a more complicated business than I thought.'

'Not at all,' says Mrs Carson. 'I've brought the ingredients for the lemon cream.'

She shows us how to beat the eggs and sugar before blending in the cream, lemon juice, and zest. She watches as Lily pours the mixture into the pastry shells and slides the tray carefully into the oven.

'Is that all?' says Lily as she straightens up. 'There must be more to it than that.'

'I'm afraid there isn't,' says her mother. 'You've avoided cooking for all these years, and it turns out there's nothing to be scared of once you face it head-on. Isn't that always the way?'

'I'll believe it when I see the final result,' says Isabella. 'And taste it, of course. Shall I make us a drink to celebrate?'

'Good idea,' says Lily. 'We could do with a cup of coffee after our hard work.'

'Coffee would be lovely,' says Mrs Carson. 'You all did very well. Could you make these again?'

'I think so,' says Lily. 'Won't Abby be surprised when she comes back to work and finds there's nothing for her to do?'

'How is she doing?' asked Mrs Carson.

'Much better,' I say. 'They're moving her to a regular ward tomorrow.'

'What a relief! I don't like to think about what Chris and her poor parents have been through. I keep thinking what if it was you, Lily? Your father and I would be out of our minds with worry.'

'I found it difficult enough when Daisy had bronchitis,' says Lily. 'I hated her being in hospital. I couldn't explain to her why we were there or why the doctors had to give her nasty medicine and stick needles into her arm. I felt I was betraying her by allowing it. I couldn't wait to get out of there. Oddly enough, it was worse when they said I could bring her home. I didn't like her being in the hospital, but I felt safer when she was there. I barely slept during her first night at home. Neither did Jack. I kept expecting a nurse to come around to take Daisy's temperature and check her pulse.'

'I wonder if it will be like that for Chris when Abby comes home,' I say. 'Hopefully not. She can talk and understand what's going on and tell him if she's feeling worse.'

Mrs Carson looks anxious. 'Lily, you must always tell Jack if you feel ill. Don't wait like Abby did and hope it will all go away. It's better to be safe than sorry. Promise me you will?'

Lily gives her a hug. 'Don't worry, Mum. I'll tell Jack if I have the faintest twinge of stomach-ache after eating too many lemon tarts. I won't even wait until morning. I'll kick him awake and give him a running commentary.'

'There's no need for that,' says Mrs Carson. 'But I'd hate to think of you soldiering on like Abby and ending up being rushed to hospital in an ambulance.'

'I'll keep an eye on Lily,' says Isabella, who has returned carrying a tray of drinks.

Mrs Carson looks doubtful. 'I'm sure you will, dear, but sometimes your mind is on other things.'

'Harsh, but true,' says Isabella. 'In that case, I don't know what to suggest.'

'Maybe I could keep an eye on Isabella,' I say. 'Then she can keep an eye on Lily, and Lily can keep an eye on me. With that number of eyes on us, we should be fine.'

'I know I'm an old fuss pot,' says Mrs Carson. 'But it's been a wake-up call for everyone. I made your father get that mole looked at last week. He's been putting it off for ages, but I told him no more! From now on, we're sorting things as soon as they arise, no matter how busy we are.'

The oven timer pings, and Lily picks up a pair of oven gloves. 'The moment of truth. I'm almost afraid to open the door.'

'You'll have to if you don't want them to burn,' says Mrs Carson.

Lily takes a deep breath. 'Wish me luck!'

She lifts out the tray of tarts and lays it on the table. We all lean forward to inspect it.

'That's amazing!' I breathe. 'They look just like real ones.'

'They are real ones,' says Mrs Carson.

'You know what I mean. They look good enough to sell – if Isabella doesn't eat them first.'

'Which is a distinct possibility,' says Isabella. 'They smell amazing too. Like a lemon grove in Amalfi.'

'They do smell good,' agrees Lily. 'When do we get to taste them?'

'Are you sure you want to eat one before your dinner?' says Mrs Carson.

'I promise to eat all my vegetables,' says Lily.

Mrs Carson laughs. 'I keep forgetting you aren't a little girl anymore. It's even more difficult to believe you're a mother of your own little girl.'

'Enough talking!' says Isabella. 'I'm going in.'

She picks up a plate and lifts out one of the tarts. 'Ouch! It's hot.'

'I'm glad to see your school science lessons weren't wasted,' says Lily.

'They weren't,' says Isabella. 'We learned all about the movement of air dispersing heat. For the non-scientists among us, that means if I blow on this tart, it should cool down enough for me to taste it.'

She gives a few quick puffs, then takes a careful bite. A look of bliss creeps over her face. 'This is incredible. And to think we did it all by ourselves.'

'We had a bit of help,' I remind her.

Isabella winks at Mrs Carson. 'Barely any. Angela only supervised. The point is we now know how to make these award-winning tarts.'

'Don't they need to win awards before we can call them award-winning?' I say.

Isabella finishes her tart. 'They won't get the chance. I'm not waiting for the judges to arrive. These should be eaten at once.'

'We can all taste one,' says Mrs Carson. 'You deserve it after your hard work. You should put the rest into the fridge. You can dust them with icing sugar tomorrow morning. It might be a good idea to serve them with a nice raspberry coulis when you make them for the ball.'

'Is that complicated?' says Lily.

'Not at all. It couldn't be simpler. You sieve the fruit with some icing sugar.'

'I thought coulis was jam thinned down with water,' says Isabella.

Mrs Carson looks amused. 'For someone who's so fond of food, you don't know much about how it gets onto your plate.'

'I'm an enthusiastic amateur,' says Isabella. 'But that's all about to change. A coulis sounds great. Add a sprig of mint, and you could serve these at The Oasis.'

'I'll put the rest of them in the fridge,' says Lily. 'Don't look so glum, Isabella. We'll have to make plenty more. For all we know, this was beginner's luck. The next batch may collapse, or the cases may burn.'

'Only if you aren't paying attention,' says Mrs Carson. 'It's a simple enough recipe. I've written it out for you. Follow these instructions to the letter, as I showed you. Don't try to be clever and add variations. Experienced cooks can tweak a recipe, but not until they've mastered the basics. You may think it's a good idea to double the lemon juice to make the filling extra tangy, but it isn't. You'll throw off the ratios of the other ingredients and ruin the tarts. Follow the recipe carefully, and you'll be fine. I suggest you practice making these each day until you're confident. Then we'll move on to the next thing.'

'Mabel has offered to help us too,' says Isabella. 'She used to work in a restaurant.'

'How kind of her!' says Mrs Carson. 'The more people we can find to help you, the better. I must be going, Lily. Your father and I are off to the cinema tonight. We're looking forward to it.'

'Thank you so much for helping us,' says Isabella. 'I hope I wasn't too difficult a pupil.'

Mrs Carson's lips twitch. 'You were born a handful. Your poor mother! But it was a pleasure to teach you. I knew you'd pick it up quickly. You're all so smart and capable.'

She kisses Lily goodbye. 'See you tomorrow morning. Daisy and your father will be planting his winter lettuce in the greenhouse. She loves that. He has to go back later and sow a few more if she's been overenthusiastic with her thumbs, but he doesn't mind.'

Lily comes back into the kitchen after seeing her mother off. 'That went well. I'm starting to feel we can do this.'

'We have a long way to go,' I say. 'But I agree. It wasn't as difficult as I thought.'

'That's because we're all such smart, capable women,' says Isabella. 'I love how your mother always sees the best in everyone, Lily. It makes me want to live up to her expectations, although I suspect I never will.'

'The three of us have managed to cope so far,' says Lily. 'We got through the filming without disaster. Then we made a plan for the party. And now we've taken the first steps towards implementing it. We should be proud of ourselves.'

'I like what your mother said about keeping an eye on each other,' I say.

'And the bit about kicking Jack awake,' adds Isabella. 'It's a great idea, Lily. It will stop him taking you for granted.'

'I mean it,' I say. 'It's how all good businesses work. Team members need to have each other's backs. They should be ready to step in and help without needing to take the credit.'

'I agree,' says Isabella. 'Abby is out of action, so the rest of us are stepping in. It's what teams do.'

'And friends,' adds Lily.

'I feel a toast coming on,' says Isabella. 'I've finished my coffee, and I don't want to make another one. And my hip flask is empty. Why don't we take the remaining tarts out of the fridge and use them to toast friendship and teamwork and all that?'

'I don't think so,' says Lily, picking up her bag. 'I have to go home for dinner. And you two should do the same.'

She fixes Isabella with a stern gaze. 'I've counted those lemon tarts, and I know exactly how many there are. If I come in tomorrow and find a single one is missing, I'm putting a lock on that fridge.'

Chapter Twenty-Four

By the time we arrive back home, I'm feeling more confident about this Christmas ball. If I'd known cooking was like this, I would have attempted it years ago. My home economics teacher first put me off the subject when she took one look at my curdled pancakes and scorched grilled cheese sandwiches and suggested I throw them away and choose a different option to study as quickly as possible.

My mother was highly amused by the thought I was following in her footsteps. She'd always been proud of the fact she could burn water. My father, seeing my downcast face, told me he far preferred shop-bought cakes, and he'd never seen anyone draw as well as me, so I might be better off choosing graphic design the following term.

I'd like to go back to Harefield High and tell Mrs Matson I'm working in a bakery now and have helped to make a batch of nearly award-winning lemon tarts. But I doubt she'd care. She ran our needlework classes too, which is why I still ask my dry cleaners to sew on my buttons for me.

'One down, four to go!' says Isabella as we drive along Compton high street. 'Abby had better watch her step. There's a new kid in town. Three of them, in fact.'

'We have a way to go before we can cook like her,' I say. 'But it was a good evening's work. If Mabel helps us with some of the other dishes, we may just get away with it. I hope so. I'd like Daniel to see how competent we are.'

I haven't told Lily and Isabella the details of my trip to the hotel. I got what I went for, which is all either of them needs to know. But I'm aware I made an absolute fool of myself, and I'd like the chance to redeem myself. It's a matter of professional pride, that's all.

I wonder whether to mention Daniel's threat to visit Honeywell. But there's no point. He was almost definitely teasing me. A man in his position doesn't have time to go running about the countryside trying to locate obscure bakeries. He has to concentrate all his energies on making sure his Christmas events run like clockwork.

Georgia is waiting for us when we arrive at the house. 'Mum's out, and Dad's having dinner with Uncle Charles tonight. I hope you're planning on cooking.'

'You're out of luck, little sister,' says Isabella. 'Grace and I have spent all day working in the bakery before spending half the evening making lemon tarts. We're all cooked out. Why can't you make us something?'

'I can't cook,' says Georgia. 'Just like you.'

'Not true!' says Isabella. 'I can bake delicious lemon tarts now. What do you have to say to that?'

'I could eat a lemon tart,' says Georgia. 'Where are they?'

'At the bakery,' says Isabella. 'Lily put them in the fridge and locked us out.'

'You could go back and fetch them,' says Georgia.

'No, I couldn't. I'm too tired. And Lily would kill me if she found out. She'd confiscate my bakery key.'

'I don't see the point of you working in a bakery when you never bring anything home,' grumbles Georgia.

'I bring plenty of things home,' says Isabella. 'They don't always make it the entire way, but I bring them.'

'Why don't I order pizza?' I ask. 'I'd offer to cook, but I'm in the mood for something more substantial than a tin of soup or scrambled eggs, which is about my limit.'

'Cool,' says Georgia. 'I'll have my usual. Thanks, Grace. Let me know when it arrives, Issy. And don't steal all my olives.'

She disappears upstairs. Isabella shakes her head. 'The younger generation has a lot to learn about manners and a hard day's work for a fair day's pay.'

'What does Georgia do?' I ask.

'She works in a boutique in Christchurch. When I say "work", she goes in each day and grumbles about having to order the stock and not being allowed to take two hours for lunch. I suspect her co-workers don't enjoy working with her as much as you and Lily enjoy working with me. I doubt there's much cheery singing as my sister goes about her work. Rather than following my excellent example and flitting about the place like a ray of sunshine, I imagine her as a little rain cloud stomping around and threatening to soak everything if no one offers it an extra-long afternoon break.'

'She seems alright to me,' I say. 'Sisters always seem to rub each other up the wrong way. Has she ever thought about working at the bakery?'

Isabella looks horrified. 'No, and please don't suggest it. Living with her is one thing. I can mostly ignore her existence. Having to work with her would be quite another. I'd be feeding her to Bernie before the end of the first day. No, she and I are better off ploughing our own furrows.'

'A farming metaphor?' I say. 'How apt. You told me the other day you help on the farm when you have time. Does Georgia help too?'

'You've met her. What do you think?'

She hands me her phone. 'If you're serious about ordering that pizza, I'd like a large pepperoni with extra cheese. I'm tempted to tell you Georgia wants a small, low carb vegetarian pizza, just to see her face. But you're paying, so I'll restrain myself. She'll have a large quattro formaggi with extra dough balls.'

'Got it,' I say. 'I was about to order myself a vegetarian pizza, but you already know my shameful secret, so I'll have a Hawaiian. Why have you given me your phone? I have one of my own.'

'It may come as a surprise to you,' she says, 'but the local pizzeria number is on my speed dial. It's number three, after Lily and Abby.'

Chapter Twenty-Five

I'm working in the shop the following afternoon while Isabella attempts a second batch of lemon tarts. The ones she made this morning were perfect, except that she turned up the oven too high and ended up by setting off the smoke alarms.

A group of women comes in, and I take an order for three cappuccinos and a hot chocolate. I switch on the coffee machine and start to grind the beans, my mind full of syllabubs and crème brûlées and almond brownies.

The shop door opens, and I hear Lily greet the customer.

'Good afternoon,' says a man's voice. 'I'm looking for Grace Andersen.'

I know that voice. I turn my head to see Daniel standing by the counter.

He catches sight of me. 'Hello, Grace.'

'I'll be with you in a minute,' I say, flustered. 'I'm just –' I break off. What was I meant to be doing?

'I'll finish making those drinks,' says Lily. 'You can talk to …?' She gives Daniel an enquiring look.

'Daniel Carter,' he says. 'I work at The Quayside Hotel.'

'Daniel is the events manager,' I say in a warning tone, and he smiles.

'Nice to meet you,' says Lily. 'I'm Lily Carson, co-owner of the Sugarloaf.'

'What were you making?' she asks me, gesturing towards the coffee machine.

'Er … four hot drinks.'

'What kind?'

I hardly hear her. What is Daniel doing here? I'd hoped he would find it impossible to locate us on a map, although I didn't think it was likely. But there were a million other things that could have happened to prevent him coming here. His car could have packed up, or he could have come down with a deadly disease. Anyway, isn't he supposed to be busy event-managing? How does he have time to spy on perfectly innocent bakeries who are simply minding their own business?

'Grace?' prompts Lily.

'Sorry. It was something with … er … foam, I think. And a hot chocolate.'

Daniel gives a tiny cough which had better not be a laugh.

'Never mind,' says Lily. 'I'll ask Mrs Parkinson.'

She walks over to the group of women and starts talking to them.

'What can I get for you?' I ask Daniel in my most professional manner.

'Nothing,' he says. 'I told you I might pop over to see your bakery at some point, and here I am.'

I wave my arm towards the cases of cakes and the cafe. 'This is it. Just a perfectly normal bakery. I'd offer to give you the tour, but you've just had it.'

'Charming,' he says with the hint of a laugh in his voice.

Lily finishes serving the drinks and returns to the shop. 'How are you getting on?'

'Daniel wanted to see our bakery,' I say. 'And now he has.'

'How nice of him to come all this way,' she says.

'Isn't it?' I agree. 'He's a busy man, especially at this time of year. I'm surprised he found the time. Or did you drop in on your way somewhere else, Daniel? Don't let us keep you.'

'It's my afternoon off,' he says. 'I have nowhere else to be. It seemed a good opportunity to visit.'

'As you can see, it's all in working order,' I say. 'Everything's running like clockwork. Business as usual.'

'I can see that.'

'Can I get you a drink now you're here?' says Lily.

'I'd love a coffee,' he says.

'What would you like?'

'I'm trying to decide between a drink with some sort of foam and a hot chocolate,' he says gravely.

'Why not split the difference and make it a cappuccino?' she suggests.

'Perfect,' he says. 'And one of those lemon tarts, please. They look delicious.'

'They are delicious,' I say. 'Our highly trained chef made them last night. You remember Abby? You met her at the hotel. She's the one who made them.'

'Great,' he says, looking slightly puzzled.

Lily waits until Daniel has chosen a seat by the window. 'What's wrong?' she whispers.

I lower my own voice to match. 'Nothing's wrong. Or it wasn't until he walked in. He threatened to come and see us when I saw him at the hotel, but I didn't think he meant it. What do you think he's doing here?'

Lily picks up the tongs and places the tart on a plate. 'At a guess, I'd say drinking a cup of coffee and eating a lemon tart. I may be wrong, but that's what it looks like to me.'

'But why here?' I insist. 'He has a perfectly good hotel he can visit if he wants coffee and cake.'

'It's his afternoon off. Perhaps he felt like trying somewhere new? Would you want to come here for lunch on your day off?'

'He's here to snoop about and find out what's going on,' I insist. 'I didn't want to mention it the other day, but when I saw him at the hotel, he seemed suspicious about what was going on here.'

'The way you're behaving is sure to put his mind at rest,' she says. 'Can you please take him this slice of cake and stop looking at him as though he's Hercules Poirot and you've just killed Sherlock Holmes?'

I take the plate over to Daniel's table. 'Lily will bring your cappuccino in a minute.'

'Wonderful,' he says. 'Would you care to join me for a few minutes?'

'I'm afraid not. We're terribly busy this afternoon.'

I follow his gaze around the nearly empty cafe. 'The afternoon rush will be starting soon.'

'I won't keep you long.'

I perch gingerly on the very edge of a chair. 'Only if Lily doesn't mind.'

She places his mug on the table. 'Doesn't mind what?'

'Daniel wants to talk to me for a few minutes.' I shoot her an agonised look, willing her to say I'm needed on the roof to clean the gutters.

'That's fine,' she says. 'It's almost time for your break. Shall I make you a latte?'

'Or something with foam,' suggests Daniel helpfully.

'Thanks,' I say to Lily. 'I won't be long. I'm due to help Abby in the kitchen when she arrives back from the suppliers. She wants me to help her make those … Bakewell slices.'

'I wish I'd waited now,' says Daniel. 'Bakewell slices are my favourite.'

Why didn't I say meringues? I have no idea how to make a Bakewell or any other kind of slice. I hope he doesn't decide to wait until they're finished so he can take one home with him. I'll have to say the oven has exploded.

'How long have you owned this place?' he asks Lily.

'A few years. It was only a bakery when we bought it. When the people next door moved out, we took on their lease and knocked their shop into ours and added a cafe. It was a huge undertaking, but we have high hopes for it.'

'I can see why,' he says. 'You've done an excellent job. And now you're looking for outside contracts? That's impressive.'

'It's all part of a balanced financial portfolio,' I inform him. 'It's basic business sense.'

'It's a one-off,' says Lily. 'But if this goes well, we're thinking of expanding into the catering business. Once Abby is –' she breaks off and clears her throat.

'I see,' says Daniel. Something about his studiously serious expression makes me think he may not have been entirely convinced by my spa story.

'Do you know Honeywell at all?' Lily asks him.

'I've driven through it a few times, but I haven't stopped. I'll make sure to do so in future, especially now I know you serve freshly made Bakewell slices.'

'I'll mention it to Abby,' I say. 'I'm sure she'll be happy to make some for you the next time you visit.'

'Couldn't you make them yourself?'

'Abby is a perfectionist,' says Lily. 'She doesn't like any of us in her kitchen when she's not here. Even though we're all completely qualified to step in at a moment's notice.'

'I'm sure you are,' he says. 'But I know what these temperamental chefs can be like. We have one at The Quayside Hotel. His langoustines are to die for, but we've learned never to go into his kitchen without an invitation.'

'How did you manage to keep him on his best behaviour when they were filming over the summer?' I ask.

'It wasn't easy. In the end, the hotel manager gave him a raise and promised him a hefty bonus if he behaved himself while the cameras were there.'

'I should have asked my bosses for a raise when the team came here,' I say. 'I could have threatened to throw a tantrum in the middle of filming. I missed a trick there.'

'I'm sure you're far too professional to do anything of the kind,' says Daniel. 'Besides, your bakery has nothing to hide. All you had to do was open your doors and welcome the team into your kitchen. You didn't need to worry your chef would start hurling saucepans and using language not suitable to be shown before the watershed.'

'Very true,' says Lily. 'I'm glad you've finally made it to Honeywell, Daniel. Maybe we'll see you over this way again.'

'I'm coming back tomorrow night,' he says. 'I want to visit your Christmas fair. I hear good things. Our hotel manager has asked me to take a look. We're thinking of holding one in the hotel grounds next year.'

'Great idea,' says Lily. 'I'm sure you'll enjoy it. People come from miles around to the Honeywell Christmas fair.'

'Have you visited it yet?' he asks me.

'No, but I've been meaning to go one evening. I love Christmas fairs. There's one near my flat in London. I go every year.'

'Perfect,' he says. 'If you aren't busy tomorrow evening, perhaps we could go together?'

Why didn't I say I've visited the fair six times already and absolutely hated it? I try to find a polite way to refuse, but I can't think of one.

'That sounds great,' says Lily. 'You and Daniel can go together and pick up some tips. Isabella and I have been talking about taking a stall there next year and selling our Christmas baked goods. You could take notes for us, Grace.'

'What do you say?' Daniel asks me.

I don't want to say yes, but neither do I want to offend him. It's important for us to stay on his good side and not allow him to suspect anything.

'Ok,' I say.

He finishes his coffee. 'Great. See you there at seven?'

'Sounds good,' I say in a strangled tone.

'It's a date. Thanks for the drink. I haven't had such good coffee for years. I especially enjoyed the foam.'

'Why did you suggest I went with him?' I hiss at Lily when Daniel has left.

'I thought you'd enjoy it,' she says. 'You told us you loved Christmas fairs.'

'I do. But it's hard enough keeping secrets from Daniel when he's ten miles away. It will be far more difficult if I have to spend an entire evening with him.'

'You'll be fine,' she assures me. 'As long as you don't drink too much mulled wine and start babbling. He's given me his card. If you really don't want to go, give him a call and tell him you're busy.'

'No, I'll go. But I'm not staying for long. And I'm not talking too much.'

'How lovely for the poor man. I expect he'll wish he'd never asked you on a date.'

'That's his problem,' I say. 'And it isn't a date.'

'What would you call it?'

'Two busy professionals taking an hour out of their evening to scope out new opportunities for their employers. Who, I might add, should consider offering their staff time off in lieu.'

'You can come in an hour later the next day,' she says. 'That's the best I can do. You shouldn't need to if you don't plan to sample all the festive drinks. But I don't want you complaining about us to the health and safety people.'

'Fine,' I say. 'I'll go. And I'll take notes. But next time an events manager comes into the bakery suggesting one of your staff accompanies them somewhere, you can send Isabella.'

Chapter Twenty-Six

It starts to snow just before closing time the following day. It's only a few flakes as yet, but the sky looks like a fat, grey, down pillow. If you slit it open, it would pour its feathers everywhere.

'It doesn't seem a good night for going out,' I say, peering along the high street to watch the last vestiges of reddish sun drain from the leaden sky.

'It's a couple of flakes, that's all,' says Isabella. 'Does everything grind to a halt in London when that happens?'

'No, but –'

'Then why are you making such a fuss? I bet it does. I expect they stop all the underground trains in case of avalanches pouring down the escalators.'

'You have an odd idea of London,' I say.

'The snow will have stopped long before you get there,' she says. 'And so what if it hasn't? No one wants to visit a Christmas fair in the rain.'

'I don't want to visit it at all.'

'Why not? The Honeywell one is lovely. I go every year.'

'Why not come with us?' I say.

'Not likely! It's a Christmas fair, not a farmer's market. No gooseberries allowed.'

'It isn't a date,' I say for the hundredth time.

'What else would you call it?'

'I don't know. A business trip?'

She gives a snort of laughter.

'A business trip? Oh, Grace –'

'Why are you laughing? Daniel wants to scope out the fair for his hotel, and Lily thinks our business might be interested in the general setup.'

'I'm sorry I laughed,' she says. 'That makes perfect sense. It's logic itself. Daniel thought the fair might interest our bakery, so he rushed over here to ask the one member of staff with no previous catering experience to accompany him. What's more, the one member of staff he knows is only here until the new year. It makes perfect sense. I withdraw my argument, your honour. I've been labouring under a grave misapprehension. The defendant is free to go.'

'I hope you don't intend to train as a barrister,' I say. 'They don't decide on someone's guilt or innocence.'

'I'd make an excellent barrister,' she says. 'I can talk for hours without running out of things to say. I can also drink a surprising amount of port. And I have an excellent sense of when someone is talking complete nonsense. Which you are. Business trip, indeed!'

'That wasn't the best description,' I say. 'But it isn't a date. That's my point.'

'And you're ridiculous. That's mine.'

'I'm not. When I met Daniel the other day, I told him I didn't know the area. He needed to visit the fair, and when he saw me here, he thought he may as well invite me to go along.'

'It sounds like a Richard Curtis film,' she says, putting on a syrupy voice. 'He was an events coordinator. She was a humble baker. But when he visited her store one day, and they accidentally happened to get talking, he thought he may as well invite her to the Christmas fair if she had nothing else to do. Little did they know the evening would change both their lives forever. Who do you want to play you in the movie?'

'I'm not into soppy romance films,' I say. 'I don't like all that boy meets girl, then boy and girl fall out over some stupid misunderstanding which could all have been avoided if they'd had the sense to talk to each other like adults. Then boy and girl get together after all is revealed, and they realise how badly they've misjudged each other. Real life doesn't happen like that.'

'Sometimes, it does,' she says. 'Even when it doesn't, it's escapism. There's nothing wrong with that. It's far more fun to watch that sort of film than the sort where boy meets girl, boy leaves girl for someone far more beautiful and wealthy, girl goes into a decline and dies of a broken heart.'

'I'd watch that,' I say. 'But only if she comes back and haunts him, and he and the other girl die of fright. I didn't have you pegged as a hopeless romantic, Isabella. Do your preferred films all have cake in them?'

'Lots and lots of cake,' she says dreamily. 'Sometimes they're set in a bakery and sometimes in a restaurant. I'm not too fussy. Sometimes, they're set in a Christmas fair. Particularly when it's snowing. Their eyes meet over the last piece of gingerbread, and he offers to let her have it. That's how she knows he's the one. Later, they sip mulled wine and warm their hands over the fire. He offers her his gloves because, for some inexplicable reason, she's forgotten hers.'

'She's a ditz,' I say. 'She deserves to have icy hands.'

'Don't be so literal,' she complains. 'It's a literary device to show he's the man of her dreams!'

'But if she accepts his gloves, he'll get frostbite. Doesn't that show us she isn't the one?'

'That isn't how it works,' she says. 'Every date like this involves someone wearing someone else's jacket. And it always ends with a kiss in the snow. That's the law. Anyway, it's time to close up. I'll give you a ride over there this evening. You can drink as much mulled wine and eggnog as you like and call a taxi to take you home. It isn't far. I promise not to comment when you stagger in at three in the morning, trip over the umbrella stand in the hall, and fall asleep in a bowl of fruit.'

'I'm meeting Daniel there at seven,' I say. 'I'll be home in time for the nine o'clock news and a nice cup of cocoa.'

'I wash my hands of you,' she says. 'Some people refuse to be helped.'

She drops me off at the village green after dinner and drives away. I'm not sure where I'm supposed to meet Daniel. He didn't specify. He merely said he'd meet me here at seven. The fair is much larger than I'd imagined. Honeywell is a small village, so I was expecting three or four stalls and a food van. This is a much larger affair. There's a reindeer carousel and about twenty log cabins standing around the edge of the green. At the furthest end is a duck pond, lightly frozen over with a skin of ice. A duck is perched on a pile of branches in the middle, watching the proceedings with interest.

There's no sign of Daniel. Was this a definite arrangement or more of a provisional one? Did I misunderstand his invitation? Did he actually say he might drop in at the fair if he had time. And if by any chance I happened to be present, there was a faint chance we might bump into each other? I wasn't too keen on coming here this evening. But it would be far worse to go home and tell Isabella I've been stood up.

I decide to investigate the stalls. If Daniel arrives, I don't want to look as though I'm standing around waiting for him. I need to give the impression I'm politely surprised to see him here, having entirely forgotten he was the one who mentioned the fair to me in the first place.

I walk towards the nearest stall and examine the painted-glass candle holders. I haven't started my Christmas shopping yet. Mum would love one of these.

The next stall looks intriguing. The sign says A Boxful of Christmas. I wonder what that could be.

'Grace?' says a voice, and I turn to see Daniel standing there wearing a thick coat and scarf.

'I'm sorry I'm late,' he says. 'I couldn't find any parking spaces. I had to leave my car outside your bakery and run over here as fast as I could. Where did you park?'

'I didn't. Isabella gave me a ride.' I don't mention this was so I could drink to excess without breaking the law.

'Do you live near here?' he asks.

'I'm staying in a nearby village.'

I don't specify which one, and he doesn't press me for details. Maybe his mother also gave him the talk about not giving out your personal details to complete strangers, no matter how plausible they may appear.

'Did it take you long to drive over from the hotel?' I ask.

'I didn't come from the hotel. I came from home.'

'You don't live at the hotel?'

'Why would you think that?' he says.

'I thought hotel staff lived on site. I worked as a chambermaid and waitress one summer during university, and they made us stay in grotty little bedrooms in the basement so we could work the late-night shifts followed by the early-morning shifts. It was like something out of Charles Dickens, only without the ghosts.'

'I see,' he says, a hint of amusement in his voice. 'I'm afraid the Quayside Hotel doesn't follow such enlightened practices. No one has yet offered me a grotty basement room. I should talk to my union about it.'

'We weren't allowed to join a union,' I say. 'I'm starting to think the Scrooge Hotel wasn't entirely above board with its employment practices.'

'I have to put up with my two-bedroom flat in Christchurch,' he says.

'How unfortunate for you. Is it at least grotty?'

'It's a new building near the water. Insulated and double glazed, with a lovely view over the water out of the living room window.'

'Never mind,' I console him. 'With any luck, there'll be a leak in the roof soon, and the building will develop a mould problem.'

'We can but hope. Did you really think I lived in the hotel?'

'I hadn't given it much thought. You probably don't work such odd shifts as I used to. It was a stupid assumption.'

'Not at all,' he says. 'They hotel is remodelling next year. I'll suggest a row of garret bedrooms for the servants.'

'I'd love to live in a hotel all year round,' I say. 'Like they do in the movies. Wouldn't you?'

'I don't think I would. Even one like The Quayside Hotel.'

'You aren't a good advertisement for your employers. What's wrong with it? The part I saw was very nice, and your office is lovely.'

'It's a beautiful hotel,' he says. 'But would you really want to spend the entire year living in one room, however luxurious? I imagine it would quickly feel artificial – as though you were playing at life.'

'It wouldn't be one room,' I say. 'I'd demand a suite of rooms for my personal use. And I'd be rolling in money, so I could mix things up. The hotel would be my base, but I'd have my luxury yacht for whenever I wanted to pop over to Biarritz or Monaco. And my Swiss chalet for the ski season. I'd find plenty of ways to fill my time.'

'You make a compelling argument,' he says. 'But that sort of lifestyle is rather out of reach for an events organiser.'

'I know it is. You need to work in a bakery if you want to afford that lifestyle.'

'They pay you well?' he says.

'Beyond the dreams of avarice. In addition to my hefty salary and annual bonus, I have free use of the company jet as long as I book it at least two weeks in advance.'

'I went into the wrong profession,' he says.

'Exactly. So, the least the hotel could do is offer you the use of the Winston Churchill Suite.'

'I haven't come across that one yet,' he says. 'But we do have the Diamond Suite. It has two large bedrooms and gold handles on all the taps. I'll make enquiries about it first thing tomorrow. In the meantime, it's cold, and I'm keeping you standing here talking. Would you like some mulled wine? We could drink it over there by the braziers.'

He nods towards a man roasting chestnuts at the far end of the green.

'I could drink some mulled wine,' I say. 'My toes are freezing. I recently had a glass at The Red Lion, and it thawed out my feet in seconds.'

'Coming up!' he says and walks over to the stall.

'One extra-large glass,' he says when he returns with the wine. 'I told the bartender you had cold feet.'

'What do you mean?'

'You told me your toes were cold,' he says.

'Oh, that.'

He gives me a quizzical look. 'Did you think I meant metaphorically?'

'Not at all,' I say, taking a gulp and choking. 'This is strong!'

'Mulled wine generally is. The vendor was adding vodka with a liberal hand, but I didn't think you'd object.'

I take a more cautious sip. 'You're right. It's doing the trick.'

'Are you really cold?' he says. 'Would you like my jacket?'

'I'm fine, thanks. Can I buy you some roast chestnuts?'

'I have a severe chestnut allergy,' he says. 'If I eat even the tiniest piece of one, my head swells up and I explode.'

'Really?'

'Not really. I was trying to lighten the mood. You seem a little tense. I'd love some chestnuts.'

We wander over to the braziers, where I buy a bag of chestnuts and some caramelised almonds. They smell deliciously of honey and vanilla.

'I had these in Germany when I visited the Christmas markets at Lübeck,' he says. 'It was an amazing experience.'

'I've always wanted to go to a real German Christmas market,' I say.

'You should add it to your annual itinerary. It wouldn't be too long a journey from your Swiss chalet. You could enjoy a few days skiing there and return through the Black Forest.'

'Maybe one day. I don't know whether it's the vodka talking, but I feel compelled to be honest with you. I don't earn enough at the bakery to finance that lifestyle. I'll have to stick to the UK for now.'

'I'm sorry to hear that,' he says. 'You told me the other day you're only here temporarily. What do you do when you're not slinging croissants and baguettes?'

'I work in advertising.'

'Oh, that's right. In London, I think you said?'

'Yes. I've been working for a firm in Canary Wharf.'

'You have been working?' he says. 'Past tense?'

I stare down at my bag of almonds. 'That's right. I went into work three weeks ago to find a redundancy letter on my desk. They couldn't even be bothered to hand it to me in person. I'd been there for four years, and I did good work for them.'

'That's rough,' he says. 'I'm sorry, Grace. Just before Christmas too.'

I wipe my eyes with the back of my glove. 'It was bad timing. But I don't want to sound like Tiny Tim. I'm not out on the street with nowhere to go. I could stay with my parents in Scotland any time I like. And I have a redundancy payment that should see me through for a while if I'm careful.'

'Don't forget your munificent bakery package,' he says. 'The taxman will be after you when he finds out about that.'

'Please don't mention me losing my job to anyone,' I say. 'I haven't told Isabella and Lily. There's no point. I hate it when people try to think of sympathetic things to say.'

'You won't hear a single kind word from me,' he says. 'I'll tell you worse things happen at sea, and you should get a grip.'

'Thank you. I appreciate it. I particularly don't want you mentioning it to anyone at the hotel.'

'I wasn't aware you knew anyone at our hotel,' he says.

'I don't. Not exactly. I mean the TV crew. Vanessa and … er … Rob.' I don't meet his eyes.

'I see,' he says. 'I don't want to downplay what's happened to you, but I doubt they'd want to put that into the programme. It's a tragedy for you, but it isn't headline news for the rest of the nation. Please don't think I'm rude for saying that.'

'I wasn't thinking of them broadcasting it on the Christmas special,' I say. 'But I'd prefer the team not to know. I knew them a little in London, and I'd rather keep it to myself until I know what I plan to do next.'

'You knew the whole team?' he says.

'Not all of them. Not Bryony. She's the camera woman. But I've met Vanessa a couple of times. And I know Rob slightly better.'

He shoots me a quick glance but doesn't comment.

'Anyway, this isn't the most cheerful subject for a Christmas market,' I say. 'It may not be Lübeck, but Honeywell is putting on quite a show for us. We should make the most of it and enjoy our evening.'

'I'm up for that,' he says, taking my glass and handing it back to the bartender. 'I haven't done any Christmas shopping this year. I thought I could kill two birds with one stone.'

'You mean you can do your research for the hotel and also get a jump on your gift buying?' I say.

'I meant spending an evening with you.'

'Oh.'

'Is that ok?' he says.

'Of course. And I'm more than happy to advise you on your gifts. I love spending other people's money for them.'

We finish the bag of almonds and move onto the roast chestnuts.

'I love these,' I say. 'I can't think why they don't sell them all year round.'

'Possibly because they're a seasonal product?' he says.

'I'm aware. You don't need to live in the middle of nowhere to understand crops.'

His lips twitch. 'Crops?'

'You know what I mean. I'm talking about how things grow. I understand chestnuts only ripen once a year.'

'I'm sure you do,' he says. 'But when you referred to them as crops, I had a vision of a combine harvester zipping up and down fields, harvesting the chestnuts.'

'They grow on trees,' I explain kindly. 'At least, I think they do. I wonder how they pick them. Do the workers climb the trees and drop them down one by one? Or do they shake the trunks and catch the chestnuts in nets?'

'I expect they use trained squirrels, like they do for the hazelnut harvest.'

'Wouldn't that be fun? The only difficulty would be how to prevent the squirrels from keeping them all to themselves.'

'I don't think squirrels eat chestnuts,' he says. 'You could trade with them for acorns. Each chestnut would be worth three acorns.'

'But who would pick the acorns?'

'Trained monkeys,' he suggests. 'You could pay them in bananas.'

'I'm starting to think you're as ignorant as I am about the finer points of British agriculture.'

'It isn't a subject that came up in my training,' he says.

'What sort of training do you need to become an event organiser? Is there a special qualification or do people just …'

He smiles. 'I'm fascinated to know what you were about to say. While you're collecting your thoughts, I'll tell you that I took a business degree, followed by a course in hotel management. I worked as an assistant manager at a Bournemouth hotel for a while. I became interested in the events side of things when we hosted a large political conference. It was quite a triumph when we pulled it off.'

'How many people attended?'

'Nearly four hundred. They didn't all stay at the hotel, but it was still a pretty full-on event. You wouldn't believe some of the special requests we had to accommodate.'

'If it was a political conference, I would. What were they?'

'I could tell you,' he says. 'But then I'd have to kill you.'

'People always say that when they don't have a reasonable answer to give. What would you do if I called your bluff and insisted you told me anyway? You couldn't kill me in the middle of a crowded fair. There are too many witnesses. Besides, how would you do it?'

'I could slip something into your mulled wine,' he says. 'Would you like another one, by the way?'

'Very subtle. No, thank you. And if I do, I'll pour my own. Your hands are tied, at least for tonight. All you can do is hope I choke on a piece of Stollen.'

'That wouldn't work,' he says. 'My professional instincts would kick in. The Heimlich manoeuvre is an early part of event planning training.'

'Do many people choke at your events?'

'It happens more often than you might think. But they devote at least half an hour to refresher training at our annual spa retreats, so I'm up to date with all the latest techniques.'

I hand him the bag of chestnuts. 'You can finish these. They're making me nervous. I thought the Heimlich manoeuvre was the gold standard of manoeuvres. Don't tell me there's a more recent one?'

'You're out of date,' he says. 'Obviously, your bakery hasn't got around to teaching you the Reverse Breathalyser or The Glottal Grab.'

'I'll have to ask Lily to update our health and safety training.'

'It must be an occupational hazard where you work,' he says. 'All those crusts ...'

'Our customers don't generally tear into their cob loaves before leaving the bakery. There's more danger of them sustaining injuries from me hurling the loaves at their heads.'

'Interesting,' he says. 'Is that all your customers or only a select few? What's your bakery's policy?'

'I don't think they have an exact policy. Or not one Isabella remembered to include in her training manual.'

'So, it's more of a random thing?' he says. 'A lottery, if you will. Should I count myself lucky to have escaped a barrage of pretzels when I visited?'

'You weren't our hundredth customer that day, so you were in no danger.'

I couldn't help observing you didn't treat the other customers to that gimlet stare,' he says. 'And neither did your co-worker.'

'Lily?' I say. 'She's lovely. I can't imagine her giving anyone a gimlet stare.'

'Just you, then. And just to me.'

'I'm sorry,' I say. 'Maybe I wasn't as welcoming as I could have been. I thought you'd come to criticise us.'

He looks taken aback. 'To criticise what, exactly?'

'The bakery. Not that there's anything to criticise!'

'But you thought that was what I was there to do?' he says. 'Do I look like a man who spends his precious free time locating small businesses to disparage?'

'I don't know. You were grumpy enough when we first met.'

He looks genuinely surprised. 'I didn't mean to be. I was extremely busy that day.'

'So was I, but I didn't look at you as though you were something the cat had brought in.'

I wonder whether I've gone too far, but he smiles. 'Very true. You were charming and professional.'

This is too much for me. 'No, I wasn't! Quite the opposite. I made a complete fool of myself that afternoon.'

'Our conversation took the odd unexpected turn,' he says. 'But all the best conversations do. I'm sorry if I gave you the impression I considered you as anything less than a fellow professional.'

'You were most restrained,' I assure him. 'In your place, I'd have called security and had me removed from the building.'

'Then I'd have missed out on the fascinating details of your chef's culinary retreat.'

'I may have got the odd detail confused,' I say.

'Such as the fact she isn't so much enjoying steam rooms and Swedish massages as lying in a hospital bed?'

It's lucky I've finished eating the chestnuts or I might have choked for real. 'You knew? How did you find out?'

'One of the TV crew told me.'

'What did they say?'

'That they'd heard your chef was ill and wouldn't be available to make desserts. I hope she's doing better now?'

'And you were alright with that?' I ask.

'Shouldn't I be? They said you had some Australian chef stepping in to take over. I looked her up, but I couldn't find her. Maybe they got her name wrong.'

'Maybe,' I say in a strangled tone. 'Did the team mention how they thought the filming had gone?'

'Weren't you there?' he says.

'I was in the shop for most of the time, and I don't know much about the TV industry. You may have noticed Vanessa isn't the warmest and most forthcoming person.'

'She seems professional enough to me,' he says.

'I'm sure she's excellent at her job. But it was all rather fraught that day, and I wasn't sure how happy they were with what they'd got.'

'They didn't mention any problems to me,' he says.

'Nothing about the cake Isabella was baking?'

'Nothing at all. But that isn't my province. All I have to do is allow them to film whatever they like around the hotel, then make it into a programme that shows the hotel in a good light.'

'Is that in the contract?' I ask.

'Not explicitly. At least, not in that form. But there was an agreement when they started filming in the spring that they wouldn't make the hotel look like Fawlty Towers.'

'I imagine there was. Do you know if that agreement covers everyone else?'

'Everyone else who?' he says.

'Anyone who might end up appearing on the show. The catering companies, for instance. Do you have an agreement they have to be shown in a positive light too?'

'I don't think so,' he says. 'I believe our contract only covers the hotel and the guests. But you could make an appointment to see Ron. He's the hotel manager. I'm sure he'd be delighted to talk you through the minutiae of your own contract.'

'Very funny. I don't plan to go anywhere near your hotel until the day of the ball. Even then, I'll stick to the kitchen area and do my best to avoid the cameras. Will you be appearing in the Christmas special?'

He pulls a face. 'I'm afraid so. I stayed out of the main show as much as possible. But this final episode is mostly about the Christmas ball. As the events manager, it was inevitable. I can't afford to hide in the hotel spa each time the crew appears, not even with our special staff rates.'

'What sorts of things have they been filming?' I ask.

'The usual. They've asked me about our general Christmas preparations. They've talked to the regular guests about what makes Christmas special at the Quayside Hotel. And they've filmed me making some of the arrangements. They were there the day your chef came over to show us what she could do.'

'You'll have to change that part now she's ill,' I say.

'That's up to them. They may decide to leave it in. We were keen for them to stress the local angle of it all. Local caterers and suppliers, that sort of thing. I've been pushing for us to go more local for a while now, but without much success. I hope Ron will see the success of this programme and decide to make the change for real. It's the right thing to do. An outfit like ours ought to be doing whatever it can to support the local community and only bringing in people from outside when absolutely necessary.'

'I agree. It's far more sustainable too. And it means a lot to local businesses. Lily and Isabella were so excited to get this contract. They told me places like ours never usually get a look in. It's a shame because their type of business is incredibly important for rural communities.'

'How are your dessert preparations going?' he asks.

'Fine, thanks. We should be on track to deliver what we promised.'

'Now that you know what you've promised?' he says. 'That was the real reason you came to see me that day, wasn't it? Your chef was ill, and you had no idea what you were supposed to be doing.'

'I was also extremely anxious to exchange views on modern hotel architecture. But yes, that's pretty much what happened. I had to come over to the hotel to …'

'Spy out the land?' he says. 'Why couldn't you have told me what had happened and asked me directly?'

'We thought you might flip your lid and pull the contract.'

'Because one member of staff was out of action?' he says. 'Hardly. We're accustomed to crises and last-minute switches in this business. Anyway, you have that other chef working for you now. If I'd kicked up a fuss, you could have mentioned her and told me to get a grip.'

'That didn't … erm … occur to me,' I say. I don't add that the entire existence of Chef Mabel was unknown to any of us until recently.

Daniel's phone rings, and he looks at the screen. 'I'm so sorry, Grace. I have to take this. I'll only be a couple of minutes.'

'No problem. See you in a minute.'

He nods and strides off towards the duck pond. I walk towards the glass candle holders. I'm about to ask how much they are when someone taps me on the shoulder, making me jump. I turn around, expecting to see Daniel, but he's still walking up and down next to the duck pond, talking earnestly into his phone.

'Hi Grace,' says Rob. 'I wasn't expecting to run into you this evening.'

Chapter Twenty-Seven

'I thought you were in London,' I say, feeling annoyed with myself for letting him know he's been on my mind, however remotely.

'I was,' he says. 'But I had to come back here for a few days.'

'With Vanessa?'

'No, just me. I've been asked to make a few final arrangements for filming the ball.'

'But you're going back to London after that?' I say.

'Unless they ask me to do anything else while I'm down here. I didn't expect to bump into you tonight.'

'I'm just here getting an oil change and my wheels realigned.'

'Good call,' he says. 'I'm buying new decorations for my goldfish tank. He's sick of swimming in and out of the same old castle.'

'I'm sure he'll appreciate it. I'm also drinking mulled wine and trying to find Christmas presents for my family.'

'How organised of you,' he says. 'I always leave mine to the last minute. I see you're looking at these candle holders. Are you thinking of buying one for your mother?'

'What makes you say that?'

'You told me she loved candles,' he says. 'You said she never turns on a light if she can help it because candles are so much cosier.'

'I don't remember that.'

'Maybe I read it when I hacked into your emails,' he says.

'That sounds more likely. Yes, I thought Mum might like this. I have to be more organised this year because I need to post everything.'

'All the way to Scotland?'

'How do you know where she lives?' I ask.

'I think you mentioned it in one of your texts to your dentist.'

'I mean it, Rob.'

'You told me your parents had moved to Scotland,' he says. 'It was the evening I cooked you a steak at my flat. Before your exclusively plant-eating days.'

That sounds possible. I vaguely remember talking about Dad's retirement, but I didn't expect Rob to remember the details. Does he expect me to remember where his extended family lives? Has he ever told me? I decide not to ask too many questions in case he has.

'I could shop online and have everything delivered to them directly,' I say. 'But this seems an excellent opportunity to look for something personal. Is that what you're doing too?'

'Not really. I'm a sucker for a Christmas fair. The cheesier, the better. This one is bigger than I expected. They must have people coming from miles around to set up their stalls. Or should I say cabins?'

'I didn't expect so much variety,' I say. 'I like the carousel with the little reindeer.'

'There's a fair near my flat in London,' he says. 'But I haven't found time to visit it this year.'

'You should take Vanessa. She'd enjoy it.'

'I expect there's one near to where she lives too,' he says. 'They're pretty popular all over the city.'

'Where does she live?'

'Wimbledon.'

'That's quite a way from Wood Green.'

'I suppose so,' he says. 'I've never thought about it.'

'If you move in together at some point, you should choose her flat. It's a lovely area.'

He puts down the ceramic snowflake he's been inspecting. 'Move in together? Why would we do that? Is she struggling with her mortgage? She's never mentioned it to me.'

I feel my face flame. 'It's usually the next step in a relationship. I'm not sure how long you two have been together, but …'

'I'm sorry, Grace. You've lost me. What makes you think Vanessa and I are together?'

'Aren't you? I'm sorry if you've broken up. I wouldn't have mentioned it if I'd known.'

He shakes his head in bewilderment. 'Of course, we haven't broken up.'

'That's good.'

'I mean, we were never together, so how could we have broken up? What put that idea into your head?'

'She did. She told me when I first met her that you and she were dating. In fact, she said you and lots of people were dating.'

He looks thunderstruck. 'Is that why you ghosted me?'

'I didn't ghost you.' I catch his eye. 'Maybe I did a bit. As I told you that night at the pub, I'm not a serial dater.'

'Are you sure you didn't mistake her meaning?' he says.

'Perfectly sure. Are you telling me you and she were never together?'

'That's exactly what –' he breaks off. 'I mean, only a couple of times.'

My heart, which had risen, sinks again. 'A couple of times?'

'That's right. I met her at some work event, and she asked me out for a drink afterwards. I happened to bump into her again the following week and we went out for dinner.'

'That sounds like a date to me,' I say.

'Not necessarily. It depends on what we ate. Would you say it sounded like a date if I told you we'd eaten jellied eels and mushy peas?'

'Did you?'

'No, we went to a Thai place near my office.'

'Thai food is definitely a date,' I say. 'It says so in the big book of dating etiquette. Any meal with noodles constitutes a date. As does red meat, caviar, oysters, and anything that involves a server lighting something on fire before charging you an arm and a leg for the privilege.'

'I set that tea towel on fire when I made you meatballs and spaghetti,' he reminds me. 'Does that mean it was a definite date?'

'Unclear. You weren't wearing black trousers and a white shirt, so it's rather a grey area.'

'Fine,' he says. 'In that case, Vanessa and I went on a date. But it didn't feel like one at the time.'

'Where did you take people on your non-dates?' I ask. 'A week in a secluded beach cabin in Acapulco? A gondola ride in Venice? Hot air ballooning over the Serengeti?'

'Nothing so exotic. Vanessa told me the following week she happened to have a couple of tickets for the theatre, and she wondered whether I'd like to go with her.'

'*Happened* to have?' I say derisively. 'And you said yes?'

'That's right.'

'Also a date,' I say. 'At least, it was if you had drinks during the interval.'

'Does a pineapple juice count?'

'You aren't making this easy for me. Did you ask them to put a shot of vodka in it?'

'I'm afraid not. Vanessa had a glass of champagne, if that helps.'

'Not only a date, but a third date!' I say. 'The dating book devotes an entire chapter to champagne and its various meanings.

It's like the language of flowers. Was it by any chance pink champagne?'

'I wasn't paying attention. Ought it to have been?'

'It depends on what message you wanted to send.'

'I didn't want to send any message,' he says. 'As soon as I suspected she wanted more than the odd evening out as friends, I …'

'You what?' I say, fascinated.

He looks even more embarrassed. 'I told her I was interested in someone else.'

'Who was that?'

'I didn't say who,' he says. 'I thought it would be easier for her to hear that than for me to say I wasn't interested.'

I'm temporarily lost for words. I recover myself at last. 'Are you serious? You thought she'd rather hear you liked someone else better than her? What planet do you live on? How would you feel if you liked someone, and they said they preferred someone else? Wouldn't it be better if they were upfront with you and said they just weren't feeling it?'

'Also not the most pleasant thing to hear,' he says.

'True, but it shows they respect you enough to tell you the truth. And it doesn't leave you wondering what this other person has that you don't have, or whether it's worth trying to change yourself in order to be in with a chance. It gives you closure and allows you to move on.'

'Maybe I ought to have told her that,' he agrees. 'But what I said was true. I had met someone.'

'Why am I not surprised to hear that? Who was it?'

'You,' he says.

'Me? But you and I only met last spring.'

'That's right,' he says. 'We met a few weeks after I first met Vanessa.'

I blink. 'Are you saying you dumped her for me?'

'No! I hadn't started seeing you properly at that point, but I'd already decided she and I weren't going anywhere. I can see now

I didn't handle it too well. But she clearly thought we had something going because she called a week later and asked me to Cornwall for the weekend. Her uncle has a weekend cottage there, and his arrangements had unexpectedly fallen through. That's when I realised for sure she was looking for something more, and I had to tell her I didn't see it like that.'

'So, you told her you were ditching her for someone else? Poor Vanessa.' I never thought I'd hear myself saying that.

'I could have ghosted her,' he says with the hint of a smile. 'But I know from experience that isn't entirely painless.'

I stare at my feet. 'I agree. It's a cowardly way to behave. But there must be a third way – somewhere between disappearing off the face of the earth and announcing you've fallen for someone else.'

'What might that be? Does the big book of dating have a chapter on it?'

'I haven't finished reading it,' I say. 'I stopped after the chapter on how to vanish from someone's life without a trace. If I had to guess, I'd say the answer was honesty. What's wrong with talking to someone and saying, "I've had fun going out with you, but I don't think we're a great romantic fit. I think we should wish each other well in our future endeavours and remain good friends?"'

'Nothing,' he says. 'Although I doubt it's as easy as you make it sound.'

'So do I, which is why I've never tried it. But I will in the future. It feels like a more straightforward way to behave.'

'Is that what you wish you'd told me?' he says. 'That you'd have fun, but you didn't see us a great fit romantically, and you thought we should wish each other well and stay friends?'

I'm wondering why I started this conversation. I'm getting myself more tangled up each time I open my mouth.

'It's more complicated than that,' I say.

'It doesn't have to be,' he says. 'No one is obliged to see anyone they don't want to, even if that other person really likes them.'

'I know. But that wasn't the reason I ghosted you.'

'I'm almost afraid to ask,' he says, his eyes fixed on my face. 'Did I do something terrible I'm not aware of?'

'If you must know, I talked to Vanessa at your firm's party. Or rather, she talked to me. She asked whether you and I were together, and she told me you were also going out with her. She said she didn't mind my being there with you that day because the pair of you weren't exclusive.'

'And you believed her?'

'It didn't occur to me not to. She's an attractive woman.'

'As are you,' he says.

I shake my head. 'Bony.'

'What?'

'And gangly,' I add. 'Like a horse.'

His face snaps in comprehension. 'I'd forgotten that conversation in the pub.'

'I hadn't. Anyway, there was no reason for me to disbelieve her. She wasn't unpleasant about it. She was very matter of fact about the whole thing. She said you weren't a one-woman guy. You were well known for it at your office, which suited her fine because she was also seeing other people. But that wasn't what I was looking for. So, I decided not to see you again.'

'Without asking me for clarification?' he says.

'What would you have said? I'm not a womaniser.'

'Exactly that.'

'But that's exactly what a sleazy womaniser would say. You weren't likely to say, "Oh, yes, I'm dating most of my co-workers and half of upper management."'

'But why would Vanessa have told you something like that?' he says. 'Was she trying to scare off the competition?'

'You'd have to ask her. If so, it was very effective. But after what you've told me tonight, I'm not so sure. Is it possible she told me what she believed to be the truth? What did you say when you told her you didn't want to go away with her for the weekend?'

He screws up his face in recollection. 'That I'd met someone else, and I wanted to see how it went with her.'

'That's all?'

'Isn't it enough? If you'd told me you'd met another man, I'd have backed off at once. I'd have realised I didn't have a chance with you.'

'I'd feel the same way,' I agree. 'But I'm wondering whether you left Vanessa with the impression you wanted to see other people as well as her, rather than instead of her. Were you absolutely clear?'

'I thought so,' he says. 'But you may be right. She didn't seem too upset. She said her uncle's cottage was often free, so maybe another time.'

'To which you replied …?' I prompt him.

'I said yes, maybe. I didn't want to be rude, not when she'd taken it so well. I thought I was being polite. She must have got the message at some point. We haven't been out since then.'

'When I saw her in the pub the other day, she made it clear you were still together,' I say.

'She can't have done. What did she say?'

'That you'd been spending lots of time together, and you were moving towards something more serious – much to her surprise.'

'But we aren't!' he protests.

'You haven't spent time together recently?'

'No! At least, only for work. Vanessa asked for me for this Christmas project when one of their editors left. She said our working styles meshed well, and it would be possible for us to pull the whole thing together at short notice. That's true. I find it easy to work with people who are direct. And she's excellent at her job.'

'I'm sure she is. So, you've been thrown together a lot over the past month. And you haven't been spending evenings together, gone out for drinks, had dinner together, visited the hotel spa wearing his and her monogrammed towels?'

He looks faintly revolted. 'I've never been to a spa in my life.'

'That last one was a joke. What about the rest of it? You arranged to have dinner with her the evening I met you.'

'No, I didn't! She texted to find out where I was because she wanted to talk to me about something. I said I was having dinner at the pub, and I'd see her back at the hotel. I was surprised when she turned up like that. Disappointed, too. I'd been hoping to spend the evening with you. But you disappeared as soon as she arrived. Was that why?'

'It was a difficult evening for me,' I say. 'Abby had been rushed to hospital, and I didn't know whether I was on my head or my heels. When Vanessa appeared, it seemed best to leave the pair of you to it.'

'I see. I wish you'd said something.'

'What was there to say? She was sitting there gushing about having stripped off in your bedroom after a pipe burst, and you didn't say anything. I thought you wanted me to leave as quickly as possible in case a pipe at the Red Lion burst and Vanessa treated to you a repeat performance.'

'It wasn't as dramatic as she made out,' he says. 'She got a little damp and came to my room to borrow my hair dryer because hers had shorted out.'

'From the way she was talking, it sounded as though you and she were sharing a room. She definitely implied you were sharing one at the Quayside Hotel. She asked whether there was a fire in the bedroom, remember?'

'That's her manner,' he says. 'She's gushy and dramatic with everyone. Plenty of people in our industry are.'

'No, she isn't,' I say. 'She's only like that with you. She doesn't like me, so she's quite rude to me.'

He smiles. 'I got the impression she wasn't too keen on you the day we came to your bakery. But the feeling seemed mutual.'

'It is,' I say. 'I doubt she and I will ever be friends. But that doesn't let you off the hook. When she arrived at the pub that night, she couldn't have made it more clear she thought you were a couple. And you didn't say a word.'

'I can see that now. But I wasn't paying much attention. As I say, she's very dramatic and touchy-feely. Most people I work with are. I was more focused on talking to you, Grace. I'd been looking for an opportunity ever since I arrived down here and found you working at the bakery. I was desperately hoping you might give me a second chance.'

'As, it seems, was Vanessa. You haven't handled this very well, have you?'

He looks uncomfortable. 'I'm obviously not very good at this relationship stuff. If what you say is correct, I need to have an honest conversation with her.'

'You do. I'm not saying she hasn't embellished out of spite. She obviously doesn't like me. But that's natural enough if she sees me as a rival. You told her you'd met someone else, and then I turned up at your firm's party. She was clearly marking her territory and making sure no one else pushed her out entirely.'

I look up and meet his eyes. 'You've behaved like an idiot, Rob. But I'm not far behind. I should have had an honest conversation with you and given you the chance to clear things up instead of behaving like a teenager and disappearing.'

'Why didn't you?' he says.

'I was hurt. I thought things were going well between us. Then I found out you were dating half of London, and I was nothing special after all.'

'Not half of London,' he says. 'Just the southern suburbs. Does that mean you would have continued seeing me if you hadn't bumped into Vanessa at that party?'

I feel a wave of embarrassment. 'I can't … I don't know. It was all a long time ago. It's hard to remember …'

He takes a step towards me. 'Grace?'

Daniel comes striding around the corner of the cabin. 'I'm so sorry! That took far longer than I expected. It was unforgivable of me to leave you standing in the cold.'

I turn in confusion. 'It's fine. Don't worry about it.'

'That's nice of you to say. I promise I wouldn't have left you like that if it hadn't been a complete emergency. Let me make it up to you with an outsize glass of mulled wine. You can watch the server pour it if you like.'

He notices Rob standing by the cabin, watching us. 'Hi, Rob! I didn't see you. Are you guys filming?'

'Not tonight,' says Rob. 'I popped in for an hour on my way to the hotel, and I bumped into Grace.'

'I'm glad she had someone to keep her company when I deserted her,' says Daniel.

Rob looks at my flushed cheeks and a look of comprehension flashes over his face. 'Am I interrupting a date?'

Daniel doesn't seem embarrassed. 'It's our first date. If you don't count the most interesting afternoon Grace and I spent at the hotel recently discussing management training techniques.'

Rob shoves his hands into his pockets and gives me an awkward smile. 'I'm sorry to have interrupted. Have a great evening.'

He nods to Daniel and turns away. I almost let him go. I can contact him tomorrow to finish this discussion. But I don't want to. I'm not some character in a bad rom com, at the mercy of someone else's whims. I don't have to wait until the final scene for all to be revealed and for me to discover my destiny. I'm a fully grown adult, and no one else is in charge of my life. I've just had this exact conversation with Rob and told him off for failing to be direct. It would be hypocritical of me to ignore my own advice.

'Rob!' I say.

He turns to face me. 'It's fine, Grace. See you around.'

'It isn't fine,' I hear myself say. 'Daniel, you're a really nice man, and you're a lot of fun to spend time with. But I don't see this going anywhere romantically. I thought I should be honest with you.'

'I see,' he says. 'Well, I appreciate you letting me know.'

'I'm sorry,' I say. 'That sounded rather abrupt. And I feel stupid saying it halfway through a first date. But I wasn't sure it was one. Now you've said it is, it seems best to be upfront about it. I'd love to spend the rest of the evening with you, as friends.'

Daniel looks at Rob. 'And will you be joining us in this evening of amicable friendship?'

Rob's eyes are alight with laughter. 'That's a kind invitation. But Grace has set the bar high regarding frankness, so I feel I should do my bit too. I met Grace in London this summer. As far as I'm concerned, she and I have some … unfinished business.'

'I see,' says Daniel. 'It may not be my place to ask, but is that how you feel too, Grace?'

I force myself to meet Rob's gaze. 'I think so.'

Daniel nods. 'In which case, would you think it extremely rude of me to leave you both here? That phone call was about tomorrow's wedding reception. The florist has sent holly and mistletoe wreaths for a Hawaiian themed reception. They seem to have misunderstood the entire concept of leis. My manager wanted me to come back at once, but I told him I was otherwise engaged, and I'd see him later.'

'That was nice of you,' I say. 'But it makes me feel even more guilty.'

'So it should!'

He sees my face. 'I'm kidding. Don't look so tragic. If you knew the number of first dates I've been on that haven't turned into second dates … Admittedly, they don't usually end halfway through the evening when someone's past catches up with them. But there's a first time for everything. It will be something for me to tell my grandchildren. If you really don't mind me ducking out and leaving you here, I ought to go and help him.'

He gives us a friendly nod and strides away across the grass in the direction of the high street. I watch him go with a mixture of guilt and relief.

'Well!' says Rob, jerking me back to reality. 'That was quite something. You really do practice what you preach.'

'I didn't with you,' I say. 'But I plan to in the future. Honesty makes everything so much easier.'

'I agree.'

He takes both my hands in his, swings me around to face him, and looks deep into my eyes.

'Grace Andersen, in the interests of full disclosure and complete transparency, there's something extremely important I have to tell you. I haven't had dinner yet, and I'm ravenous. I see a stall over there selling hot dogs. Would you care to join me?'

Chapter Twenty-Eight

He takes my hand, and we walk over to the hot dog stall and join the queue. The smoky scent of roasting sausages and barbeque sauce drifts through the frosty air.

'Hungry?' says Rob.

'Surprisingly so, considering I've recently eaten half a treeful of roasted chestnuts.'

'The little-known British roast chestnut tree?' he says. 'A heritage variety, I believe.'

'Farmers seem to have moved towards the vacuum-packed varieties these days,' I say. 'I hear they're more resistant to disease.'

He looks at the sign hanging outside the cabin. 'Just roast vegetables for you, I assume?'

'I'd like a hot dog with all the extras to start with. I may finish with a pulled pork sandwich.'

'I wasn't sure whether today was one of your meat-free days,' he says. 'I don't know how it works. Do you alternate days or make exceptions on days starting with T?'

'Have you finished amusing yourself at my expense?'

'You know how it is,' he says. 'We make fun of those we feel are superior to us, in order to bring them down to our level.'

'It must be difficult for you to spend time with someone who's so nearly achieved sainthood.'

He squeezes my hand. 'I'm glad to be here with you, Grace. I've missed you.'

'It's nice to see you again,' I admit.

We reach the front of the queue, and he points to the sign. 'Sausages and pulled pork. No lobster tarts, I'm afraid.'

'I told you before. I wouldn't touch those with a barge pole.'

'Two of your finest hot dogs, please,' he says to the stall holder. 'And load them up. We're celebrating.'

We walk back to the brazier to eat our hot dogs.

'What exactly are we celebrating?' I ask, retrieving a piece of fried onion from the wrapper and dumping it on top of my hot dog. 'Is it your birthday or something?'

'Not until June. But it feels as though it is.'

'What, then?'

He smiles down at me and gently tucks a strand of hair back under my hat. The expression in his eyes makes me catch my breath.

'Lobster Tart Day,' he says. 'It's the first thing I mark on my calendar each year. I'm sorry. That was insensitive of me. I should have asked first whether you celebrate.'

'This is a cultural thing, I take it?'

'That's correct,' he says. 'It's a huge thing in some of the Pacific Islands. My great-great-grandfather first –'

'Don't tell me. He was born there and brought the tradition to our shores. And your family has passed it down to each new generation.'

He rolls his eyes. 'Don't be ridiculous, Grace. My great-great-grandfather came from Croydon. He started out as a grocer, but he rose to become town mayor before he died. They put up a plaque in his honour.'

'What does it say?'

'I'll take you to see it sometime, and you can read it for yourself. You must remember to bring a wreath.'

'Lily is convinced there'll be a plaque outside our bakery once we've gone multi-national,' I say. 'But if your great-great-grandfather didn't come from a Pacific Island, why did he celebrate Lobster Tart Day?'

'He was once shipwrecked there. He didn't escape for a decade. They're known as "The Lost Years" in our family. No one knows what he did or what happened to him there. He refused to talk about it. But he eventually returned with a huge appreciation for seafood. He insisted we all celebrate Lobster Tart Day each December.'

I scrunch up my wrapper and toss it into a nearby bin. 'Imagine if he'd met and married someone out there. You would never have been born, and you and I would never have met.'

'What a dreadful thought,' he says. 'But he was already married by the time he was shipwrecked, and my great-great-grandmother had given birth to my great-grandfather and several other children.'

'Was your great-great-grandmother shipwrecked with him? She must have been a remarkable woman.'

He shakes his head. 'Thankfully, she was safely at home while all this was going on. I'm not sure why he was on that ship in the first place. It may have been for his health. I hear he was prone to bronchitis. No one knew about the voyage until he returned. In fact, there were several scurrilous rumours about him and a certain Enid Higginsbottom of Putney. All anyone knew was that he disappeared for ten years. By that time, my great-great-grandmother was about to have him declared legally dead so she could marry Albert Matching from down the street. Then up popped great-great-grandfather again, safe and sound and rather less sunburned than one might have imagined in someone who'd spend all those years perched on a coral atoll. Still, there he was. His family was most relieved to hear about his time in the Pacific Ocean after all the unkind stories that had been flying around. To cut a long story short, he insisted his family should celebrate Lobster Tart Day from that day onwards. And so we have, out of respect to that fine old gentleman. He also put it into his will that his vast fortune would only pass down to his successors if we continued to celebrate.'

'What fortune?' I say. 'You told me he was a grocer in Croydon.'

'He came from humble origins. But while he was unavoidably absent for a decade, he managed to found a successful seafood import business. I believe they supply Harrods to this day.'

'I look forward to seeing the programme about your family's genealogy in the near future,' I say. 'I'm sure your production company has optioned it?'

'They've attempted to several times. But my father refuses to sign the release forms. If he ever changes his mind, my company will be on it like a flash. They can come and film our annual celebrations – the lobster hat parade, pin the tail on the lobster, and of course the traditional lobster tart dance. Shall I demonstrate for you now?'

'Not here, thanks. You might knock over the brazier and start a fire. I assume it's an energetic sort of a dance?'

'No, it's more of a quadrille.'

'You win,' I say. 'Thank you for the fascinating history of your family heritage. Speaking of making TV programmes, I haven't thanked you for not giving the game away that day at the bakery.'

'What game?' he says. 'Oh, you mean your chef. How is she now?'

'She's doing a lot better, thanks, although she was very ill for a while. They let me visit her last night for the first time. It was a shock to see her looking so pale and thin. She's such a lively person, always busy with something.'

'I'm glad she's ok,' he says. 'I expect she'll pick up quickly now she's turned the corner. I remember what a shock it was when I saw my father after his quadruple bypass a few years ago.

But he was home within the week, and he's back to hiking in the Lake District whenever he gets the chance. The doctors told him exercise and healthy food was the key.'

'Plenty of lobster tarts?' I say.

'Don't be ridiculous, Grace. They contain far too much cholesterol.'

'Perhaps I should order a few from Harrods and take them into the hospital for Abby. Chris says she isn't eating much yet. Isabella was horrified when I told her. She's busy drawing up elaborate plans to smuggle in baskets of baked goods.'

'Does the hospital have a ban on people bringing in food?' he says.

'Not at all. I tried to explain that to Isabella, but she wouldn't listen. She was having far too much fun searching online for the hospital building plans. She was muttering about tunnels and diversionary smoke grenades when she dropped me off here tonight.'

'Isabella seems an ingenious sort of woman,' he says. 'I was rewatching the footage we took when we were with you. When Bryony zoomed in on Isabella mixing that cake, I'm almost sure I saw an olive flying past Vanessa's head.'

'You aren't including that?' I say anxiously.

'Don't worry. That part got conveniently left on the cutting room floor.'

'Do you still use film?'

'I meant metaphorically,' he says. 'I should have said those particular pixels are no more. They're whirling through space somewhere, waiting to be reassembled into a different form.'

'Abby would hate it if we made the bakery look ridiculous,' I say. 'She's worked so hard to build up the business. Lily and Isabella have too. But Abby's the one who's developed all the new recipes and signature dishes. If she saw Isabella prancing about making olive and candied peel cakes, she'd end up back in intensive care.'

'I get it,' he says. 'Don't worry. The footage of our visit to your bakery only takes about thirty seconds. We have a lot to pack into the final episode. Most of it will take place at the hotel. We've been filming the run-up to Christmas for the past few weeks. We'll cut away a few times to show you and the other caterers and your preparations. But that won't take long. The final segment will be the ball itself. That's the highlight of the programme. It's a great way to finish the series.'

'I wish we'd known that when you came to the bakery the other day. You can't imagine what a panic you threw us into when you arrived with almost no notice.'

'I often have that effect on people,' he says. 'I have no idea why.'

'I'm serious. We didn't dare tell Vanessa about Abby in case she decided to make us look incompetent on camera.'

'That may have been wise,' he says. 'Vanessa is extremely good at what she does. She'd have been onto that like a shot.'

'She was onto us,' I say. 'You can't tell me she didn't realise something was going on.'

'She had her suspicions,' he says.

'But then Chef Mabel magically appeared to save the day?'

He opens his eyes wide. 'Grace Andersen! Are you telling me it was all a put-up job, and Chef Mabel was a work of fiction?'

'Not at all. She's as real as your great-great-grandfather.'

'I'm delighted to hear it,' he says. 'I personally never doubted her story. But it was mildly amusing to see Vanessa searching for her name on the way back to the hotel.'

I give a shout of laughter. 'She didn't! Did she find anything?'

'A cleaning company in Perth. She also got a possible hit in the Northern Territories, but it turned out to be nothing.'

'I wish I'd been there,' I say.

'It was best you weren't. I had to stare out of the window when she started searching for Wombat Wallow. She asked Bryony whether she thought it was spelled with two Ls or one.'

'Was Vanessa very angry with us?' I ask.

'I think her professional pride was wounded.'

'She can't have swallowed all that nonsense Mabel came out with.'

'No, but she thought there might be a grain of truth in it somewhere. She thought Mabel was a proper chef who decided it would be fun to exaggerate her Australian heritage.'

'I'm glad Mabel refused to sign the release,' I say. 'I don't think the wider world is ready for her yet.'

'All the great ones are unappreciated in their time,' he says. 'Like my great-great-grandfather. Apparently, his wife never fully trusted him again.'

'Poor woman. Are you really coming back on Christmas Eve to film us preparing the desserts?'

'I believe so. You may have bought yourself some time with your Antipodean friend and her antics, but we're giving you another chance to mess things up.'

I bite my lip, and he smiles. 'I don't mean that. I should have said you'll have another chance to display your astounding talent and expertise.'

'I don't have any. Neither do Lily and Isabella. But we're learning fast. Our lemon tarts are a thing of beauty and wonder. And Mabel came in and taught us how to make brownies and crème brûlées last week. She may not be world-famous outside of Wombat Wallow, but she can certainly cook.'

'Will she be there on the day we film?' he asks.

'I'm not sure Vanessa's blood pressure could take it. If all goes well, we should be expert enough by then to pass muster. We're keeping things simple. Mabel says good quality uncomplicated desserts are far better than inexpertly produced complicated ones. Abby planned to make individual chocolate soufflés with Chantilly cream. But we switched those for chocolate mousses.'

A thought strikes me. 'You won't repeat all this to Vanessa? Should I have said this was off the record before we started talking?'

'I can promise you I don't have a hidden microphone concealed about my person,' he assures me. 'And when no one jogs it electronically, my memory is conveniently flexible.'

He slips an arm around my shoulders. 'Stop worrying and take the night off. Let's look at the rest of the fair.'

We set off towards the stalls, still with his arm around me. Maybe he thinks I'll get lost in the crowd if he doesn't hold on to me. There are plenty of people here now, so he may have a point.

We walk across the frozen grass to a stall selling handmade Christmas ornaments.

I pick up a delicate glass sphere painted with poinsettias. 'Isabella says her family are putting their tree up this weekend. I think her mother would like this. She grows poinsettias. She says they're the only positive thing about a British winter.'

'I'll take the one with the holly tree,' says Rob, handing it to the stall holder, who wraps it in tissue paper. 'My mum will love it.'

'Is your tree up yet?' I ask.

'I don't have a tree.'

'Not even a tiny one? You must have. It's practically the law.'

'I have a plastic one somewhere in my loft. I didn't bother getting it down this year as I'm down here almost until Christmas. How about you? Did you say you were staying with Isabella?'

'I moved into her house last week. I couldn't keep inflicting myself on Chris while Abby was away. It felt too awkward. And I couldn't afford to stay at the hotel like you.'

I remember my discussion with Daniel about servants' basements and feel a fresh pang of guilt. I didn't intend tonight to go like this. Daniel didn't seem too put out, but it wasn't ideal.

'The hotel offers us a bed whenever we're filming,' he says. He catches my eye and grins. 'Single bedrooms!'

'No roaring fires and huge spa baths?'

'Not so much as a fan heater. And I had to bring my own dressing gown. It's quite a comedown from my luxury London flat, with its private library and wine tasting room.'

'You must have forgotten to show me over that wing. All I saw was an extremely tiny kitchen and bathroom.'

'Are you enjoying staying with Isabella?' he says.

'Somewhat to my surprise, I am. She made her family sound a lot weirder than they are, which meant I was nervous about meeting them. But they've made me really welcome. I'm not sure her father really knows who I am. Isabella says they have visitors coming and going all the time, and he gets them confused. He's very nice though. He talks about sheep a lot. I don't have much to contribute to the conversation, but I can now tell a Welsh mountain sheep from a Texel.'

'Which is more than I can,' he says. 'Speaking of sheep, what do you think of those woollen gloves? I never know what to buy for my sister, but she's always complaining her hands are cold.'

'Great idea. How about some matching socks? I like those reindeer ones.'

'I'm getting through my Christmas shopping at top speed,' he says. 'How much do you have left to do?'

'All of it. I'm not too organised at the best of times. But this year has been so full on that I haven't given it a thought.'

'Your parents like gardening, don't they?'

'How do you know that?' I ask.

'You told me. And I listened. You also told me your favourite flowers are peonies because they remind you of your grandmother's garden when you were small. Your favourite drink is gin and tonic. And you can recite pi to sixty decimal places.'

'Congratulations,' I say. 'You now qualify for your official stalker's badge. You completed the practical section when you ambushed me in the car park that night. And now you've passed the theory section of the exam by demonstrating a thorough knowledge of your subject's likes and dislikes. I had to subtract a few points for the gin and tonic. If you'd been listening carefully, you'd have heard me say I like vodka and tonic. But overall, it was a pretty good effort.'

'I'm sorry about that car park thing,' he says. 'In my defence, I identified myself immediately this evening when I saw you, and I made sure there were plenty of people around.'

'I appreciate that. Don't look so worried, Rob. I was joking! They don't appear to serve vodka and tonic here, but Isabella told me to be sure to taste the eggnog.'

'I'm up for that. It will be my first one of the year.'

'Mine too,' I say. 'I've already tasted the mulled wine, and I can recommend it.'

We walk over to a stall called Snowball Saloon, and I order us both a glass of eggnog.

'Rum or Bourbon?' says the stall holder.

'I have no idea.' I turn to Rob. 'What do you think?'

'Bourbon,' he says without hesitation, and the stall holder nods.

'It's the only way,' adds Rob. 'My family drinks it every Christmas Eve. It's an old family recipe.'

'Of course it is. Passed down from your great-great-grandfather. Using a recipe he developed during his stay in the Pacific.'

'Actually, it was given to him by the captain of the pirate ship who rescued him and gave him a ride home,' he says.

'Then it ought to contain rum!'

He shakes his head. 'That particular pirate had a rum allergy. It made life difficult for him and held him back his entire career. He was never promoted beyond middle management.'

'Poor man. I hope he found himself a more suitable profession at some point.'

'I believe he became an aromatherapist and lived out his days selling a successful line of coconut-scented products.'

I finish my eggnog. 'I'm happy for him. Would you like another glass of this?'

'I'd better not. I drove here.'

'What would you like to do next?'

He considers. 'How about a ride on the carousel?'

'It's a nice thought, but how will you get past the height restrictions? It's for children up to the age of about ten.'

'Shall we sue them for age discrimination?' he says.

'Knock yourself out.' I point to a stall selling home-made fruit cakes in Christmassy tins. 'In the meantime, I want to get one of those for Isabella.'

'That's kind of you,' he says. 'But doesn't she have access to as much fruitcake as she can eat?'

'Not even close. Lily doesn't let her touch the ones Abby baked. She says they're too expensive. Isabella's family are bound to have a cake on Christmas Day, but I think she might appreciate one all to herself. She can keep it in her bedroom and eat a slice whenever the midnight munchies strike.'

We select a tin with a picture of Honeywell on it.

'In case she forgets where she works,' says Rob.

'It's either that or an angel with a golden harp. She'll like this one. She can keep sweets in it when she's finished the cake. Georgia won't think to look there.'

Rob helps me to choose a packet of peppermint bark and some cosy bed socks for Abby. I select two hand-painted wineglasses for Lily and a bottle of gingerbread scented bubble bath for Daisy.

A man shouts to us as we pass his stall. 'Three rings for a pound! Win a giant snowman!'

Rob stops. 'I love those things. I used to win prizes all the time when I was a child. Can you hold these?'

He hands me his parcels and strides over to the stall. 'What do I have to do?'

The man points to the wooden poles. 'Toss your rings over those. If one of them goes right over, you win a prize. If all three go over, you win one of those snowmen.'

'Easy!' says Rob. 'I'll only need one go.'

The man hands him the three rings. 'Show us how it's done, mate!'

Rob frowns in concentration, then throws the first ring. It misses the poles entirely and falls at the stall holder's feet.

He picks it up. 'Try again. You can still win a prize.'

Rob squints at the poles and throws the second ring. This time it hits the pole but bounces off.'

'I used to be able to do this,' he mutters. 'I was the Merryfield Primary School fete champion back in the day.'

'But that wasn't done after a visit to the Snowball Saloon,' I remind him.

'If I could do it after three ice cream floats, I can do it after a glass of eggnog. Stand back, Grace. I don't want to hit you when I throw this next one. I've been too tentative so far. That's my problem. A sport like this takes commitment.'

He whirls his arm in wild circles before launching the final ring towards the pole. It hits the stall holder on the shoulder, and he winces.

'I'm so sorry,' says Rob. 'Are you alright?'

The stall holder picks up the ring. 'Hazard of the trade. I've been hit far harder than that.'

'Is that a challenge?' says Rob. 'Here's five pounds. I'd like fifteen more rings, please.'

'You really want that snowman, don't you?' says the stall holder.

Rob points to me. 'She tells me she won't see me again if I don't win it for her.'

'I'm more likely not to see you again if you do,' I say. 'I'm staying at Isabella's. Where do you expect me to keep a giant snowman?'

'That's your problem,' he says. 'First, I have to win it for you.'

He makes the whirling gesture again, and the stall holder retreats to the back of the stall.

Twenty minutes later, I touch Rob's arm. 'It may be time to accept defeat.'

'Never!' he says. 'If there's one thing I've learned from my family history, it's that perseverance pays off. If my great-great-grandfather hadn't kept trying to escape from his island, no one would ever have seen him again.'

'Even Enid Higginsbottom,' I say. 'But there has to be a limit. You could have bought several giant snowmen with the money you've spent at this stall. And you haven't got a single ring on any of the poles.'

'The night is young,' he insists.

'Actually, it's not,' says the stall holder. 'We'll be packing up in a few minutes. Better luck next time, eh?'

Rob sighs. 'I think the game is rigged. I may have to report your stall to the ombudsman. I'm sorry, Grace. I tried my best.'

'You've been my best customer tonight,' says the stallholder. 'I can't let you have one of the giant snowmen, but how about one of these snow globes?'

'What you think, Grace?' says Rob. 'I don't need a pity prize.'

'They're awfully nice snow globes,' I say, inspecting them. 'It would be a nice reminder of your great-great-grandfather and everything he taught you.'

'You choose one,' he says.

'I can't. They're all so lovely. Which one do you like?'

He looks at them carefully, and his face creases with laughter. 'This one,' he says, handing it to the man, who wraps it in tissue paper. Rob puts it into his pocket.

We walk towards the main entrance, hand in hand.

'I wasn't sure about coming here tonight,' I say. 'But I've had a lovely evening. Thanks, Rob.'

He looks down at me, and the expression in his dark eyes makes my heart beat faster.

'I'm glad I found you again,' he says.

'Me too.'

He glances up at the sky. 'Right on cue. I was about to ask for my money back.'

I follow his gaze and see the first few snowflakes drift down past the Honeywell streetlights. A swirl of wind catches them as they fall more thickly, dancing around us like cherry blossoms.

Rob leans in and brushes his lips against mine. For one perfect moment, we stand there in the silent snowfall. His lips are soft and warm, and I can feel his heartbeat against my body as he pulls me closer.

He draws away at last. 'That was … unexpected.'

'Not to Isabella,' I say. 'She told me tonight would end with a kiss in the snow. She just didn't know it would be with you.'

'Even Isabella isn't infallible,' he says.

'Don't tell her that. She'd be devastated.'

'Those were her exact words?' he says. 'A kiss in the snow?'

'As I say, she fancies herself as a bit of a prognosticator.'

'She shouldn't give up the day job,' he says, lifting his hand to stroke my cheek. 'First, she got the wrong man, and now she's got the wrong number.'

'What do you mean?'

'A kiss in the snow implies just one kiss,' he says. 'She's way off there.'

'Is she, indeed?'

'Completely,' he says, reaching for me again. 'I may not have succeeded in the sport of ring tossing tonight. But I intend to set a whole new record for kissing someone in the snow before either or both of us freezes to death.'

Chapter Twenty-Nine

Isabella knocks on my bedroom door the following morning.

'I can't wait any longer! How was it? I said you could roll in at 3 a.m. but I didn't expect you to take me literally.'

I sit up and push my hair out of my eyes. 'It wasn't 3 a.m. It was closer to midnight.'

'Just like Cinderella!' she says.

'I came home in a taxi.'

'Which is the modern-day equivalent of a carriage. It wasn't by any chance Pumpkin Cabs Inc?'

'No, it was Mitchell and Sons. It clearly said so on the side of the taxi. Contrary to popular belief, I wasn't too drunk to read it.'

'Which makes you even more like Cinderella,' she says. 'At least, the stories don't tell us whether she got drunk. But they wouldn't be suitable for young children if she did.'

'And I didn't break your umbrella stand,' I add.

'Again, neither did she. That may be because they hadn't invented umbrella stands in those days. Or had they? Maybe she bumped into a wig stand or a doublet press.'

'We've established I'm nothing like Cinderella,' I say. 'For one thing, I didn't dance, which we know for a fact she did.'

'Not even a festive jig around the fire with the merry villagers?' she says. 'That's disappointing.'

'Not even that. And I was wearing jeans and a thick sweater and a waterproof coat, which I'm fairly sure she wasn't.'

'She may have done in the winter,' she says. 'I expect she did. They didn't heat those castles very well. I'm more disappointed about the dancing. Are you sure you didn't take part in a small one? How about when the speakers played a romantic song and it started to snow?'

'As far as I remember, all they played was Frosty the Snowman and Rudolph the Red-nosed Reindeer.'

'Frosty can be a romantic song in the right circumstances,' she says. 'All that stuff about traffic cops.'

I swing my legs out of bed. 'I'm getting up.'

She heaves a sigh. 'Poor Daniel.'

I blush. 'About that.'

Her eyes widen. 'What about that? You're holding out on me, Grace. I can tell. What about Daniel? Did you run away with him for a quickie Vegas wedding? Tell me at once!'

'We wouldn't have had time to get to Vegas and back.'

She gives an impatient shrug. 'Gretna Green, then. Or maybe the market had a marriage celebrant dressed as Santa to add to the festive atmosphere. Is that what happened? Did you think you were visiting Santa to sign your Christmas list, only to realise when he handed it back that you were married?'

'No,' I say. 'And who signs their Christmas list?'

'I do! Georgia and I post ours to the North Pole each year. It's important for us both to sign them or he won't know which bedroom to deliver them to. It was probably less important for you if you saw him in person.'

'But I didn't. Not even at a distance. So, there was no chance for Santa to marry us.'

'Poor Daniel,' she murmurs again.

I stop laughing. 'Well, actually …'

She fixes me with a steely gaze. 'Don't leave me hanging. Explain yourself at once.'

I reach for my hoody. 'We don't have time right now. I have to take a shower, and you and I are opening up this morning. We mustn't be late. Lily is taking Daisy for her check-up this morning. We'll have customers queueing up outside complaining. We can't leave them standing in the snow. They'll storm the bakery, led by that Wendy woman. It must be almost time for her to return something or other.'

Isabella narrows her eyes at me. 'I'm perfectly prepared to leave them standing in the snow the entire day, even if the queue stretches all the way to the Red Lion. I'm not leaving this room until you've explained to me what you mean by, "Well, actually …"'

I pick up my wash bag. 'There was a small change of plan at the last moment.'

Her face falls. 'He didn't come after all?'

'I mean I didn't spend the evening with Daniel. I spent it with Rob.'

I ignore her startled look as I march towards the bathroom and turn on the shower.

Isabella is waiting for me when I arrive downstairs. Mrs Campbell is frying bacon, and Georgia is sitting at the table spreading butter onto several pieces of toast.

'Can I help you with that?' I ask Mrs Campbell.

She flaps her hand at me. 'Sit down, Grace. I won't be a moment. My daughters have eaten all the bacon I cooked for myself, so I'm preparing another batch. Would you like some?'

'Just toast for me, thanks.'

'Are you sure?' says Isabella. 'Bacon sandwiches are excellent for hangovers.'

'I don't have a hangover.'

'You weren't too coherent when I saw you this morning.'

'Yes, I was.'

'No, you weren't,' she insists. 'You couldn't even remember who you'd spent the evening with. If that isn't a sign of drunkenness, I don't know what is. I blame myself. I should never have told you to visit the Snowball Saloon. They serve excellent stuff, but it isn't for amateurs. I see how it was. You tried to run before you could walk. You had one glass, and it went straight to your head. Which eggnog did you choose?'

'Bourbon.'

She clicks her tongue. 'That's the worst kind. No doubt you gulped it down, thinking what a delicious creamy drink it was, like a milkshake. "More, please, my good man," you said, holding out your cup to the stallholder. Instead of realising he was dealing with an amateur and cutting you off, he recklessly agreed. He suggested you tried the rum next. By the time you'd knocked that back, it seemed a good idea to sample their brandy eggnog too, and the rest is history.'

'I'm afraid I only had one glass,' I say. 'Although I did have a glass of mulled wine with Daniel when I first arrived.'

'I'm confused,' she complains. 'You told me you spent the evening with Rob.'

'I did.' I crunch my toast, ignoring her look of agonised entreaty.

'If you don't stop talking gibberish and tell me right now what's going on, I'll … I'll …'

'Don't talk with your mouth full, dear,' says Mrs Campbell placidly.

Georgia looks up from her plate. 'If Issy didn't talk with her mouth full, she'd never talk at all.'

'Nonsense,' says Mrs Campbell. 'Your sister has lovely manners. What's the matter, Bella?'

Isabella waves an accusing piece of toast at me. 'It's Grace. She knows I'm not at my best in the morning, yet she insists on torturing me.'

I relent. 'I'm sorry. It's all perfectly simple. I arranged to visit the fair with Daniel, but about half an hour after we arrived, Rob appeared. He and I had a talk, and I realised I hadn't been quite fair to him in London.'

Isabella's eyes widen. 'Are you saying you dumped Daniel for Rob?'

'Cool,' says Georgia, looking at me with fresh interest.

I try to maintain my composure. 'I wouldn't put it quite like that. But I realised things couldn't go anywhere romantically with Daniel, so I decided to be honest about it.'

'How did he take it?' says Isabella.

'Very well. Anyway, there was a genuine emergency back at the hotel, so he said goodbye, and I stayed at the markets with Rob.'

'Poor Daniel,' she says for the third time.

'I know. It wasn't ideal. But it was better than pretending.'

'Would you have told him if Rob hadn't been there?' she says.

'I expect I'd have waited until he asked to see me again, which would also have been awkward.'

'Who is this Rob guy?' says Georgia. 'One of your customers?'

'Someone I knew in London. He's a part of the film crew covering the Christmas party.'

'Cool,' she says again, returning to her breakfast.

Isabella scrutinises me carefully. 'So, you no longer hate and despise Rob as a rampant womaniser?'

My cheeks flush. 'I may have got slightly the wrong end of the stick there.'

'And he's not seeing Vanessa anymore?' she says.

'Again, that may not have been entirely accurate.'

'You're a dark horse, Grace. Just wait until I tell Lily!'

'Don't you dare! I can't imagine what you'd say to her, but there wouldn't be more than a grain of truth mixed with your usual flights of fancy. I'll tell her myself – if I continue to see Rob.'

'If?' she says. 'Are you telling me you ditched that lovely Daniel for someone you may not see again?'

'How do you know he's lovely if you've never met him?'

'Lily said he was. And he *sounds* lovely.'

'I'll have to introduce you some time,' I say. 'And I am seeing Rob again. He's taking me out for dinner tomorrow evening.'

'Not at the hotel?' she says.

'That might be awkward. He mentioned a place called The Wild Horse.'

'Lovely!' says Mrs Campbell. 'Henry and I go there all the time. Mention our name, and they'll give you a good table.'

'Don't forget to order the Cointreau Mousse,' says Isabella.

She drops her plate into the sink. 'We can't afford to sit around here all morning gossiping about your love life. I'm surprised at you, Grace. As a new employee, you should be trying to make a good impression, not mooning around talking endlessly about your new boyfriend. Get a move on! You know how I hate keeping our customers waiting. It isn't professional.'

There are several people outside a bakery when we arrive.

'I'm so sorry,' Isabella greets them. 'One of our staff members had a crisis, and I needed to help her deal with it.'

'Not Abby, I hope,' says one of the women.

'Not Abby,' Isabella reassures her. 'Come on in. It's freezing out here. May I offer you all the drink of your choice as a small recompense for making you wait?'

She ushers everyone inside and shows them to their tables.

'Who had a crisis?' I ask her in a low voice.

'You did. First, you had to deal with your terrible hangover. Then you had to burble on for hours about how dreamy your new boyfriend is.'

'I wouldn't have mentioned him at all if you hadn't been so nosy. And he's not my boyfriend!'

'No?' she says. 'What would you call him – your suitor, your gentleman caller, your beau? Don't look so embarrassed, Grace. We've all been there. Young love is a beautiful thing.'

I leave her making lattes and march off to the kitchen to prepare the dried fruit. Mabel is coming in at closing time to teach us how to make syllabub. It's the last dish we need to learn. After that, all we can do is practise like mad and hope for the best.

Things quieten down after lunch. Lily stays in the shop while Isabella and I look after the cafe.

Bernie arrives mid-afternoon and gives a delighted bark when he sees me.

'Shh, darling!' says his owner. 'You want your lovely biscuit, don't you?'

'Hello, Mrs Ogilvie,' I say. 'Did you walk all this way in the snow?'

'Bernie doesn't mind,' she says. 'He's dressed for the weather, as you see.'

Bernie is indeed wearing a wonderful tartan coat and little fur boots.

'He looks extremely cosy,' I say. 'But I really meant you.'

'Oh, I'm fine,' she says. 'This is a thick coat, and Mabel brought me a pair of sheepskin boots back from Australia. I must say they're lovely and warm.'

I'm tempted to ask whether Mabel bought them from the Wombat Wallow corner store. But I don't dare. For all I know, Mrs Ogilvie has never heard of Wombat Wallow. Mabel is entitled to her secrets, just as the rest of us are.

'My sister will be here at five o'clock,' she says. 'I believe she's helping you with your desserts?'

'That's right. She's an excellent cook.'

'She is. Although she's rather slapdash about the washing up afterwards. I often have to go in and clean up when she's finished. I don't want to serve Bernard his food in a dirty kitchen. He wouldn't like it.'

I'm surprised Bernie doesn't eat his meals sitting up at the table with a dainty napkin tucked around his neck. But I don't say so. It's nice to see a pet so well cared for and loved.

By four thirty, the last of the customers has left the cafe. I'm wiping the final table when the bell jingles and a customer comes in, letting in a blast of cold air. I turn to greet them and see it's Rob.

Isabella winks at me. 'Grace, would you like to serve our customer? Lily is in the office, and my hands are full cleaning the coffee machine.'

I walk over to the counter. 'Hi, Rob. I didn't expect to see you today.'

Isabella clears her throat and gives me a meaningful look. I roll my eyes at her. 'Fine! Hello Mr Marshall. Welcome to The Sugarloaf Bakery. How may I help you today?'

'Very professional,' he says. 'You could have been doing this for years.'

I lower my voice so Isabella can't hear. 'No, I couldn't. I'd have murdered my boss long ago. What brings you here today?'

His answering smile sends the blood rushing to my cheeks. 'I came to see you. It's been too long. But I do need to talk to you. I have to go back to London this evening. Vanessa isn't happy with the way the editing is going, and she wants me to take charge.'

'I see. Did you and she have that discussion we talked about last night?'

'We did. But I don't think it's anything to do with that. There are some technical issues I have to sort out as quickly as possible or this Christmas special may have to be cancelled.'

'Is it as bad as that?'

'I think so,' he says. 'I'm sorry about our dinner tomorrow night. I'll take you another time if you'll let me.'

'These things happen. How did Vanessa take it, by the way?'

'She was surprisingly fine with it.'

'You didn't tell her about me?' I ask.

'No, I told her the truth. I said I'd enjoyed spending time with her, but I wondered whether I'd been unclear about where I saw things going. So, I'd like to clarify I see us as good friends.'

I give a choke of laughter. 'Don't tell me you wished her well in her future endeavours?'

'I'm not sure. I don't think so. But this honesty thing of yours is great. I think it could catch on. If I were you, I'd patent it before someone gets hold of it and writes a bestseller. You could call it, *I Wish You Well*.'

'Maybe after Christmas,' I say. 'Thanks for letting me know in person. Honeywell is rather out of your way. You could have called me.'

'I still don't have your number. I hinted at that in the pub that night, but you fobbed me off. I thought you might have a policy not to hand it out until you'd known someone for at least a year.'

'I changed provider when I came down here, and they gave me a new number. Give me your phone.'

He hands it to me, and I add myself to his contacts. 'There you go. You can stop complaining about it now. The bakery has a landline. You could have called me on that.'

It's his turn to lower his voice. 'Isabella might have answered, and I'm terrified of her.'

'You aren't the only one. Let me know when you're coming back down. Maybe we can have dinner then.'

'I doubt I'll see you before we come over to film your final preparations,' he says. 'You, your co-workers, and the elusive, camera-shy chef Mabel. For someone with so many hit TV shows under her belt, she's oddly reluctant to appear on screen. Anyway, I didn't want to call. I wanted to give you these in person.'

He reaches into his pocket and hands me a gold edged envelope.

I open it and pull out two tickets. 'Are these what I think they are?'

'It depends on what you think they are. They're tickets to the Quayside Hotel Christmas ball. Daniel gave them to me this morning. He said he thought I might like them.'

'That was nice of him. But won't you be at the ball, anyway? You're filming the whole event.'

'I don't do the actual filming,' he says. 'Vanessa will be there to keep an eye on things. You mentioned you'd be using the servant's entrance, which seemed a shame. Once you've delivered your desserts, you'll have the rest of the evening free. I'd be delighted if you would accompany me.'

'I'd love to,' I say. 'Thanks, Rob. I've never been to anything like that before. I'll have to buy myself some new jeans especially for the occasion.'

'Me too,' he says. 'On second thoughts, maybe I'll rent some. I hear Armani has a good line in this year with diamante encrusted hems. We'll be the John Travolta and Olivia Newton John of the ball.'

He looks at his watch. 'I must go. Sorry again about tonight. But I'll see you very soon.'

He glances over at Isabella.

'Don't mind me,' she says. 'I'm just wiping this smudge off the wall.'

She ostentatiously turns her back and starts wiping at a piece of non-existent dirt.

'How tactful,' murmurs Rob. He leans across the counter and kisses me gently. 'See you next week.'

Isabella doesn't turn around again until Rob has left the shop.

'He's gone,' I say. 'You can stop pretending to clean that wall.'

'Don't say I'm not tactful,' she says.

'Or embarrassing. How did you know he wanted to kiss me? Maybe he wanted to break up with me, and you made it impossible for him.'

'Even you can't break up with two people in twenty-four hours,' she says. 'Did I hear something about tickets?'

I wave them at her. 'It appears I will be taking part in this event after all. I wasn't expecting that.'

She claps her hands. 'That's so exciting. Do you have something to wear? It doesn't matter. You and I are a similar size.

You can borrow one of my dresses. Or Georgia's. She has an amazing Jenny Packham dress. She bought it last year for some charity thing one of her boyfriends took her to.'

'She won't want to lend that to me.'

'She won't have any choice,' she says. 'Otherwise, I'll tell our parents about the time she borrowed Dad's old Bentley to go off-roading. Mum will do your hair for you. She's surprisingly good at it. She'll do your make up too –'

She breaks off, and a slow smile spreads over her face. 'I told you this morning this was like a fairy tale, and I was right. Look at you! A humble shop assistant, slaving away all hours of the day and night at the whim of your evil employers. But now the tables have turned. All we need is a pumpkin and a few mice. We don't have any mice here at the bakery because we're an exemplary establishment. But my uncle has a few barns. We're bound to find a few there.'

She warms to her theme. 'Lily and I are obviously the ugly sisters. Georgia can be your fairy godmother and provide the dress if she doesn't want to end up grounded for a year. And Rob will be Prince Charming in his sequined jeans. This is all working out perfectly. Grace Andersen, you shall go to the ball, or I'll know the reason why!'

Chapter Thirty

We decide to close the bakery on Friday morning for the second round of filming.

'It's a shame, but it has to be done,' says Isabella. 'We need all hands on deck while the team is here. We can't allow ourselves to be distracted by Grace hurling bread rolls at any of the customers she takes a dislike to.'

'Stop worrying,' I say. 'The last time the team was here, we were frantically trying to hide the fact that Abby was in hospital, and none of us had the faintest idea what we were doing. Things are completely different now. Abby is almost better and, against all the odds, we three have learned to cook, and we're about to put The Sugarloaf Bakery on the map with a triumphant display of sugary goodness.'

'Ignore Cinders here,' says Isabella. 'She's delirious. All she can think about is pumpkins and glass slippers and kissing Prince Charming at midnight.'

'Don't be ridiculous!' I say hotly, and Lily laughs.

'I'm perfectly serious,' I insist. 'Everything is different this time. It makes it so much easier now we have nothing to hide.'

'It helps that you're dating the producer,' adds Isabella.

'Leave the poor woman alone,' says Lily. 'Don't take any notice of her, Grace.'

'Rob isn't the producer, and I'm not dating him,' I say.

'And you didn't kiss him at the Christmas fair in front of half of Honeywell?' says Isabella. 'I have to say I was shocked when I heard about that. The fair is a family event, not one of your London raves. And you haven't been mooning around the bakery all week humming love songs and getting the customers' orders wrong?'

'Definitely not,' I say. 'I can't sing in tune, for one thing. If you heard someone humming, I expect it was Lily.'

'Not guilty,' says Lily. 'I may have sung along to the odd Christmas carol while I was in the kitchen, but that's all.'

'This wasn't carols,' says Isabella. 'There was nothing about wassailing and throwing figgy pudding at carol singers. This was all about nightingales and roses and chocolate hearts.'

'It was probably one of the customers,' says Lily. 'Mrs Ogilvie, perhaps. Anyway, Grace is right. We're in a far stronger position this time. I watched her piping the cream onto the chocolate mousses yesterday afternoon. Even Abby couldn't have done it more professionally.'

'Don't tell Abby that,' says Isabella. 'She feels bad enough about not being able to cater this party without hearing we're fine without her.'

'She doesn't need to worry,' says Lily. 'It takes the three of us working full time to achieve one tenth of what she does. And she doesn't have to throw half of it away.'

'I wish she didn't have to miss all the fun,' says Isabella.

'Me too,' I say. 'But she should be back at work in the new year. And there's always next Christmas.'

'And Valentine's Day,' adds Lily, glancing at Isabella.

'Ah, yes, Valentine's Day,' says Isabella, clasping her hands. 'Always such a special day at The Sugarloaf Bakery. It's how Lily and I first met. I walked into the bakery, and she thought she'd never seen such a beautiful woman. Unfortunately, I was seeing her ex-boyfriend at the time, so she had to make do with Jack.'

'I remember it rather differently,' says Lily. 'But I don't have time to argue. The team will be here in an hour, and we haven't yet grated the chocolate for the mousses.'

'You and I can do that,' says Isabella. 'Grace will want to take some time to re-do her make up and check her hair is smooth. You can use my office if you like, Grace.'

'I'm not telling you again,' says Lily. 'Leave the poor woman alone.'

'I'll do some crème brûlées,' I say. 'I'm not confident enough to prepare those with the entire team watching, but they would look nice in the background. I'll do about twenty of them. Mabel is coming in as soon as the team has gone to help me finish the rest. We've been allocated a fridge at the hotel, so I'll take them over later. We can caramelise them tomorrow.'

'Sounds good,' says Lily. 'Isabella and have prepared some of the tarts. The team can film us making the coulis. I still wish we didn't have to do it with someone looking over our shoulder and capturing it for posterity. I have the feeling Vanessa would like us to fail.'

'Me too,' says Isabella. 'I can't think why, but she doesn't seem to have warmed to us as much as I expected.'

The van pulls up outside the shop at eleven o'clock sharp, and we look at each other in sudden consternation.

'This is it,' says Lily.

'I suppose so,' I say.

'We'll be fine,' says Isabella. 'We're a team, and there's no us in team.'

Rob climbs out of the driving seat and slams the door. He glances over at the bakery and sees us watching. He raises a hand in greeting and gives me a tiny smile.

I smile back before catching sight of Vanessa, who has emerged from the passenger side and is giving the bakery her usual supercilious look.

'Open the door, Grace,' says Isabella. 'You're the one he's come to see, not us.'

'Not a word more, or I'll stuff you bodily into the fridge and lock the door,' warns Lily. 'At least, I would if I didn't think you'd enjoy it.'

'I'll be good,' promises Isabella.

Vanessa opens the door, and Rob follows, carrying Bryony's camera gear.

'Nice to see you again,' says Lily. 'Can I get anyone a hot drink before we start?'

'We're in a hurry,' says Vanessa. 'We're filming over in Aldchurch after this.'

'Is that Kit's Catering?' says Lily. 'They're really good. Are they ready for tomorrow?'

'I have no idea,' says Vanessa. 'They seem a very professional outfit.'

Her eyes sweep across the counter and over the empty cafe. 'You don't seem too busy.'

'I know,' says Isabella. 'It's very odd. I heard about the zombie apocalypse on the news last night, but I thought it wasn't due to arrive in Honeywell until this evening.'

She catches Lily's eye and coughs. 'Sorry. We decided to close the shop while you were here. It felt rather crowded last time, with people coming in and out of the kitchen. We'd prefer to give you our undivided attention while you're here.'

'Whatever,' says Vanessa. 'I'll help you set up in the kitchen,' she tells Bryony. 'I wasn't happy with where we put that light last time. It threw too much shadow over the table.'

She doesn't wait for an answer but walks to the kitchen. Bryony follows her.

'I'll be through in a second,' says Rob.

Isabella takes Lily's arm. 'I'll show you the discrepancy in the accounts I found this morning.'

'Discrepancy?' says Lily. 'What do you mean?'

'I'm sorry to hear about that,' says Rob. 'I hope it isn't too large.'

'I'm afraid so,' says Isabella. 'Several thousand pounds has gone missing, and I have no idea where it's gone. Come on, Lily. You need to see this.'

Lily smiles at me and Rob. 'Goodness! A discrepancy, you say? How awful. Just before Christmas too.'

The pair of them disappear.

'I apologise for my co-workers,' I say. 'I have no control over them. They were here when I arrived in the village.'

'I'm sorry about your financial woes,' says Rob. 'I hope things aren't as bad as they seem. Meanwhile, as we seem to have the place to ourselves ...'

He pulls me into his arms and kisses me. 'I've missed you.'

'You too. Although we've been so busy that I haven't had time to think about anything other than desserts.'

'One more day,' he says. 'And then I'll have you all to myself. Are you ready for the ball?'

'As far as the catering goes. How about you?'

'I've done the editing for everything we have so far. It's looking good. I'll spend this evening working on the footage we take today. Then I'm just about finished, except for the footage we take at the ball.'

He kisses me again. 'How about you? When does the bakery close for Christmas?'

'We're open until lunchtime tomorrow. Then I'm free until the 27th.'

'And where will you be spending Christmas Day?' he says. 'You aren't flying up to Scotland?'

'Not a hope. My parents live several hours from the nearest airport. I'd have to leave as soon as I arrived. Isabella's family has invited me to spend Christmas with them. I'm sure they don't really want an extra person, but her mum insisted. Apparently, they go up to the Manor House for Christmas lunch, and it's like something out of Downton Abbey. How about you?'

'Rob!' shouts Vanessa. 'What on earth is keeping you so long? I've already told you we're in a hurry.'

He releases me, and I take a step back in case she decides to come and find us.

'Does Vanessa know you're taking me to the ball?' I ask.

'I was hoping you might agree to wear a disguise,' he says. 'A wig and a moustache should do the trick.'

Vanessa appears. 'What are you doing in here? And where are the other two? I want to get started.'

'They're sorting out an urgent financial matter,' says Rob. 'And Grace was explaining to me that Chef Mabel was hoping to be with us today, but she's been unfortunately detained.'

She gives an exasperated sigh. 'Don't start all that again. Chef Mabel doesn't exist, as you well know. I don't even believe she's a chef.'

'She is,' I say. 'She's extremely talented. She may have exaggerated her story a little to add colour, but she cooks very well.'

'I don't have time to listen to nonsense,' she says. 'Can you fetch the others so we can get started? They'll have to sort out their accounting problems another time.'

I knock on the office door as I pass, and Isabella opens it.

'Are you ready?' I ask.

'Your hair is ruffled,' she says. 'Honestly, Grace, we've been through this several times. Professional appearance is key to a successful business.'

'I hope your financial discrepancy wasn't too serious,' says Rob.

Vanessa stops dead. 'Financial discrepancy?'

I give Isabella a warning glance. If Vanessa gets a hint of a juicy story concerning the bakery, she'll want to include it in the programme.

Isabella gives me a faintly mocking grin in return. 'It turns out there was nothing to worry about. Lily double checked the accounts and pointed out that I'd transposed a few zeros. It's easily done when you're as busy as we are.'

'Transposed a few zeros?' queries Vanessa.

'And a couple of decimal points,' says Isabella. 'Still, all's well that ends well. The accounts are once more in perfect order, and the bakery is back in profit. Shall we get this show on the road?'

Vanessa doesn't say any more, but she doesn't look pleased. If Isabella has been counting on an invitation to the production company's summer party next year, she may be disappointed.

We find Bryony in the kitchen. 'I can't move the light any closer to the table,' she says when we come in.

'It will be fine there,' says Vanessa. 'The main thing is to avoid that band of shadow across the food preparation area. Let's make a start.'

Lily and Isabella wash their hands and put on their hair nets. I take up my usual position in the shelter of the doorway and observe the proceedings.

'Aren't you joining them?' says Vanessa.

'You'll have to make do with me and Lily,' says Isabella. 'Grace prefers to take a more backseat role – but no less crucial for all that. If you look at that counter – she waves her hand to where I've left the first batch of crème brûlées cooling – you can see some of the outstanding work she did for us this morning. It's a joy to have such a skilled member of staff working alongside us.'

'Are you working here permanently?' Vanessa asks me.

'Grace is here with us over the Christmas period,' says Lily. 'She's been invaluable. We couldn't have done this without her.'

I give her a grateful smile but don't speak. The less I say at this point, the better. I don't want to mention anything that might hurt or damage the bakery.

'Only I heard that PDT was laying off staff,' pursues Vanessa. 'That's your place, isn't it, Grace?'

'That's right,' I say briefly.

'So, were you one of them? Is that why you've ended up down here working in a bakery?' She manages to make it sound like septic tank maintenance.

'I'm not sure why you're so interested,' I say. 'But yes, as it happens, I've been made redundant. Which turned out to be excellent timing because it enabled me to take a job in this bakery. And it isn't just any bakery. It's the most wonderful bakery in the world. It started out as practically nothing, and these incredible women saw its potential and turned it into what it is today – the heart of the community. It's been a huge privilege to work here. Losing my job at PDT is no great matter. If anything, it's given me the opportunity to discover how decent businesses treat their staff. They care about who they are as people. They don't dump a redundancy notice on their desks after four years and forget about them. I'll easily find myself another job in the new year. But I doubt it will be anywhere with one tenth as much heart and integrity as this place.'

I don't exactly expect Vanessa to burst into tears when I say this, so I'm not disappointed.

She shrugs. 'Did you get any of that, Bryony? Can we use it in the show?'

'No!' I almost shout. 'You can't use it. I've already told you I haven't signed a release. And I have no intention of appearing on your … show.'

I almost say stupid show but restrain myself. I don't want to annoy her in case she gives less favourable coverage to Lily and Isabella. They've worked so hard to get where they are, and they deserve the world to see it.

'We should make a start,' says Rob. 'What will you be doing this morning, Isabella?'

'Lily and I will be making chocolate mousses,' she says. 'We have sixty of them to prepare by this afternoon. We'll finish the lemon tarts this evening, and tomorrow will be even busier.'

'Is anyone else helping you?' he says.

'If you're referring to Chef Mabel, I'm afraid not. As I mentioned earlier, she's been unavoidably detained.'

She starts to whisk the eggs, and Bryony zooms in on Lily as she melts the chocolate.

I hate to admit it, but Vanessa knows what she's doing. She asks all the right questions and leads Isabella on to give a brief history of the bakery, while Lily talks about her memories of growing up in Honeywell.

'That's plenty,' she tells Rob an hour later. 'You should be able to work with that. It's only a short segment.'

'No problem,' he says. 'I'll have it done by tomorrow morning.'

He squeezes my hand as he walks past me. 'Well done,' he says in an undertone.

He accompanies Vanessa into the shop, talking about lighting and match cuts.

'Do you need help with the camera bag?' I ask Bryony.

'Don't worry,' she says. 'I'm used to it. Besides, Vanessa would go mad if I let anyone else touch the technical equipment. She's very strict about that.'

'She seems very strict all around,' says Isabella.

'She's ok,' says Bryony. 'She works hard, and she expects everyone else to do the same. But she's good at her job. I've learned a lot working for her.'

She closes the kitchen door behind her, and Lily collapses into a chair. 'Thank goodness that's over! I can't believe we didn't drop anything or smash anything. I was terrified we'd have a repeat of yesterday when you dropped that tray of mousses.'

Isabella sinks into a chair next to her. 'Whipped cream all over the floor wouldn't have sent the right message, would it? It's difficult to pretend you're a professional setup when half of your desserts end up ruined.'

'All's well that ends well,' says Lily. 'I can't believe we've made it through in one piece. We had no business taking this contract. I realise that now. We ought to have called Daniel as soon as we knew Abby was out of action, not pretended we knew what we were doing. The entire ball could have been ruined.'

'It was a bit of a risk,' says Isabella. 'But it was worth taking. The Sugarloaf Bakery's reputation is about to soar.'

'If anyone had known what we were doing, it would have plummeted,' says Lily. 'And we would have deserved it. Thank goodness we had a professional chef helping us out, even if she was somewhat fictional!'

'We'd have been fine,' says Isabella. 'Grace was our secret weapon. First, she dated the events manager, and then the editor. Talk about devotion to duty!'

'I really like Rob,' says Lily. 'He seems like a good guy.'

'He is,' I say. 'But don't tell him I said that. He'd get too big for his boots.'

'And what you said about the bakery was lovely,' she says.

'I meant every word.'

'Why didn't you tell us you'd been made redundant?' she asks. 'If anyone would have understood, it's me. It's how I ended up here in the first place.'

'I didn't want to think about it, I say. 'I'm not too worried about finding work. But it was difficult to realise I'd given four years of my life to a company who don't see their staff as human. Coming here was exactly what I needed to restore my faith in human nature. And I reconnected with Rob. If I'd stayed in London, I would probably never have seen him again.'

'It's funny how things work out,' she says. 'I didn't expect to meet the love of my life when my mum got me a temporary job here.'

'So, is this true love?' Isabella asks me. 'Does the glass slipper fit?'

'You're getting ahead of yourself,' I say. 'All I can tell you is that I really like him, and I hope things work out between us.'

'And he's clearly crazy about you,' says Lily. 'Don't look like that, Grace. It's obvious how he feels from the way he looks at you. He –'

She breaks off as the kitchen door opens, and Bryony walks back in.

'I forgot my other bag. Good luck with the rest of your preparations. I may see you at the hotel tomorrow. Gotta run! Vanessa is chomping at the bit.'

'I'll open the shop,' says Lily. 'I told as many customers as possible that we were closing this morning. But the message won't have got out to everyone. I hope we don't have disgruntled customers lined up all the way down the high street.

'I hope we do,' says Isabella. 'It would show the team how popular we are. There's nothing like angry customers beating down your door to demonstrate you're a successful business.'

'Looked at a different way,' I say. 'There's nothing like an angry mob to show we don't take customer service seriously.'

Isabella opens the kitchen door and peers out. 'No angry mob that I can see. I don't know whether to take that as an insult or a compliment. But Bernie is sitting outside in the snow, looking chilly. I can't tell which of his owners has brought him in today, but I expect he's hoping for a biscuit either way.'

Chapter Thirty-One

Lily wants to close the bakery the following morning, but Isabella refuses.

'We're always open until lunchtime on Christmas Eve. Our customers expect it. We can't let them down.'

'It's a special occasion,' pleads Lily. 'They'll understand.'

Isabella is adamant. 'Our customers are the most important part of our business. They'll be here when the TV crew has gone. We can easily manage for the morning.'

In the end, I look after the shop while Lily and Isabella whip the cream for the syllabubs and bake the final batches of brownies.

We say goodbye to our final customers at noon and breathe a sigh of relief.

'We have time for a quick sandwich before we start on the lemon tarts,' says Lily. 'I promised Daniel we'd have everything there early in case of any last-minute hiccups. I don't know how Abby copes with the pressure.'

'We'll be fine,' says Isabella. 'The crème brûlées are safely in the hotel fridge. All we need to do is caramelise them. The syllabubs are done, and we have one hundred brownies cooling on their trays.'

'Ninety-nine brownies,' says Lily, and Isabella laughs. 'Who's counting?'

'I'll finish the chocolate mousses,' I say. 'I did the first batch yesterday evening and put them in the fridge. I have thirty more to make. One of you can pipe the cream onto them when we get to the hotel.'

Lily collapses into a chair. 'I'm glad you're going to the ball and not me, Grace. I'm dead on my feet. The thought of dancing into the early hours doesn't appeal.'

'Grace doesn't have to get up with a toddler at the crack of dawn,' says Isabella.

'She has to get up with you,' says Lily. 'I can't imagine you sleeping late on Christmas morning.'

'Santa brings me a special stocking to keep me quiet until the sun is up,' says Isabella. 'Grace can sleep until I've opened that and played with all my presents.'

We eat a quick lunch, after which Lily helps me finish the mousses.

'Did you ever think we'd manage this?' she says, grating chocolate over the final one. 'I didn't.'

'There were times when I felt less sure than others. But somehow, I always had faith we could do it. You and Isabella are quite a team, even with Abby out of action.'

'I'm glad you're here,' she says. 'We couldn't have done it without you.'

We finish the mousses, and Lily volunteers to take them over to the hotel.

'You should go home and start getting ready for the ball,' she tells me. 'It starts at seven o'clock.'

'That's almost four hours from now,' I say. 'Half an hour will be more than enough for me.'

'You have to be joking!' says Isabella. 'This is the biggest night of your life. Even if we go home now, it will be tight.'

'It isn't the biggest night of my life,' I say. 'It's a Christmas party, that's all.'

'First of all, it's a ball, not a party,' she says. 'And it isn't just any ball. Prince Charming will be there!'

'Is that right?' I say. 'Remind me to introduce him to Rob.'

'Lily and I weren't invited to this shindig,' she reminds me. 'So, we want to live vicariously through you. We'll be spending the evening in the kitchen. We need to know at least one of us is having the most perfect night of their lives.'

'So, no pressure,' says Lily.

'I'm calling Rob and asking whether he wants to go to the cinema instead,' I grumble.

Isabella picks up my bag. 'If that's your attitude, I'm keeping your phone until you're ready. Time is slipping away as we speak. Get your coat, and let's get out of here. See you at the hotel, Lily!'

Three hours later, I'm sitting in front of the triple mirror in Mrs Campbell's dressing room while she twists my hair into a knot and pulls out a few strands to frame my face.

'Now for the dress!' says Isabella. 'It's a good thing it fastens up the back or we'd have to do your hair all over again.'

Mrs Campbell considers me carefully. 'That should hold until the end of the night. Perhaps I'll give it another spritz of hair spray, just to make sure.'

I hold up a protective hand. 'No more, thanks. There may be lighted candles there tonight, and I don't want to go up in flames.'

She laughs. 'Alright, I'll leave it like that. You look lovely, Grace. Doesn't she, Bella?'

'She looks amazing,' says Isabella. 'Who would have guessed she'd scrub up so well?'

She helps me into the dress and fastens it up at the back. She turns me to face the mirror. 'You'd never think you were the same person who was running around the bakery earlier today, covered in flour. What do you think?'

I study my reflection. 'Is that really me? I look so …'

'Gorgeous?' she says. 'Stunning? Elegant?'

I look at the stranger in the mirror. She looks back at me with a faintly surprised expression.

'Grown up,' I say at last.

'It's a lovely dress,' says Mrs Campbell. 'It could have been made for you.'

Georgia puts her head around the door. 'Well, it wasn't. It was made for me. At least, I bought it. It had better come back in one piece.'

'I'll be careful,' I promise.

'Don't listen to her,' says Isabella. 'The last time she wore that dress, she spilled a pint of beer down it and sat on a chicken vol-au-vent. She had to have it dry cleaned.'

'I'll run screaming from any vol-au-vents I encounter,' I promise. 'And I'll stick to champagne all night.'

Georgia snorts and disappears.

'I'll get it dry cleaned for her,' I say.

'No need,' says Isabella. 'She'll only spill something on it again. Seriously, what do you think of the dress?'

I look at myself in the mirror again. The dress is a deep red satin, with a fitted bodice and a flowing skirt that falls in graceful folds to my feet. A diamante clasp at the waist sparkles like a captured star.

'I love it,' I say. 'It's exactly the sort of dress I'd have chosen for myself. I hate fuss and flounces. And I love the colour. It's perfect for a Christmas ball. Do you think Rob will bring me a holly corsage to wear with it?'

'Not unless he wants to feel the full force of Georgia's wrath,' she says. 'Don't mention anything spiky to her or she'll make you take it off and wear those sparkly jeans instead.'

Mrs Campbell goes to her wardrobe and selects a silver wrap. 'This matches Georgia's shoes perfectly. Don't tell her I have it, or it will disappear into her room, and I'll never see it again.'

'We should get going,' says Isabella. 'We're taking some of the desserts with us, and they need lots of space. Grace may have to sit in the boot.'

Rob is waiting in the lobby when we arrive.

I walk over to greet him, feeling remarkably self-conscious. 'Hi, Rob.'

For a moment, he doesn't appear to recognise me. Then his face breaks into a smile. 'Is that really you? You look amazing.'

'There's no need to sound so surprised.'

'I'm not. You always look lovely. But that dress is something else!'

'Borrowed feathers,' I say. 'This dress has to be back in Georgia's wardrobe at the end of the night or I'll be uninvited to the family Christmas.'

'We'll have to make sure it enjoys its evening,' he says. 'It sounds as though it doesn't get out much.'

'Your tuxedo is very nice too,' I say. 'Does it get invited to many occasions like this?'

'I haven't asked it any personal questions. We only met for the first time this afternoon when we were introduced at the rental store.'

'I look forward to getting to know it better,' I say. 'I've just seen the TV crew. I plan to hide behind you whenever they come near me tonight.'

'I'll protect you,' he says. 'I was about to suggest we went to the ballroom, but I think Vanessa is trying to catch my eye.'

I look over and see Vanessa making her way through the crowd of people streaming through the foyer.

'Why are you wearing a tuxedo?' she asks Rob. 'I told everyone they needed to be smart and blend in, but there was no need to –'

Her gaze falls on me, and she breaks off. Then her eyes narrow.

'Aren't you supposed to be in the kitchen? I saw your friends carrying stacks of dishes in earlier. And why are you dressed like that?'

'Isabella has upgraded our uniforms,' I say. 'She felt our current overalls didn't adequately reflect our status as purveyors of fine desserts to the cognoscenti.'

Her eyes narrow even further as she takes in my dress and upswept hair.

'Grace is off duty tonight,' says Rob. 'Daniel gave me a couple of tickets last week. They had a cancellation, and he thought I might like to use them. I asked Grace to be my guest.'

Vanessa frowns. 'Wasn't there a waiting list?'

'To be Rob's guest?' I say.

'To attend this ball!' she snaps.

I don't answer. There's no point in putting her back up even more than I already have. She and I will never be friends. We're too different. But she's only doing her job. This must be a stressful night for her, and there's no need for me to make it worse.

'I'll check in on Bryony and make sure she has everything she needs,' says Rob.

'No need,' says Vanessa in a surprisingly friendly tone. 'You should enjoy a break. You've been working hard.'

'So have you,' he says. 'You'll be glad when this is all over.'

'I'll be relieved,' she says. 'I've told my bosses never to expect me to work to such a ridiculous deadline in the future.'

'But it looks as though you've pulled it off,' he says.

'With your capable help,' she says. 'Did you finish last night's editing?'

'All done and dusted.'

She looks pleased. 'And did you follow my instructions?'

'Absolutely,' he assures her. 'The Christmas special should be a successful programme. It's a great way to round off the series.'

Vanessa's eyes slide towards me and away again. 'That's what I'm hoping. I look forward to seeing your final splices. Will you be watching the Christmas special, Grace?'

'I will. I haven't seen the original series, but Daniel tells me it was very good. Great … er … production values,' I finish lamely.

'I'm sure you'll enjoy it,' she says. 'I must go. Have fun!' She disappears back into the crowd.

'I shouldn't have been so snarky,' I say. 'This must be a stressful night for her.'

He smiles. 'Isabella had the right idea. Your previous overall was practical, but nowhere near as attractive as that dress. I'm sure you'll have an influx of customers once the word gets around. You may need to turn up the heating in the bakery, though. The colour is a bold choice too, but it works. Will you be expected to wear your hair like that every day?'

'I hope not. I'd never get a hairnet over it. Isabella's mother did my hair, and she insisted on using an entire can of hairspray so it didn't fall down halfway through the evening.'

'She did an excellent job,' he says. 'You look beautiful.'

'It was chaos this evening,' I say. 'Georgia was lurking in the doorway, threatening me with all sorts if I dared to spill anything on her dress. Isabella was darting in and out talking about desserts and telling her mother she was using the wrong shade of eyeshadow. Just as we were about to leave, she came rushing in to tell us she'd got a puncture and needed to borrow Georgia's car. Georgia flat out refused because she was going out tonight too. We ended up bringing half the desserts over here in Uncle Charles' new Mercedes. He was reluctant to give Isabella the keys, but she charmed him into it.'

'How exciting for the desserts,' he says. 'They deserved to arrive in style after all the hard work you've put into them. I'm surprised Isabella didn't hire a stretch limo. And what was Mrs Campbell doing while all this was going on?'

'She was a beacon of calm,' I say. 'I suspect she's inured to chaos. She kept spraying my hair with more and more hairspray and telling me about the time she and Isabella's father went to a Hogmanay party in Scotland and got snowed in. The guests weren't able to leave for five days, so they all made the best of it and had a weeklong party.'

'Maybe that will happen tonight,' he says. 'It's already snowing quite hard. And where better to be stranded over Christmas than a five-star hotel?'

'I don't want to be snowed in. It's all very well for the people staying here, but I don't have a change of clothes. And I can't wear this dress for the next five days. Georgia will kill me if it isn't back in her wardrobe tonight.'

'You could borrow a dressing gown from the spa,' he says.

'No thanks. I'm going home at midnight even if I have to dig my way out with a cake slice.'

'Glass slippers and all?' he says. 'Wouldn't they slide around in the snow?'

'I'll take my chances. And this dress had better not turn to rags, or Georgia will tear me limb from limb.'

'Spoilsport,' he complains. 'It would be fun to be snowed in until the new year. We could organise a giant murder mystery event for the guests.'

Isabella appears in the lobby and bobs a curtsey to me. 'Please, ma'am, the tweeny has broken one of the plates. Should I give her notice?'

'It's Christmas,' says Rob. 'Everyone deserves a second chance at Christmas. Even Lily.'

'Fine,' she says. 'But don't blame me when half the china is broken and you're eating off the floor. Why aren't you dancing?'

'We're planning a murder mystery instead,' Rob tells her. 'Stay alert for when the lights go out.'

He takes my hand. 'But until that happens, you're right. This is a ball. Grace and I should go and enjoy it.'

Chapter Thirty-Two

We walk across the lobby and through the large double doors into the ballroom. I'm taken aback by the transformation. I saw the space yesterday when we delivered our first batch of desserts, but this could be an entirely different room. Garlands of fresh pine and twinkling lights adorn the walls. They could technically be described as fairy lights, but they're nothing like the ones I use to decorate my tree each year, which flash in time to whatever music I'm playing.

There are several crystal chandeliers above our heads containing what look like real candles. Closer inspection shows them to be electric. But they're incredibly realistic and cast a soft glow across the polished wooden floor. There's a string quartet on a dais playing carols, and an elegant Christmas tree decorated with white lights and silver ornaments. Someone has arranged an enormous pile of beautifully wrapped presents around its base.

'Do you think they're real?' I ask Rob.

'I expect they're catering boxes of gravy wrapped up in festive paper. Otherwise, the guests would hide them under their fur coats when they left.'

'Why would they do that?' I say. 'Everyone here looks as though they earn more in a year than you and I will do in a lifetime.'

'Appearances can be deceptive. I'm sure there are plenty of high-class jewel thieves here tonight. This is just the sort of event they love. Shall we try to spot them? I vote for that woman in the green dress.'

I follow his gaze and see an elderly woman with beautifully coiffed hair talking to a man wearing an expensive looking tuxedo.

'You're joking,' I say. 'She's the real thing. Definitely a Lady Something-or-Other, if not a Duchess. That looks like a real tiara in her hair.'

'Paste,' he says without hesitation. 'Or else she stole it from one of the other guests.'

'She did not!'

'You're wrong. Lady Dorothea waited until Mrs Blenkinsop had gone down for dinner. Then she let herself in with the pass key she stole from Daniel this afternoon while she engaged him in discussion about the hotel's grouse shooting facilities. She slipped inside and purloined the tiara and hid it in the Harrods carrier bag she keeps her dirty laundry in.'

'But why hasn't Mrs Blenkinsop recognised the tiara and called the police?'

'She doesn't dare. She stole it last week when she attended the Hunt Ball over at Ditchling. She's stymied. If she reports the theft to the police, they'll discover the tiara is stolen and arrest her. Lady Dorothea has played a blinder.'

'You've convinced me,' I say. 'What will Mrs Blenkinsop do about it? A hardened criminal like that surely won't give up without a fight.'

'She won't,' he says. 'She'll wait until midnight when everyone is distracted by kissing everyone else. That's the moment she'll strike. Her accomplice will sneak downstairs to the fuse box and switch off all the lights. And Mrs Blenkinsop will seize the opportunity to sneak up behind Lady Dorothea and rip the tiara out of her hair. By the time the lights are back on, Mrs Blenkinsop will be nowhere to be seen. As the chandeliers flicker back to life, the guests will be greeted by the sight of Lady Dorothea's lifeless form lying on the ballroom floor.'

'Lifeless?' I object. 'She only lost a tiara. That can't have come as much of a shock to her. It must be a hazard of the trade.'

'True,' he says. 'But in the commotion, one of the chandeliers will have come loose and fallen on her head!'

'Poor woman. She didn't deserve such a fate.'

'Teach her to keep her hands to herself,' he says heartlessly.

'But she wasn't stealing it for herself,' I say. 'Her great-aunt has just died, leaving Lady Dorothea to support several indigent nieces and nephews.'

He gives the woman a considering look. 'Lady Dorothea must be almost eighty. She's doing well to have had a living great-aunt until so recently.'

'She only thought it was her great-aunt,' I say. 'It was actually her younger sister. But it was a complicated family set up. Lady Dorothea's mother didn't like to admit she'd had a baby out of wedlock, so she told her children it was their great-aunt.'

'That makes sense,' he says. 'I hear it happened quite a lot in previous generations.'

'And Lady Dorothea is only forty-five,' I add. 'She's prematurely aged by the stress of her great-aunt's untimely death and the burden of caring for her ten so-called great-nieces and-nephews.'

'You mean uncles and aunts?' he says. 'What a tragic story. I'm sorry now that I judged her so harshly. When Mrs Blenkinsop's accomplice switches off the lights, one of us should stand near to Lady Dorothea to fight off attackers.'

'You do that. In the meantime, I'll find Daniel and warn him his maintenance team has been slacking off, and they need to fix the chandelier.'

The woman in the green dress says something to her companion and walks in our direction. She gives us a friendly smile as she passes. 'Are you enjoying yourselves?'

'Very much,' says Rob.

'I'm so glad. I've been coming here for the past ten years, but they've outdone themselves this year. I must remember to thank the organiser.'

She nods pleasantly and moves towards a group of people at the side of the room.

'I feel terrible now,' I say.

'You shouldn't,' says Rob. 'That was a cover story. They've only been holding this ball for the past four years.'

'Really?'

'I have no idea. But I can find out.'

'Please don't. She seemed so nice. I feel guilty about what we were saying.'

'Don't be,' he says. 'She and her companion were making up equally scurrilous stories about us when they were talking just now. She told him you're a professional tennis player who's been forced to retire because of a drink problem.'

'She did not!'

'I'm afraid so. She said you'd started on the sports drinks, telling yourself you could take them or leave them. As your ranking increased, you began to feel the pressure. You started to add a nip of something to your water bottle during major tournaments, increasing the dosage each time, until at last you were drinking neat vodka between the sets. They ended up having to carry you off court on a stretcher halfway through the Wimbledon quarter finals, thus destroying our country's hopes of having a British women's champion in the next few years.'

'And how do you know all this?'

'I can read lips,' he says. 'They taught me during my time in the French Foreign Legion. I rarely use the skill, but it comes in handy at times like this.'

'You've never mentioned this part of your life to me,' I say.

'I haven't mentioned it to anyone,' he says. 'I try to forget my painful past. I wish you hadn't brought it up tonight.'

'My apologies if it's a section of your family history you prefer not to publicise. Like your great-great-grandfather's Caribbean travels.'

'Pacific,' he says. 'Sometimes, it feels as though you don't listen to a word I say.'

'But why did you join the French Foreign Legion? I'm almost sure there's a British one. Why didn't you join that?'

He sighs. 'The clue is in the name. French *foreign* legion. I'm foreign as far as the French are concerned. The British branch doesn't want any locals joining. If we try to insist, they direct us to the home guard.'

A server stops and offers us his tray. 'Would you like to try the blinis?'

'Do you have any lobster tarts?' says Rob.

'I don't know, sir. I could check with the kitchen.'

'Please don't bother,' I say. 'These look delicious.'

We help ourselves, and he moves away.

'You have to rid yourself of this lobster tart fixation,' I tell Rob. 'I recommend a course of cognitive behavioural therapy.'

'Only if you agree to see someone for your sports drink addiction,' he counters.

'I'll think about it. In the meantime, why don't we forget about the life histories of our fellow guests and our own sad memories and enjoy this party? I've never attended anything like this, and I may never do so again.'

'Not until you become head chef at The Sugarloaf Bakery,' he says. 'Would you like to dance?'

The orchestra has struck up a waltz, and several couples have taken to the dance floor.

'Maybe when a few more people have joined in,' I say. 'I'd feel conspicuous if we started dancing now. Also, I've never learned to dance.'

'Me neither,' he says. 'But I thought we could join the throng and give them our best Saturday Night Fever impression.'

'I'd need more to drink before I attempted that. Ask me again at midnight.'

'That will be too late,' he says. 'I told you – everyone will be kissing everyone else at midnight.'

'This is a Christmas party,' I remind him. 'You're getting confused with New Year's Eve.'

'I'm aware of what kind of party this is,' he says. 'I've been filming the preparations for long enough. But I have every intention of kissing you at midnight.'

'In front of everyone?'

'If need be. Otherwise, out on the terrace. This is your official notification.'

He looks at his watch. 'On second thoughts, midnight is still three hours away. What do you say to bringing my plan forward? We should at least practise for the big moment. Shall I fetch your wrap?'

I see Vanessa pushing her way through the crowd towards us.

'Too late,' I say. 'You've missed your chance.'

Rob turns his head to look at her. 'I'm sure it won't take long.'

'I wish I could share your certainty. She looks quite worked up about something.'

Vanessa dodges past a group of servers. 'There you are, Rob! I've been searching for you everywhere.'

He raises an eyebrow. 'I wouldn't have thought I was difficult to find. This is a ball, and I'm in the ballroom. Perhaps you were searching for us on the terrace instead? A moment later, and you would have been proved correct.'

She doesn't appear to be listening. 'I've had a call from Gareth. He's in a state about the first lot of edits. I told him I'd find you, and we'd call him back.'

She holds out her hand to him. 'Hurry up!'

'I'm sorry, Grace,' says Rob. 'I'll be as quick as I can. Will you be ok?'

'I'll be fine. I may take the opportunity for a chat with Lady Dorothea. I'd like to fill her in with a more accurate version of my back story.'

'If the conversation flags, you could tell her about my great-great-grandfather,' he says. 'You'll probably find they're related somewhere on her great-aunt's side.'

'Rob!' says Vanessa impatiently.

'See you in a minute,' he says to me and follows her towards the main doors.

I debate whether to track down a server and get myself another glass of champagne, which is dry and delicious and obviously expensive. I suspect it's one product Daniel didn't source locally for this event. Not only will the shipment have come from the Champagne region of France, but the grapes will have been grown in Monsieur Champagne's own back garden.

'Grace?' says a voice, and I turn to see Bryony lifting her camera onto her shoulder.

'Don't point that thing at me!' I warn her. 'It appears to be loaded.'

'It's digital,' she says. 'Did you think we still used film?'

'It was a joke. But not a very good one. How are you getting on? Are you gathering plenty of footage and achieving all the right angles?'

'It's going well,' she says. 'It's a shame they'll only use about fifteen minutes of it. I've filmed lots of interesting discussions. And I got some great shots of that couple over there dancing a tango earlier. They looked like professionals.'

'I hope you get some shots of our desserts too,' I say. 'I don't want to brag, but they look amazing.'

'I will,' she promises. 'Your bakery will get plenty of coverage in the final programme. Vanessa will make sure of that.'

'She will? I thought they were only using the catering parts as background scene setting.'

'That was before –' she breaks off, confused.

'Before what?'

'Nothing. Never mind. Forget I said anything. It doesn't matter.'

'You can't leave me hanging like that,' I say, laughing. 'What were you about to say?'

She looks even more embarrassed. 'I was talking about the conversation you all had after we finished filming.'

My stomach does a flip, and I stare at her in dawning horror. She can't mean the discussion we had after Rob and Vanessa left. I want to ask, but I don't dare. She may be talking about something else entirely. I don't want to give the impression I'm trying to hide anything and prompt her to ask awkward questions.

I force myself to speak lightly. 'I'm afraid you've lost me.'

'What you were all saying about not knowing how to cook,' she says. 'And how you tricked Vanessa and the hotel so you didn't lose the contract.'

'But that was –' I clear my throat, fighting the urge to let out a frenzied scream which would shock Lady Dorothea and her friends.

'That was a private conversation,' I add more calmly. 'It was after you'd finished filming.'

'That's right. But I forgot to switch off the back up audio. We always have that in case there's any problem with the sound on the video. It's come in useful on more than one occasion.'

I close my eyes, thinking back to the day of the shoot. Rob and Vanessa went into the shop, and the three of us talked about the filming and what a success it had been. Fragments of our conversation come back to me, and my stomach goes into freefall. What did we say? Something about it having been an enormous risk to take the contract because none of us knew what we were doing. Then more clearly, coming into focus as though I'm watching a black and white movie, I see Bryony opening the door and walking in, telling us she'd forgotten her bag. The back up recorder must have been in there. And from what she's saying, it caught everything we said.

I open my eyes to see her looking concerned. 'Are you ok, Grace?'

'I'm fine,' I say in a squeaky voice. 'I was wondering … about that audio … are you sure Vanessa plans to use it?'

'Definitely! She was really pleased with it.'

I'll bet she was. She wasn't able to use the footage of Mabel, but she's had her revenge. I can't bear to think of Lily and Isabella's faces when I tell them about this. They'll be devastated.

A thought strikes me. Vanessa isn't putting the edits together. Rob is. A wave of relief washes over me. All I have to do is to find him and ask him not to include any of that conversation.

I give Bryony a relieved smile. 'I'll have to be on the lookout for that in the future. But I doubt any of it will make the final cut. It was a pretty boring conversation. It wouldn't add anything to the programme.'

'Vanessa didn't think it was boring,' she says. 'She was really excited about it. She told Rob to make sure he included every word.'

'And what did he say?'

She considers. 'At first, he said he wasn't sure there'd be time for it. But Vanessa was adamant. She said it was up to her what went into the final production, and he was only a contractor. He'd be breaking his contract if he refused to do what the producer told him.'

'Poor Rob,' I say. 'What did he say to that?'

'I don't think he minded too much. Vanessa kept saying it was a fantastic opportunity. She was pleased with me too. Rob agreed with her in the end. He said it added a human element to the production, which was a good thing.'

I swallow hard. 'You don't think he said that to keep Vanessa quiet?'

'Not at all,' she says. 'The more he thought about the idea, the more he seemed to like it. Vanessa said she wanted him to include the entire conversation, and he said he would. He promised not to leave anything out.'

The ballroom feels as though it's spinning around me, and it isn't because of the champagne. I can't believe Rob has agreed to do this. He must know how bad this is for the bakery. I understand it's his job. But in his place, I would have refused to do what I was asked and braved the consequences.

'Are you sure you're ok?' says Bryony.

'Fine. I just need to … I'll see you later.'

Without waiting for her answer, I turn and push my way through the crowds towards the double doors.

Chapter Thirty-Three

I start to run when I reach the entrance hall. I almost skid on the shiny floor as I pass the reception desk. I stop and pull off my shoes. They aren't too high, but the heels are slippery. I pick them up and resume running. If anyone tries to stop me, I feel capable of hurling the shoes at them. Particularly if it's Rob and Vanessa. I have enough shoes for them both if I aim carefully.

Daniel is standing next to the Christmas tree talking to a tall man with red hair.

'Grace?' he says as I jog past him. 'Is everything alright?'

I don't break my stride. 'Not remotely. Sorry, Daniel. I can't stop!'

He looks alarmed. 'Is someone ill?'

'Nothing like that,' I call over my shoulder. 'And nothing's on fire. This is … personal!'

Without waiting for an answer, I run downstairs to the kitchen area. I hope Lily and Isabella are still here. They may have gone home once they were sure everything was good with the desserts.

But they haven't. They're standing next to the fridges, talking to a couple of people I don't immediately recognise. The woman turns when I burst in, and I realise it's Abby.

I stop dead. 'Abby? What are you doing here?'

'Checking up on us,' says Isabella.

'Not at all,' says Abby. 'Chris brought me home from the hospital this afternoon, and I persuaded him to bring me here for an hour so I could see what you've all been up to in my absence.'

'What did I tell you?' says Isabella. 'Checking up on us.'

'I wasn't keen,' says Chris. 'The doctors told us Abby should rest as much as possible over the next week.'

'I wouldn't be able to rest without seeing everyone and congratulating them,' says Abby. 'Doctor Burton only meant I shouldn't start training for the next Iron Man competition.'

'Can I give you a hug?' I say. 'A gentle one. Or will I burst your stitches?'

'Isabella has already given me a far from gentle hug, and I'm still in one piece.'

She walks towards me, and I hug her gingerly. 'I'm so happy to see you, Abby.'

'Not as happy as I am to be here. Lily and Isabella sneaked me into the dining room to see the buffet. I couldn't believe it when I saw what you'd done.'

'Always the tone of surprise,' says Isabella. 'I don't know what all the fuss is about. So, we ran our bakery at the busiest time of the year while throwing together enough desserts for one hundred and twenty people. It was barely a challenge for three such competent women as us.'

'We had a lot of help,' says Lily.

'Hardly any,' says Isabella. 'Your mum popped in and out, and Mabel offered the odd comment. To be honest, they were more in the way than otherwise. I didn't like to say anything while they seemed so enthusiastic, but that's how it was.'

'Lily tells a different story,' says Abby. 'I've been hearing all about Chef Mabel. If I'd known we had such an exceptional international talent in the village, I would have hired her on the spot.'

'I'm glad you've brought that up,' says Isabella. 'We've been discussing hiring Mabel and letting you go, Abby. I'm sorry to land this on you right before Christmas, but it's just business. Once the show has aired, people will be coming from miles around to beat down our door and demand to taste our amazing products. Chef Mabel may not appear on camera, but she's an integral part of our operation.'

In the excitement of seeing Abby again, I'd almost forgotten why I'm here. 'Isabella!' I say.

'I'm joking,' she says. 'Lily and I would never fire Abby. Far too much paperwork, for one thing. And no one, even Chef Mabel, makes biscuits the way Bernie likes them. I wouldn't say he's been wasting away exactly, but he –'

'Grace?' says Lily. 'What's wrong?'

To my annoyance, I feel tears spring to my eyes. 'I'm sorry to do this tonight, especially with Abby here. But you have to know some time.'

'Sit down,' she says. 'You're as white as a sheet.'

'I'm fine. I've been talking to Bryony. She told me –'

My voice cracks, and I can't go on.

Chris pulls out a chair for me. 'It's ok, Grace. Tell us what's happened, and we'll do our best to help.'

'No one can help,' I say. 'We've messed everything up. We should have cancelled this contract as soon as they took Abby to hospital.'

'But why?' says Isabella. 'The desserts are great. They've turned out even better than we expected.'

'It isn't the desserts!' I wail. 'It's the filming. Bryony says she left the audio running when the team were at the bakery, and they recorded our entire conversation after we thought they'd left.'

Lily looks appalled. 'In the kitchen?'

'That's right.'

'About us not knowing how to cook?'

I nod. 'And the rest. They caught it all.'

'That isn't good,' she says, recovering herself. 'But it doesn't mean they'll use it in the show. Vanessa was saying they were tight for time, and they had to edit most of it out –'

'They're making time for this. It's all gone in. Bryony says Vanessa was really excited about it.'

The smile has disappeared from Isabella's face. 'But Vanessa isn't editing it. Rob is. He won't include anything that makes us look bad.'

I wipe my eyes. 'He already has. Bryony told me Vanessa was thrilled when she heard the tape, and she insisted he use the entire thing.'

'That doesn't mean he has,' says Lily. 'Isabella is right. Rob wouldn't do anything to hurt you, Grace. Ask him not to include it.'

Isabella looks more cheerful. 'Lily's right. Find him and ask him. Beg if you have to. But it won't be necessary. He'll be too busy thinking about how sensational you look in that dress to think about anything as boring as work. If the worst comes to the worst, you can sneak into his room tonight with a large magnet and wave it over his suitcase. That should erase any tapes he may be hiding in there.'

'You don't understand,' I say. 'Rob was happy to use the footage. Bryony said he agreed with Vanessa it was too good to leave out, and he told her he would use it all. He said it added human interest. I'm so sorry. I should never have agreed to go out with him, let alone come to this stupid ball.'

'I don't see what difference that would have made,' says Lily. 'Rob would have still been there for the filming, and they would still have recorded that conversation. This is on us. We should have checked they'd finished recording.'

'What did you all say?' says Abby. 'Maybe it wasn't that bad.'

'It was worse,' says Isabella.

'Can you threaten to sue them?' says Abby.

'What for?'

Abby shrugs. 'I'm not a lawyer. Damage to reputation, maybe? Defamation of character? Loss of earnings?'

Isabella shakes her head. 'We signed a contract to say they could use what they filmed in any way they liked. That's why we were so terrified of making fools of ourselves the first time they came to the bakery. We weren't so worried the second time. We thought we'd got through the worst of it without disaster and we now knew what we were doing. That must be why we let our guard down so easily.'

'I should take Abby home,' says Chris. 'The doctors said she should avoid stress as much as possible.'

I lift my head from my arms. 'I'm so sorry. I shouldn't have said anything tonight. But as soon as Bryony told me what had happened, all I could think of was to come and find Lily and Isabella.'

'I'm not going anywhere!' says Abby. 'If the bakery is in trouble, that concerns me too. Besides, this isn't the sort of stress they said I should avoid.'

'They said any over-exertion,' insists Chris, his brow furrowed with anxiety.

'He's right,' I tell Abby. 'You don't want a relapse right before Christmas.'

'I'd be more stressed at home, not knowing what's going on. I'm staying here in case there's anything I can do to help.'

The kitchen door opens, and Rob appears, accompanied by Vanessa and Andrew, the second cameraman.

'There you are!' Rob says when he sees me. 'You disappeared from sight, and I couldn't find you anywhere. No one seemed to know where you were. It was a complete mystery. It wasn't midnight, so I didn't think you'd have rushed away to your pumpkin Uber. Then I bumped into Daniel, who told me you'd last been seen running down the stairs to the scullery, clutching your glass slippers. I almost expected to find you dressed in rags. But here you are, looking as lovely as ever.'

He breaks off, noticing the other four huddled at the end of the table. 'Hi, Lily. Hi, Isabella. Congratulations on an amazing job. You must be proud of yourselves.'

I've been staring at him, unable to speak. But this speech jerks me into action.

'How dare you? Don't think you can come in here, being all charming, when you've behaved as you have. You're a snake, Rob Marshall. I should never have had anything to do with you.'

I point to Vanessa, who's watching us with a faint smirk. 'She told me exactly who you were when I first met her, and I should have listened. I never want to see or speak to you again.'

To my horror, I start to cry in earnest.

Rob starts towards me, but I throw up a hand to stop him.

'Don't! You can't expect everyone to fall for your act like they usually do. You've talked me around once with all your stupid family history and stories about lobster tarts. But not this time. You're a vile, despicable creature, and I'm better off without you. Why don't you get lost and leave us all alone? You've done enough damage for one lifetime.'

'Way to approach him tactfully,' murmurs Isabella.

Rob looks thunderstruck. 'I don't understand. If I've done something to upset you, Grace, tell me what it is, and I'll do my best to fix it.'

'Oh, will you? Does that mean you won't be using that footage after all?'

He's taken another step towards me, but he stops at these words. 'Footage? From yesterday?'

'Don't play dumb with me! It doesn't suit you. I mean, it does suit you. Because you're stupid,' I clarify.

His lips twitch. 'So I've been told many times.'

'I imagine you have. Give me a straight answer, Rob. You owe me that at least. Have you heard that audiotape?'

'Yes, but –'

'And do you plan to use it in the programme?'

I will him to say no, to tell me Bryony misunderstood the conversation. That, instead of Rob saying it was a good idea to include it, he'd told Vanessa it was the most stupid idea he'd ever heard. And if she thought something like that was interesting, he hoped someone would fire her.

He doesn't. He looks from me to Vanessa and back again.

'Don't look at her!' I say. 'You can't hide behind someone else's decisions. Tell me straight out. Do you intend to use that footage in the show?'

He nods. 'I do.'

I swallow hard. 'Every single word?'

'Pretty much. I can explain –'

I try to speak calmly. 'No explanation needed. I thought you were different.'

I jerk my head towards Vanessa. 'This is exactly what I would have expected from someone like her. But I believed you were better than that. Obviously not.'

Vanessa looks like the cat who's swallowed the cream. I look away again. I have nothing to say to her.

'I think you should leave,' I tell Rob.

He doesn't move. I pick up a whisk and wave it threateningly. 'Get out before I hurl this at you!'

I expect him to turn away, but he doesn't. 'I'm not going anywhere. You can throw as many whisks at me as you like. There's a potato masher on that table. You're welcome to throw that too.'

Lily lays a hand on my arm and gives a tiny shake of her head. I know she's right. The last thing we need is for me to be arrested on Christmas Eve for culinary-related assault.

'Grace is upset,' she says to Rob. 'I don't blame her. We're all pretty disappointed in you. You should leave.'

'I'll leave,' he says. 'But only if Grace comes with me.'

'Back to the ball?' I say. 'You have a nerve!'

'Back to my room.'

Isabella gives a derisive snort. 'You don't know when to give up, do you? If that wasn't so offensive, I'd laugh.'

A tiny smile plays around his mouth. 'You can come too. And Lily. I'm inviting you all.'

I've never yet seen Isabella lost for words. But there's a first time for everything. She gives him a withering glance.

'I mean it,' he says before she can speak. 'There's still half an hour before they're serving the food. There's something important I need to show you.'

He gives me a more serious look. 'Give me half an hour. If you're still mad with me after that, you can whisk me or blend me or caramelise me to your heart's content. I can't say fairer than that.'

Lily surprises me. 'I think you should give him a chance, Grace. We'll all come with you.'

'Thank you,' says Rob.

I follow him towards the door, ignoring Vanessa's smirk as I pass her.

I glare at Andrew, who is standing in the doorway watching us. 'You'd better not have been filming any of that!'

I push past him and follow Rob up the stairs, with Lily and Isabella bringing up the wake.

Chapter Thirty-Four

Daniel is standing in the entrance hall when we reach the top of the stairs. He looks surprised to see the procession of people. 'Is everything alright?'

'Not really,' says Lily when I don't answer. 'But there's nothing anyone can do about it.'

'We're heading up to my room,' says Rob. 'You're welcome to join us if you like.'

'For what?' says Daniel.

'We're watching a movie.'

Daniel looks surprised. 'We're serving the buffet soon.'

'That's fine,' says Rob. 'It's an extremely short movie.'

He leads the way up the next flight of stairs and down a corridor, where he taps his card on one of the locks.

'Welcome to my humble abode,' he says, gesturing for us to go inside.

Vanessa follows me. 'It's a beautiful room, isn't it, Grace? It even has a whirlpool bubble bath.'

'Don't bother!' I snap. 'I doubt you've ever seen the inside of this room before.'

Rob laughs and hastily turns it into a cough. 'I'm afraid there's not much space on the bed. But if you don't mind squashing up a little, this won't take long.'

He opens his laptop and puts it on a small table in front of the bed. 'Can you all see well enough? Great. I brought you up here because I thought you might like to be the first ones to watch the final cut. You're fairly central to it, so it only seems fair.'

I'm about to burst out angrily, but Lily stops me. 'I'm sure we're all very interested.'

'Time's short,' says Rob. 'And they'll be serving the food soon. I'll skip the introductory section.'

He consults a small notebook. 'Let me see now … ah, yes. You first appear at eleven minutes and twenty-eight seconds.'

He presses a couple of buttons, and the screen springs to life. I don't want to watch it, but I can't look away. It's like watching a car crash in slow motion. Or a fleet of giant lorries driving at top speed towards the edge of an impossibly high cliff.

Daniel appears on the screen. He seems to have been talking about the preparations for the ball. '… which is why we've made it our main priority this year to source everything as locally as possible.'

The scene cuts to an outside shot of the bakery. We hear Isabella's voice saying, 'It was a huge amount of work, but it's been more than worth it. We set out to make this a community project. And I believe we've achieved that.'

I glance at Isabella, who's turned pink.

We switch to the interior of the bakery, which looks beautiful. Lily and Isabella have done a wonderful job with the décor and the lights.

'How much extra work do you have at this time of year?' says Vanessa's voice.

This time it's Lily who answers. 'A tremendous amount. But we don't mind. Isabella and I both love Christmas, and so do our customers.'

The view switches to the kitchen, and I give an involuntary choke of laughter as I see Isabella, with several smudges of flour on her face, busily stirring her mixing bowl. The camera zooms in on Lily as she opens the oven and takes out the mince pies. They're crisp and golden and remind me I haven't eaten since lunchtime.

A banner appears on the screen – *The Sugarloaf Bakery's Biggest Challenge Yet!*

We hear Rob's voice. 'Just as everything appears to be going well, the bakery is hit by an unexpected setback. Their head baker has been taken ill. Will the team be able to pull together and save the situation?'

To my astonishment, Mabel appears. She's wearing a bright pink twin set and the biggest diamante earrings I've ever seen. She beams at the camera.

'This place is extraordinary, and it's run by extraordinary women. They aren't the sort to be put off by a minor setback.'

We hear Lily's voice again. 'I can't believe we made it through in one piece.'

'It was a bit of a risk,' says Isabella.

'They may have been worried,' says Mabel's voice. 'But no one else had any doubts. Their customers have every faith in them.'

'And you should know what you're talking about,' says Rob.

'Thank goodness we had a professional chef on hand,' says Lily's voice.

Mabel reappears. 'They're too kind. I was able to offer the occasional piece of advice, but they would have managed fine without me.'

'Grace was our secret weapon!' we hear Isabella say. 'Talk about devotion to duty.'

'They all worked extremely hard,' says Mabel. 'Teamwork – that's the thing. And loyalty to your staff.'

'We didn't drop anything or smash anything,' says Isabella's voice.

'Of course, they didn't,' says Mabel's voice. 'I'd employ them in my restaurant in Wombat Wallow in a heartbeat.'

'The entire ball could have been ruined,' says Lily.

'Not a chance,' says Mabel. 'And here's someone who agrees with me.'

The camera pans back, and we see Bernie sitting by the counter, laughing up at the camera.

'This little fellow is the bakery's mascot,' says Mabel, bending to pat him. 'He's always believed in his friends here at the Sugarloaf, haven't you, boy?'

Bernie gives an excited yap, and we hear Rob laugh.

'Thank you so much for giving up your time to talk to me today,' he says. 'I know you're a busy woman.'

'No worries, mate!' says Mabel. 'They did a bonza job, and I'm happy as a kookaburra to have been involved.'

The camera cuts back to the outside of the bakery, and we hear Lily's voice saying, 'All's well that ends well.'

Rob leans over and switches off his laptop. No one moves. I don't dare raise my eyes and look at him directly. I have no idea what to say to him.

Lily is the first to break the silence. 'That was amazing, Rob.'

Her voice seems to jerk Vanessa back to reality.

'It most certainly was not! I clearly told you to use that footage exactly as I gave it to you.'

'And so I did,' he says. 'You know how this works. You can't expect me to use sections of dialogue without adding some context. That's all I've done.'

'The context was perfectly clear,' she says. 'You've deliberately edited it to make them seem competent.'

'Did you want him to edit it to make us look incompetent?' says Isabella.

'There was no need!' Vanessa shoots back. 'You did that all by yourselves.'

'That's unfair,' says Isabella. 'We've worked incredibly hard to pull this off. And we've managed it. Look what a success tonight has been. It will be even more of a success when the guests see our food.'

She turns to Daniel. 'You're happy with what we've done, aren't you?'

'Perfectly happy,' he says. 'You've fulfilled the contract to my complete satisfaction.'

'You see?' Isabella says to Vanessa. 'What's the point of making us look bad in a programme like this? It's a Christmas show. It makes a far better story for the viewers to see a plucky local business struggling with adversity and triumphing. Rob can see that, even if you can't.'

'She's right,' says Rob. 'It doesn't seem in the Christmas spirit.'

'I'll decide what's in the Christmas spirit!' says Vanessa, and Lily gives a choke of laughter.

'I imagine you've deleted what you didn't use,' Vanessa tells Rob. 'But you're right. We don't need that footage.

Rob looks startled. 'You agree with me?'

'I do. It seems a shame to waste our viewers' time with something so minor.'

'Thank you,' says Isabella.

'Viewing minutes are precious,' says Vanessa. 'We need to reserve them for the most engaging and compelling content. We've taken far more dramatic footage tonight. And not just the audio!'

It takes me a second to realise what she means. Then I see her triumphant smile and realisation dawns.

Rob catches her meaning at the same time as I do, and his face darkens. 'Absolutely not! I mean it, Vanessa.'

'Why not?' she says. 'The show could do with it after the syrupy schmaltz you've given us.'

'None of the film crew is contracted to appear on camera,' he says. 'I won't give you permission to show me.'

My heart, which has been slamming in my chest so hard I can't breathe, gradually returns to normal.

'And I'm not signing a release,' I say. 'So, it looks as though you can't use any of that scene in the kitchen.'

'Thank goodness for that,' says Isabella, uncurling herself from where she's wedged in between Abby and Lily. 'I'm glad we've got that sorted out. It must be nearly time for the buffet. I'm starving!'

Daniel is watching her with an amused smile. 'Technically, the food is for the party guests.'

'I'm aware,' she says with dignity. 'But there were a few less than perfectly shaped desserts when we prepared them earlier. I'm not too proud to eat them. I don't believe in wasting food. And even scullery maids must eat. So, if that's all …'

'Not by a long shot,' says Vanessa.

'I've already told you,' I say. 'I won't sign a release.'

'You don't need to. You aren't here tonight in your capacity as a bakery employee. You're here as a guest. And every guest has agreed to be filmed as a condition of purchasing their tickets. Ask him!' She jerks her head towards Daniel.

'Is this true?' Lily asks him, and he gives a reluctant nod.

'Don't take it personally, Grace,' adds Vanessa. 'It's my job as a producer to give our viewers an optimum viewing experience. It would be remiss of me to cut or deceptively edit scenes which might interest and entertain them. Unprofessional, too!'

She darts a look at Rob, who doesn't react.

Isabella swings her legs off the bed and slips her feet into her shoes. 'If you'll all excuse me, there's something I need to check up on. I'll be right back.'

No one seems to notice her departure. Rob and Vanessa are engaged in a heated discussion. Chris is making sure Abby is alright. And Lily is talking to Daniel, who's shaking his head as he answers her.

I stare numbly at Rob's laptop. How could I have been so stupid? We were ridiculously unguarded during our discussion last week, but this is a thousand times worse. And it was entirely avoidable. All I had to do was ask Rob what was going on. Instead, I lost my temper and lashed out. And this is the result. After all our hard work, I've made the bakery look terrible.

I'm aware I've made myself look even worse. I'll be a laughingstock. I won't be to show my face in public for years – perhaps decades. I'll have to move abroad and live out my days in obscurity in some tiny country where there's no chance of running into anyone I know. Even that may not work. Knowing my luck, I'll walk into some remote beachside bar to see a shot of the Quayside Hotel and hear my voice yelling at Rob.

I may as well stay in my own country. At least I speak the language. I can hide in my flat all day, only venturing out after dark to find food.

My gloomy thoughts are interrupted by a knock at the door. Rob stops arguing with Vanessa and opens it. Isabella is standing there, accompanied by an elderly man wearing a tuxedo.

'Everyone, this is Harry Davies,' she says. 'Harry, this is everyone. Harry is my uncle's lawyer. I remembered Uncle Charles telling me Harry would be here tonight. So, I went downstairs to find him. I felt we needed some expert advice.'

'We don't need a lawyer,' says Vanessa dismissively. 'I have every right to use tonight's footage as I see fit. And Daniel agrees with me.'

'There's no harm in getting a second opinion,' says Isabella. 'It's what they do in all the TV shows, which is what we appear to be living in at the moment. So, I thought why not pop down and fetch Harry so he can tell us one way or another? I've explained the issue to him, haven't I, Uncle Harry?'

'Uncle Harry?' says Vanessa. 'Is this man even a lawyer?'

'Of course, he is,' says Isabella. 'You don't think I'd make up something like that?'

Rob gives a cough that sounds suspiciously like *Chef Mabel!*

'Twice,' finishes Isabella.

Harry gives Vanessa a cold look. 'I most certainly am a lawyer. I work for the firm of Stoughton and Fry. I'm not accustomed to having my word doubted.'

He looks around the room. 'Are we being filmed?'

'Andrew's camera is switched off,' says Rob. 'I've double checked that.'

'Very wise,' says Harry.

He peers at us over his spectacles. 'The point at issue appears to be one of competing contracts. The Sugarloaf Bakery has been functioning under one contract, while the guests at the ball have been operating under another. The problem we have here is that one of the employees –' he breaks off and gives Isabella a questioning look.

'That's Grace over there in the red dress,' she says.

Harry nods to me. 'This young woman has been functioning as an employee of the bakery. To the best of my understanding, she has not signed a release to say she agrees to appear in that capacity. On the other hand, she is also a guest at this ball and has therefore agreed to appear on camera at the discretion of the production team.'

'We know all this,' says Vanessa. 'Perhaps you could hurry things along. Bryony is down there all alone, and I don't trust her not to miss things.'

Harry holds up his hand. 'Isabella has shown me the contract she and her partner signed. It appears to be valid until December 24th, at which point it ceases. One could make a strong argument that, as an employee, Grace is covered by this contract. In which case, it covers her until midnight tonight. It is an interesting point of law whether the superseding contract with the hotel takes precedence. I am inclined to think it does not. In which case, I am minded to advise that unless the tickets were purchased prior to the signing of the bakery contract, the initial contract remains in force until midnight tonight.'

'They weren't,' says Rob. 'Daniel only gave me the tickets last week.'

'I did,' says Daniel. 'And I would be prepared to testify in court to that effect.'

Vanessa looks annoyed. 'You aren't in an episode of Law and Order!'

'You're quite right,' says Daniel. 'I've been living with TV cameras for so long that it's difficult to tell what's reality and what's fiction.'

Vanessa bites her lip. 'My company may well take the view that tonight's contract is binding. I'm sure they will.'

Harry gives her a benign smile. 'That may be so. And it would certainly be possible to make that argument. But it would be a long and costly legal battle and would do your production company's reputation no good. If Grace were to win, she would be entitled to heavy damages. My firm would be delighted to represent her on a contingency basis.'

For a moment, it seems as though Vanessa is about to argue. Then she collapses. 'Fine! We won't include the footage. I still believe we have the right to do so, but I have better things to do with my time than engage with frivolous lawsuits.'

'Do we have your word on that?' says Isabella eagerly.

Vanessa shoots her a look of pure dislike. 'You do.'

'That's good enough for me,' says Daniel. 'I'm reliably informed that verbal contracts are binding in the state of Hampshire.'

Vanessa isn't listening. She gestures to Andrew. 'Hurry up! We have to get downstairs to film the buffet.'

She stops in the doorway and gives Rob a nasty look. 'You needn't think our firm will be putting any more work your way in the future.'

Rob holds the door open for her. 'The loss is mine. Merry Christmas, Vanessa.'

The door closes behind her. There's a stunned silence before the room erupts.

'That was amazing!' shrieks Lily, flinging her arms around Isabella. 'I can't believe you did that.'

'It wasn't me,' says Isabella. 'It was all Uncle Harry.'

Rob looks at Harry, a tiny smile playing about his mouth. 'Would you think me impertinent if I asked you a question? The cameras have gone, and there's no backup audio in this room. So, you're quite safe to answer.'

'Certainly,' says Harry.

'It doesn't really matter either way,' says Rob. 'But are you actually a lawyer?'

'Certainly, I am,' says Harry. 'I have worked for the Campbell family for many years.'

'I can't think why no one trusts me,' complains Isabella. 'I hardly ever pretend someone is something they aren't.'

'I do not, in fact, practice contract law,' says Harry. 'I have spent the greater part of my career focused on property law.'

'I see,' says Rob. 'So, your offer to represent Grace in court was …'

Harry's face doesn't flicker. 'Perfectly genuine. It has been a long time since I studied statutes, but I would have done my best.'

'I'm sure you would,' I say. 'I'm extremely grateful for what you did tonight. I thought for a moment I was toast.'

'Put it out of your mind,' he advises me. 'I may not be as up to date as I might wish on contract law, but I know enough to sound knowledgeable. And any lawyer will tell you that's nine-tenths of the law.'

'I thought that was possession,' says Isabella.

'It's the same thing,' says Lily. 'Rob is no longer in possession of the footage of our conversation in the bakery. And Vanessa is no longer in possession of the right to use Grace's … erm … forceful representation of her feelings.'

She catches my eye. 'Don't look like that. Nothing terrible has happened.'

I'm not so sure. I look over at Rob, but his face is inscrutable.

'Who's coming down to the kitchen with me?' says Isabella. 'I stashed plenty of food in the fridge. We should celebrate.'

'Not for us, I'm afraid,' says Chris. 'Abby needs some rest.'

'I wish he wasn't right, but he is,' says Abby. 'I almost fell asleep during the documentary. Sorry.'

'Perfectly understandable,' says Rob. 'I get that all the time.'

Abby hugs us goodbye and wishes us a Merry Christmas, and she and Chris leave.

'If my legal services are no longer required,' says Harry, 'I should be getting back to my wife. She will be wondering where I am.'

'Lily and I will escort you downstairs,' says Isabella. 'After everything you've done for us, you deserve a guard of honour.'

She and Lily follow Harry out of the room.

I stare at the carpet, not wanting to meet Rob's eyes. Is he waiting for me to leave too? Should I sneak out of the back entrance and take a taxi home?

'Grace?' he says at last.

I look up to see him watching me. The usual smile has disappeared from his face.

I clear my throat. 'I'm really sorry, Rob. I should never have flown off the handle like that without giving you a chance to explain. Can you ever forgive me?'

He considers me carefully before answering. 'That depends.'

'On what?'

He takes my arm and leads me towards the door. 'On the buffet, which I am reliably informed is about to be served. If the quality of desserts is sufficiently good, I may be persuaded to overlook your behaviour just this once.'

'And if not?' I ask.

'That's difficult to answer. But there's only one way to find out. Shall we go and taste this syllabub of which I've heard so much?'

Chapter Thirty-Five

Neither of us speaks as we walk down the flight of stairs to the lobby. My brain is spinning after the events of the past hour. I need to apologise properly to Rob, but I don't know how. I made him look like a complete fool in front of everyone, unaware he was risking his job to protect me. I made myself look an even bigger fool, but that isn't his problem. If I'd appeared on the show, screaming and threatening to throw whisks, it would have been entirely my own fault.

Even worse, I didn't trust him. My first thought was to suspect him of betraying us. In his place, I would find that difficult to forgive. Vanessa has lost tonight's battle, but I may have lost something far more important. And it's my own stupid fault.

I stop in the middle of the lobby. 'Rob?'

'Yes?'

'I really am sorry. I know it doesn't help, but I wanted you to know. Lily and Isabella are having their supper down in the kitchen. It might be better if I joined them. Isabella can give me a ride home later.'

'You want to eat your supper among the ashes?' he says.

'Not exactly. The hotel kitchen is spotless. But that's the general idea.'

'And what about me?' he says. 'Are you planning to abandon me to the horrors of making conversation with the local landed gentry? You'll be stuffing your face with all the leftover tarts and syllabubs with your friends, while I have to make small talk with people I don't know. Not a hope. If I have to do it, so do you. Consider it penance.'

The band around my heart loosens. 'That isn't very chivalrous.'

'Neither is threatening to whisk me into a thousand pieces.'

'Or mash you,' I remind him. 'I'd have offered you the choice.'

'I'm not entirely chivalrous,' he says. 'If you get caught on film spilling syllabub all down that beautiful dress, don't look to me to save you.'

'I won't. You've already saved us twice. First, when you didn't tell Vanessa that Abby was in hospital. And then when you edited the film to make us look good. I can't believe you did that for us.'

'Not for you. For the viewing audience,' he says. 'Having deprived them of the wonder that is Chef Mabel, I felt it was my duty to give them a heartwarming experience with which to start their new year.'

'They almost had a very different experience,' I say. 'I came within seconds of hurling a chocolate mousse at your head.'

'That would have made great television. Why didn't you?'

'Isabella had eaten them all.'

'Remind me to thank her later. I've already told you this is a rented tuxedo.'

'It's lovely,' I say. 'Although I was disappointed you didn't turn up in your sparkly jeans, as promised.'

'They'd all gone when I reached the shop. I'll have to get there earlier next year.'

'Are you expecting to buy tickets next year?' I ask.

'Only if you come with me.'

My heart unclenches further. 'After the way I behaved, I didn't think we'd make it to the end of the evening, let alone next year.'

'That's because you don't know me very well,' he says. 'Something I intend to remedy as quickly as possible.'

He pulls me towards him, and I look into his eyes, no longer caring we're in a crowded lobby or that Bryony and Andrew may appear at any moment holding a camera.

Someone crashes into me, almost knocking me to the floor.

'Sorry,' apologises a large man in a badly fitting tuxedo. 'It's an awful crush in here. Are you alright?'

'I'm fine,' I say, rubbing my elbow.

'Perhaps this isn't the place,' says Rob. 'It's like trying to sing an aria in the middle of a herd of stampeding buffalo. We'd better join them, or the lobster tarts will have gone, and we'll be stuck with boring desserts.'

I take his hand and we follow the crowd to the dining room. Rob's phone beeps, and he pulls it out of his pocket and glances at the screen.

'Everything ok?' I ask. 'You aren't being called back to work?'

'I think I've burned that particular bridge.'

'I'm sorry.'

'Don't be,' he says. 'My firm wasn't too keen for me to do this in the first place. But Vanessa made a point of it, and she's friendly with our managing director.'

'Will she tell them what you did?'

'I doubt it,' he says. 'I adhered to the letter of the law and included the scene she asked me to include. It isn't my fault if it showed you all in a better light than she'd hoped.'

'How did you get Mabel to give that interview?' I ask. 'I'm surprised she was willing to be filmed.'

'I went over to see her this morning. She took some persuading. But she was anxious to help you as much as she could, even if it meant signing a release. I promised to "lose" the earlier footage of her so Vanessa couldn't decide to use it later.'

'She did a tremendous job,' I say. 'I must remember to thank her.'

'Mabel's sister insisted her dog appeared too,' he says.

'Bernie is wonderful. He added a cute touch to the whole thing.'

'That isn't a universal opinion,' he says. 'Mabel referred to him as the hellhound at one point. I thought Mrs Ogilvie might cancel the interview.'

'Poor Bernie,' I say. 'I hope he knows she doesn't mean it.'

We reach the dining room, which is lit by more chandeliers. They appear to be safely anchored to the ceiling, but you never know.

'Hungry?' says Rob as we reach the first table.

'Starving! It's been a long day.'

He hands me a plate, and I fill it with food. There are mini beef Wellingtons and bacon wrapped dates and chilli and lime scallops. At the far end of the table, I see a pile of coconut shrimp and chicken satay skewers. This is an impressive display. I hope the guests aren't disappointed when they reach the desserts.

'I don't see any lobster tarts,' says Rob, scanning the table.

'I asked Daniel to make sure there weren't any. You may think you can take them or leave them, but it's becoming increasingly obvious you have a problem. I'm cutting you off. Try one of those roasted pepper and goat cheese bruschetta. I'm coming back for them as soon as I've finished this lot.'

'Thank goodness, my family has already celebrated Lobster Tart Day this year,' he says.

'Speaking of your family, are you spending Christmas day with them?'

'I half promised to join them at my sister's house,' he says. 'But I've received a better offer.'

'To do what?'

'That text was from Isabella inviting me to spend tomorrow with you all at her uncle's house.'

'Are you sure?'

'Look for yourself.' He hands me his phone.

Miss Isabella Campbell requests the honour of your company at Compton Manor tomorrow at noon. No RSVP required. Sparkly jeans optional.

My heart gives a bound. 'Do you plan to accept?'

'I'll have to ask my girlfriend first and see what she thinks. She can be quite difficult when she wants to be.'

'I know she can,' I say. 'But she's working on it. She'd be delighted if you said yes.'

'So will my sister,' he says. 'I heard her tell my mother she had enough to do with cooking for her in-laws without me turning up and causing her more work.'

A wave of happiness sweeps over me. 'I'm glad you'll be there.'

'So am I,' he says. 'I could give you my Christmas present tomorrow, but I brought it with me tonight, so I may as well give it to you now.'

He reaches into his pocket and hands me a small parcel. I tear open the paper and see it's the snow globe he won at the Christmas fair. I didn't get a chance to see which one he chose. I study it carefully. It's a tiny pirate ship sailing towards a desert island, complete with a miniature coconut tree.

'I love it!' I say. 'Thank you so much, Rob. It makes me feel a part of your family history.'

'You remind me of my great-great-grandmother,' he says. 'The same willingness to believe the best of everyone.'

'I've given you ample demonstration of that tonight,' I agree, and he laughs.

'Let's say the same willingness to put up with a member of my family. Anyway, it's time we got to work on this buffet. The locals have excellent appetites, and I'd like to try one of those smoked salmon things before they all disappear.'

We eat as much as we can, then move on to the dessert table. It looks even more tempting than I remember. Lily and Isabella have dredged the white chocolate brownies in icing sugar and piled them high on the silver platters. The lemon tarts glisten alongside the delicate glasses of chocolate mousse and crème brûlée, while the Christmas syllabubs stand in their crystal glasses like a group of snow-capped soldiers.

'It's a work of art,' says Rob. 'I can hardly bring myself to spoil it.'

'If you don't, the landed gentry will. They have no scruples about that type of thing.'

He selects a syllabub and dips his spoon in. 'Incredible. Did you really make these?'

'We ordered them from the supermarket.'

'I see.' He points to the chocolate mousses. 'How about those?'

'Packet mixes.'

'I hardly dare ask about the lemon tarts and brownies.'

'The tarts came from that frozen food warehouse on the bypass,' I say. 'And I bought the brownies from the Christmas market last week. They'll be a bit stale by now, but I expect the guests will be too drunk to notice.'

'Why didn't you tell me any of this before?' he grumbles. 'I could have put it all into the programme.'

'If you think Vanessa would let you anywhere near the editing suite after this ...'

'I imagine tomorrow's invitation might be rescinded if I made your bakery look bad,' he says.

'You'd be washing up in the basement with the footman and the boy who does the boots. I suggest you let it go.'

He picks up a plate. 'In the meantime, I want to try one of your frozen lemon tarts.'

'Thawed-out lemon tarts,' I correct him. 'We aren't complete amateurs.'

'Indeed, you aren't. Should I be worried about the fact you aren't sampling your own product?'

'I can't face them,' I confess. 'I've been eating nothing else for two weeks. Isabella made us taste all the failed batches so we could learn from them.'

He tastes all five desserts while I watch in fascination.

'Do you need to take a nap to recover?' I ask when he's finished.

'They barely touched the sides,' he says. 'I had to try them all after the work you've put into them. You should be proud of yourself.'

'We are. It seemed such a huge mountain to climb when we first started out. But it got easier as we went along. And our customers have been very patient over the past few weeks. They've bought all our spare desserts to take home or ordered them in the cafe. Isabella's also done her best, but she's only one woman.'

The band strikes up a lively rendition of Jingle Bell Rock.

Rob holds out a hand to me. 'I love this song. It's so romantic that it's often moved me to tears. Would you like to dance?'

'I've always preferred Grandma Got Run Over by a Reindeer,' I say. 'It reminds me of my mother's driving.'

'I'll ask them to play that next. Hurry up, before the song finishes.'

He leads me onto the dance floor where, to my surprise, I see Isabella performing what looks like a syncopated quick step with Daniel. She waves when she sees us.

'What are you doing up here?' I say as she passes. 'Aren't you supposed to be washing up in the scullery?'

'I'm here as a guest of the management,' she says.

'That would be me,' says Daniel. 'It seemed a shame to leave her all alone in the kitchen once Lily had gone home.'

'I can understand that,' says Rob. 'Although it appears to be her natural habitat.'

'There's plenty of food up here for a few extra people,' says Daniel. 'We're heading back to the buffet after this dance.'

I watch them disappear into the crowd of dancers. 'Finally, a man who really gets her.'

'She's very lucky,' says Rob.

'He's the lucky one,' I say. 'That's if they're even a thing. She may only be using him for his event planning credentials.'

'He looks happy enough about it,' says Rob.

'True. I'd like him to be happy. He's a nice man. Look how he stuck up for us tonight. He deserves someone nice like Isabella.'

'If he couldn't have you?' he says.

'No one deserves me. Especially not after the way I've behaved tonight.'

'Stop beating yourself up,' he says. 'Who among us can honestly say we've never threatened someone with a whisk and called them a snake on TV?'

He pulls me into his arms. 'Now stop talking or we'll miss the bit about dancing and prancing.'

We set off across the floor together.

'This takes some practice,' I gasp as we nearly collide with an elderly couple expertly jiving to the music.

'I'm willing to put in the hours if you are,' says Rob.

The song finishes and the band starts playing Have Yourself a Merry Little Christmas.

'Now this one, I like,' says Rob. 'Just the thing for a fiery Latin tango. However, in light of the enormous quantities of dessert I've eaten, maybe we should try something less vigorous?'

He puts his arms around me, and I rest my head on his shoulder as we sway in time to the music.

'How long until midnight?' he says.

'About ten minutes, I think.'

'Too long. I can't wait until then. I'm afraid I may have to kiss you now.'

'Here on the dance floor?' I say.

'It's too far to the terrace. Besides, it's snowing. I'd get cold, and you don't have a jacket to lend me.'

'But what about Lady Dorothea?'

'I'm definitely not kissing her,' he says. 'But I saw her dancing nearby a minute ago. I'd hold onto your jewelry if I were you.'

'I'm only wearing earrings.'

'You should be safe then. But I'll keep an eye on my pocket watch. It's the most valuable thing I own. Solid platinum and encircled with five carat diamonds. It's a family heirloom. My great-great-grandfather brought it back from his travels.'

'Of course, he did. A gift from the Emperor of the Pacific Islands?'

'Not even close. He found it inside a shark.'

'What was he doing inside a shark?' I ask.

'He never told us. Taking shelter, perhaps? The point is that he found this pocket watch, and it's been passed down through the generations. My father gave it to me last year and told me not to lose it.'

'Can I see it?'

He pats his pocket and pulls a face. 'I appear to have lost it. No doubt Lady Dorothea swiped it when we were chatting earlier. I'll have a word with her before she leaves.'

'I would. Things like that tend to carry curses. If it leaves your family, you'll have a hundred years of bad luck.'

'In which case, she can keep it,' he says. 'Who needs that?'

His eyes soften as he looks down at me. 'I have all the luck I need, Grace Andersen. I found it the day I met you.'

'That's very sweet,' I say. 'But I'd like the watch as well.'

'I didn't expect to find you so mercenary. Fine, we'll go and talk to her in a minute. In the meantime, the clock is about to strike twelve, and I promised myself weeks ago that I'd kiss you on Christmas Eve as well as Christmas Day.

His hand is warm on my back as he draws me closer. This kiss feels different to the others we've shared. It's familiar, yet somehow brand new. I know him better now and trust him in a way I didn't before. I feel as though I've been found by the person I knew all along would come looking for me, even before I knew I was lost.

I'm startled when the huge clock on the wall chimes twelve.

Rob's grip tightens on me. 'You aren't going anywhere. I don't have time to chase you the length and breadth of the country to return those very expensive shoes you've borrowed. Besides, I promised I'd kiss you on Christmas Day, and I plan to keep that promise.'

I smile up at him. 'I couldn't run anywhere even if I wanted to. Glass slippers would be comfortable compared to Georgia's shoes. I can't think why she bought them.'

'Give them to Lady Dorothea,' he advises. 'That should stop her running off with my great-great-grandfather's watch.'

'Happy Christmas!' says Isabella, appearing at my shoulder. She looks from me to Rob. 'I'm not interrupting anything, am I?'

'Not at present,' says Rob, brushing his finger over my cheek and smiling into my eyes. 'But if you hang around for five more seconds, I'm afraid that will no longer be the case.'

I hope you enjoyed this book. If you did, please consider leaving a review on Amazon. It helps new readers find my books, and I really appreciate it.

Join my mailing list to receive a free story about a reluctant bridesmaid and be the first to be notified about my upcoming books.

rosemarywhittaker.com/signup

Also by Rosemary Whittaker

The Sugarloaf Bakery series

Available now in paperback and Kindle ebook

A Tale of Two Christmases

Available now in paperback and Kindle ebook

The Year Away series

Available now in paperback and Kindle ebook

Made in the USA
Monee, IL
15 March 2024

55156470R00164

50/-

Moh & Maya